Tales From an Endless Summer

A Novel of
The Beach

by Bruce Novotny

A Cormorant Book
Down The Shore Publishing

The final chapter in this book, "Labor Day," previously appeared, in somewhat different form, in a column in the *Beachcomber*.

For information, address:
Down The Shore Publishing, Box 3100, Harvey Cedars, NJ 08008.
The words "Down The Shore" and the Down The Shore Publishing logo are registered U.S. Trademarks.
Printed in the United States of America. First printing, 1996.
⊛ *This book is printed on recycled paper — 10% post-consumer content.*
10 9 8 7 6 5 4 3 2 1

Library of Congress Cataloging-in-Publication Data
    Novotny, Bruce, 1962-
      Tales from an endless summer : a novel of the beach / by Bruce
    Novotny.
        p.   cm. -- (A cormorant book)
      ISBN 0-945582-30-7 -- ISBN 0-945582-31-5 (trade paper)
      I. Title. II. Series.
      PS3564.0927T34 1996
      813'.54--dc20   95-30737

                                                  CIP

This story is dedicated to
Louis Novotny, Jr., my father.

He surely would have shaken his head at
some of its contents, but I believe he
would be proud of me for writing it.

Any project as long in the making as this one will come to owe a hefty list of debts by the time it is completed. Many thanks to:

Anna Leadem
my brother Jeff
Marion Figley
Rich Youmans
Ray Fisk
Leslee Ganss
the insights of Bob McKee
Linda Opdyke and Mary Lechleidner
Laura Kingsbury (and P. G.)
Anyone who ever partied at or remembers fondly the surf shop
in a special way, Lauren Aquino
and the love and inspiration I get every day from Nina

Tales From an Endless Summer

A Novel of
The Beach

Chapter 1

Bloodstained Surfing Magazine

The surfer found himself awake on his couch. He lay there, his eyes open in the darkness, and could not tell if it was near dawn or still the middle of the night. "If it's morning," he thought, "I've got to go surfing." He listened for traffic noise on the Boulevard a few blocks away, tried to gauge the activity of the birds outside. The breathless hum of quiet was all he heard, and it told him nothing. "I really ought to get a clock," he said to himself and then retreated under his coarse wool army blanket, hiding from the possibility of morning. His feet rubbed together. There was warmth trapped down there; it felt good. He didn't want to leave this comfort, wanted very much to drop back into sleep. He closed his eyes.

But ...

What if there are waves?

Shit. What if there are — what if it's actually a quarter to six and a four-foot swell is pumping and it's glassy and no one else is out there? What if you miss it?

What if you miss it.

The surfer rolled from his side to his back and covered his eyes with his arm. He pictured Buddy's greeting: "Where were ya, Kring? It was classic, all-time." Of course it was. And of course by the time Kring arrived the tide would have come in and the wind would be sideshore and the magic was gone.... It had happened to him before.

Kring got up. He tugged a pair of sweatpants over his legs and butt, a T-shirt over his shoulders, and he pushed open the side door of the garage that served as his home. He stepped into a gray morning, his momentum pushing him onto his rusty bicycle. He pumped the clattering pedals and guided the bike toward the beach, straight into a mystery zone of fog, a heavy atmosphere of chilly perspiration that had settled over Long Beach Island and kept the streets to itself.

When he got to the beach, Kring discovered that the fog was in control here too, allowing at most twenty-five feet of visibility. Kring could see the bubbles churned by the ocean's thrusts onto the sand, and watch its retreats, but that was all. Everything beyond the water's very edge melted into the mist. Kring exhaled forcibly. This was a frustrating discovery. Now that he was up he wanted to surf, dammit, and it seemed like lately shit was always getting in the way. His job. Crowds. Flat spells. Now it was a thick ground layer of fog. He couldn't even tell if there were waves out there. He picked up a shard of a clamshell and pitched it into the unknown. It made no sound, just disappeared. There was nothing he could do except shrug his shoulders and return to his still-warm bed. Maybe he could steal a few more minutes of sleep until the fog lifted.

The garage apartment was silent when he returned and gray light filtered through the dusty windows. Kring stepped into the room and the aluminum door slammed behind him. Outside, the fog moved slowly past the door with chilly breaths of ocean breeze. Kring shuffled to the TV and switched it on, powering up the monotone of the NOAA marine forecast that played in a continuous audio loop on cable channel 13. He bent toward the couch and stretched gratefully into its folds, pulled the musty blanket up past his eyebrows and exhaled into the wool. The low hum of the weather report was the only sound. "Periods of patchy ground fog," it said. Tiny points of dust floated upward in the air before the windows and vanished out of the dim light's path. Kring closed his eyes. He was comfortable again. He could barely hear the TV.

The door to the apartment swung open with a crash and before Kring had a chance to mumble, "What the hell," someone was screaming "Que pasa!" in his ear. "Que pasa, dude! You got a job yet? What time is it? Got any food?" the intruder yelled. "Kring! You got a job yet, dude?"

Kring didn't know who was haranguing him but he did know it was too damn early for this shit. Without opening his eyes, he reached under his couch and pulled out a small handgun that sometimes worked and sometimes didn't. He was tired, frustrated, aware of only a voice, bugging him while he was trying to sleep. Kring pointed the weapon in the direction of that voice and pulled the trigger.

The suddenness of explosion rang through the morning. It silenced the intruder and satisfied Kring. A thin, swirling film of blue-grey smoke hung heavily in the lightstream before dissipating. The weapon had worked this time. The silence returned.

The smell of gunsmoke burned his nostrils and he threw the blanket off his face. Kring looked at the unpainted ceiling and, as far as he was capable, considered things. Random violence wasn't a normal feature of his existence, but it certainly had its place, he thought.

There on the floor in front of the refrigerator was what looked like the twisted body of Mark Space. Space was a summer person here on Long Beach Island, maybe eighteen years old, a guy Kring knew from summer parties as one who did little with his time but drink other people's beer and badger other guys' girlfriends. He didn't surf, yet he still thought he was cool. "On the Jersey Shore, I guess, he thought he could get away with that," Kring sneered, "but he was wrong."

Damn, Kring almost said aloud when the realization hit him that Space had owed him five dollars for a share of a pizza bought at Crank's last party.

The kid would have been good for it too, if only Kring had been a little patient. It occurred to him that the body might have the five bucks on it, that Space may have unwittingly walked into an ambush when he wanted only to pay his pizza debt and clear his name. But if that was the case, Kring's own moral code decreed that he'd forfeited any right to the money by his savage act of violence. And anyway, if that's why Space was here, why was he talking that shit about a job?

Kring sighed and looked at the scene before him; Space's body was on the floor, the gun half under the couch, a bloodstained surfing magazine half-covered by Space's head. Kring's digital clock had gone dead, its face now black where bright red numbers should glow. Kring's attention was drawn back to the surfing magazine. And the blood on it. This bothered him, and so did the clock and the silence. He lay back down and covered himself with his blanket, felt something jab his shoulder. He rolled up on his elbow and reached awkwardly behind. He pulled out a tiny silver ball-and-dagger. One of Lissa's earrings. He rolled it between his fingers, staring, then focused beyond it. There was no body on the floor. There was no bloodstained surfing magazine. The NOAA report droned on from the TV speaker.

"Man, that was weird," Kring said uncertainly. "It was so real." He knew he was awake now. Kring looked at the earring in his hand and told himself that he had to return it, if he ever saw Lissa again. He was glad she hadn't stayed the night. He was glad she hadn't had sex with him.

He pretended to push the earring post through his earlobe, not sure if he wished his ear were pierced or not. When he lay back and dropped his hand to the floor, he let the earring drop out of his palm and bounce along the cement. It came to rest in just about the same spot as the bloodstained surfing magazine had been, as if it were ready to disappear too, if the surfer fell back asleep. But he didn't fall asleep. He just lay there in the early morning warmth, brushed a curly black hair off his stomach, and said, barely aloud, "Another one of those fucking dreams."

His eyes drifted back to focus on the spot where the bloodstained magazine had been, as if to convince himself for good that it really was not there. He felt relief that the cement floor was bare. Bare, except for the earring and a computer form and return envelope crumpled together in a ball under the chair across the room. "Fucking alumni office," he muttered as he regarded the trash. "What business is it of theirs how I'm living? Just one more recent graduate who'll be listed Missing in Action for a few years. Big fucking deal."

Sunlight was hitting his refrigerator. He realized that the fog had lifted.

He tossed the blanket aside and pulled himself with a struggle to his feet. On the wall next to the door was an old rotary phone, his landlord's line actually, but Kring picked it up and patiently dialed Buddy's number. He counted eleven rings and hung up. "Shit, I hope I didn't sleep for hours," Kring moaned. "I hope it's not past eight." He grabbed his wetsuit and shed his sweats, pulled the neoprene over his feet and body in a series of motions. When he was fully wetsuited, Kring grabbed his six-foot-four Romantic tri-fin surfboard and strode out the door. His bike was a little trickier to ride with his board under his arm, so he just took it slower. At the Boulevard he paused. The bank clock read 6:14, and Kring was relieved. Not only had he not wasted a slot of time sleeping — what a weird dream, he thought again — but he still had almost four hours before he had to be at work at Sportswater jet ski rentals.

By the time he reached the beach, Buddy was already out in the rolling waves, a black shape like a gull only bigger, bobbing in the glare. The surf, Kring saw right away, was mediocre. It was waist-high, and broke inconsistently. Typical Jersey Shore trash, but Kring would have been upset if he'd missed it. Buddy would have told him about it, and even stories of sloppy surf made Kring want to get out there.

He didn't know Buddy well, but for most of May and June he had been a pretty dependable surfing companion. He'd shown up on the island in early March, and since then lived alone in an apartment above a store in Ship Bottom. No one knew where he came from, and Buddy never said. He didn't have many friends. Kring knew him only from surfing.

12

Kring shook his head vigorously to wake himself up, wrapped his leash around his ankle, and charged into the chilly surf.

"Another weird dream today," he told Buddy when he reached the spot where his friend waited for one of the infrequent waves to offer itself.

"Yeah? What about this time?" Buddy replied laconically.

"That spaz Mark Space slammed my door open, yelling at me to get a real job."

"Ya killed him?"

"Yeah."

"Handgun or blunt instrument?"

"Handgun. It was pretty cool. I must have wanted to do that, y'know, subconsciously, ever since he snaked me on his boogie board that time."

"When was that?"

"Couple weeks ago. That Memorial Day south swell. Little shit cut me off on the wave of the day! Then he didn't even do anything on it. Just slid down and rode the whitewater."

"He deserves to get shot for that," Buddy said half-seriously.

"Yeah. But until I woke up and realized it was a dream, I was afraid I wouldn't get back the five bucks he owes me."

"Still, that's not worth passing up the chance to blow him away."

"Why? Because he's a snake?"

"Sure. Or just because he rides a boogie board. So what's it mean, Doctor?"

"What's the dream supposed to mean?" Kring asked. "I don't know, just latent hostility toward Space, I guess. And it means that *I want waves.*"

"How you figure?"

"That's all anything means, man," Kring said with a laugh as he dug for a small wave that carried him away.

Many rides later, the sun was a few hours higher in the sky, and Kring announced casually, "Next wave I'm heading in. Gotta get to work."

"Come on, dude, it's early yet. I thought all you wanted was waves. What's this *work* shit?"

"Greg is ready to fire me if I don't show up. One more time, man, that's what he said. Surfing is life, but it don't pay no bills. And *these* waves aren't worth poverty."

With the next surfable peak, Kring was off, riding it for all it was worth, crouching low then hopping on his front foot when it was dying. He scrambled pathetically for the last few yards. At last he sank, still standing on the board. He paddled in without a look back.

Once on the beach, Kring unwrapped his ankle cord and tucked his board under his arm. He watched Buddy for a moment, a silhouette again floating alone out in the mediocre surf. Kring turned and headed up the beach, on his way to work.

Chapter 2

Wetsuit Rash

Kring leaned back against the front wall of the High Point Volunteer Fire Company building and watched a steady trickle of surfers, surf babes and wannabees make their way past him into the firehouse. Next to him, Spill coolly checked out each passing bro and betty, a boyish smile on his face and carefully tended dark hair pushed to the side. They were waiting for Crank to show up for the movie. Kring had known Spill for maybe ten summers, bodysurfing together as kids and then, as teenagers, working at an amusement park in Beach Haven. Kring worked the Skee-Ball booth and Spill ran the Dragon ride. That's where Kring met Crank, who was from Spill's hometown. When Kring got into surfing, Spill and Crank went no further than boogie boarding. It never meant to them what it meant to Kring. To them, it was just something to do. Spill even became a lifeguard.

Now Spill peered into the darkness with disinterest and matched looks with each girl who passed. Each time, he smiled. He was skilled at such matchings. Most gave him a second look back. A few smiled, Kring noticed.

This Long Beach Island showing of *Wetsuit Rash*, the latest underground surf movie making the rounds on both coasts, was a social event. It was one of the few real opportunities throughout the summer for this crowd to gather in one place, from up and down the island, and the atmosphere was loose and celebratory. It was soaked in summer, early summer, possibility-filled freedom. Everyone seemed to glow with early tans and, laughing and stoked, they caught up with friends not seen since the summer before. They were free again of school and the suburbs and shoes; they were at the beach. Hundreds of curious, joyful naked toes marched past Kring and Spill in the warmth of the late June evening.

Kring saw many people he recognized. But many in the surfing crowd, he knew, sported the same look, and that probably accounted for most of the familiar faces. The hair was part of the look, cut short with a little tail at the back, already streaked by the sun, or even bleached white. The face of untroubled youth was there with sunburned highlights, and, in the eyes, the moral duty to rebel against something. They had been there once, he and Spill, eager to prove that they were one of this crowd, but they outgrew that a few years ago.

"Spill, dude! What's up! You go out today?" they heard an unsteady voice blurt behind them. Kring looked up to see California Bob by the door, tipping a beer can to his mouth. He let Spill answer. He just watched. To ask Spill about the waves, he thought, was absurd. Spill wasn't a surfer, he only rode a boogie board which, to Kring, didn't count at all.

"Dude, 'sup," Spill replied. "Nah, I didn't bother. I heard it was good this morning, but it flattened right out. It was small and crumbly when I checked."

Bob looked at Kring, "Yo, K, didn't see ya there in the dark, brah." He turned again to Spill. "Yeah? Where'd you check it at?"

"Behind the 7-Eleven. It was high tide, though."

"Yeah? I was out up here all afternoon and it was like head-high and barreling."

Kring immediately understood that meant small and crumbly. California Bob's penchant for telling tall tales, especially about wave heights, was common knowledge. Once that habit was understood, Bob was fun to have around. Spill was good at that game, too, at least as good as Bob. Spill was sneakier about it.

"Oh yeah," he said, "a few good sets rolled through in Ship Bottom, but I got out of the water when I saw the shark."

Bob's eyes widened at the word *shark* and he shouted "No wa-hay!" with an incredulous grin. Behind him, in the shadows, Kring smiled.

"You didn't hear about it, dude? It was heading south, so I figured it swam by you-all up in Cedars already. I thought the Northenders would all be talking about it tonight."

"No-ho way, dude! How big?"

"I don't know, maybe six, eight feet. I saw the fin cut the surface and I just turned and paddled in, y'know, trying not to splash too much. I didn't even tell the other dudes out there that I saw it." Spill laughed with an *Ain't I bad?* timbre.

"Really, dude," Bob agreed, shaking his head. "Wow." He paused.

"Dude, you wanna get high?"

"Sure," Spill replied quickly.

"Got any substance?"

"No, man, ain't carrying," he said as a pine branch shook behind them. They turned to see Crank emerge into the building's light, draped in a colorful Baja poncho.

"What's the word, you wave gods?" Crank said in greeting.

California Bob addressed Crank in his wavering crazy voice, "Hey dude, where you been? Around or what?" And in the next breath, "Got any buds?"

"No, man, but Miller might be able to hook you up. I heard he scored some abusable stuff," Crank replied in a put-on voice meant to poke fun at Bob.

"Cool. He's here, I saw him go in already — ah, his girlfriend doesn't like me," Bob said. He pondered this with the gravity of a judge. "I'll be cool," he finally decided. "No problem-o." He slipped in the door, behind the line, without paying for the movie.

Crank gave his Billy Idol-blond hair a toss and pulled a few bills from the pocket of his knee-length shorts. One of the bills floated to the ground and Crank captured it with his bare foot. He pulled a beer out of the belly pocket of his Baja and handed it to Spill. "Dude, you want a beer?" he asked Kring, who just shook his head.

Spill turned to take the can Crank offered and said "Cali-Bob told me it was overhead and hollow in Cedars."

"He's so full of shit," Crank responded. "It wasn't even waist high and it was sloppy."

"I know. I told him I saw a shark off Ship Bottom. Heading from Cedars."

Crank laughed out loud. "That's cool," he said between breaths, "totally cool. He believed you of course."

"Of course."

They headed for the door and were inside before the movie began. A great collective hoot went up from the crowd when the lights went out.

The audience was partying, Kring noticed, buzzing, excited at the prospect of a new surf movie. The younger kids, the grommets, were stoked to have something to do at night besides hang out at the arcade. They had a chance to hang out with the real surfers, the guys they knew from the shops and the contests.

The crowd seemed built of heads turning and bobbing, arms flailing in demonstration. The room was alive and rustling under the flickering images on the wall. The crowd's long hoot at the first image of a wave onscreen drowned out the film's narrator, and similar hoots arose with each of the first dozen rides shown. The noise drowned out the music. The bad speakers and alternative-rock soundtrack took a few minutes to assert themselves over the room.

By the intermission, the continuous footage of surfers riding perfect waves began to bore Kring and Spill and, it appeared, many others in the audience too. But while the lights were on, they all insisted to one another that it was a totally hot flick.

As the first reel of film was rewound and the second was being loaded onto the projector, Spill looked around for friends and good-looking babes. Kring watched as California Bob led Miller outside with an expectant look on his face. A minute later he saw Miller's girlfriend leave, swinging her car keys defiantly.

When Mark Space leaned over from his seat behind Crank and asked if there was a party anyplace, Crank reported, "I heard there might be one at this house in North Beach; you ought to check it out."

"Could I get a ride from you guys?" Space asked.

"We're not going. We're going out to the bars after the movie, probably to Beach Haven," Crank said, undoubtedly aware that Space lived in Surf City and would have a tough time getting back from the other end of the island at the end of the night. As he listened to the exchange, Kring was relieved that he felt no urge to shoot Mark Space.

Spill turned to Crank and whispered, "Think he'll figure out that we pass North Beach on the way to Beach Haven?"

"Not the Space Pilot. Not a chance. And I don't want to get stuck with the geek if there's no party."

After a minute of confusion, Mark Space said aloud, "That's cool," and Crank breathed a small sigh of relief.

"Hey, you guys hear about the shark scare in Cedars?" Space added as the lights went out again. Another predictable hoot arose from the crowd. A second later the lights came back on and one of the sponsoring shop owners announced, "Hey, we forgot to pick the winners of this new surfboard, and we got some T-shirts to give away too, real nice T-shirts here."

Kring knew the guy who won the gleaming new board, knew him as a boogie boarder who would sell the prize as soon as he could. The guy gathered up the armful and left in a hurry. "Fuck the rest of the movie," Kring heard him say on his way out the door. Crank complained the fix was in because he again failed to win anything, and he warily pulled another Coors Light from the pocket of his Baja. "It's a little warm," he apologized as he handed it to Spill. He pulled out another for himself and they cracked them open just as the lights went out a second time. The two of them settled into a dull torpor, rebels sipping warm beer as Kring sat nearby, trapped by a lack of options. Crank was his ride. He didn't see any other friends in the audience so it was either Crank's ex-haust-leaky Malibu or hitching.

The second half of the movie wasn't much different from the first, ex-cept that the audience no longer competed with the narration. Crank liked the Claymation interludes and cheered wildly each time the figures appeared. The rest of the crowd was sedate except for an uproar during a segment fo-cusing on big-wave wipeouts. The end of the movie came as a relief to many, and the firehouse emptied slowly of wearied gremmies and surfers. They were all talking about the guy whose board got bit by a shark in Harvey Cedars. Kring and Spill laughed together, then climbed into Crank's car and swal-lowed exhaust fumes as they headed for Beach Haven, fourteen miles south and what seemed like a hundred traffic lights away.

"Lotion's going to Touché?" Crank asked.

" 'S what she told me," Spill said. Kring sat in the back and said nothing.

"Cool," Crank said. "I'd love to nail her. She's a headliner. She's a prime-timer."

"Yeah, she's like gorgeous, but I don't think she'd give either of us a tumble. I get that feeling, ya know?"

"You never know. It's a new summer, and I personally am looking better than ever. By the way, where's your van?"

"Some kid at work wanted to borrow it. He thinks he's finally gonna get it from this girl he's been dogging. I think he's wrong, but he's filling it up with gas for me."

When they got to Surf City and Crank swung a hard squealing turn onto Central Avenue, Kring spoke up from the back seat. "Hey, could you guys drop me off at the Gateway? I don't feel like going all the way to Beach Haven."

As the warm air rushed through the window, harassing his face, Kring thought about Beach Haven, thought about Lotion. He remembered the first time he ever saw her. Before they became friends, before he had even spoken to her for the first time at that party on the beach, he had seen her wandering through Beach Haven one early summer evening and fol-lowed her. She was the very image of the seventeen-year-old beauty play-ing at the shore. She seemed to possess the power to order her own universe, and he had followed her as she ducked into the shops of Schooner's Wharf, one by one, humming to herself, looking for nothing to buy. The sky, he remembered that day, had been an overcast dusk long before nightfall, but as he followed this entrancing girl with the long chest-nut hair, the clouds seemed to part all at once from the horizon, and an ethereal glow spread across the water. It reflected off the bottom of the cloud cover and the dark surface of the bay. The girl seemed drawn to the water, to the small bay beach in front of the shops. She slowly danced around the tourists, gazing to the west, and Kring trailed a few yards behind her, also mesmerized by the brilliant reds and purples that seemed to hang in the air like dust in a lonely room. She walked to the water's silvery edge and admired her world. Kring stood a few yards away, and a guy next to her turned and said, "Red sky at night, sailor's delight." She smiled politely at him and returned to her sky without comment. Kring felt foolish then for following her, and he slipped away and returned to the amuse-ment park. The image of her remained in his mind for days afterward. And he met Lotion not two weeks later at a surfer's party. He never got over his foolish feeling and so never tried to romance her. They discov-ered a shared love of the ocean and of sunsets and became great friends, but he never told her about the first sunset they had shared, the first sunset he had really appreciated.

As they approached the big intersection in Ship Bottom and were slowing down for the red light, Kring opened his door and prepared to step out onto the street. But the light turned green as they were saying their catch-ya-laters. Crank yelled, "Jump!" and put his foot on the gas. Kring was just clear by the time the car surged away, and he stood in the empty roadway as the Malibu sped through the streetlights and the glow of the gas station, the door still hanging open. Kring watched as the door was taken care of with a sharp swerve, and the car disappeared down the avenue. Kring cursed his friends and walked to the Gateway Lounge.

When he arrived he sat at the corner of the bar and ordered a long-neck Budweiser. On a small stage behind him Lloyd Hubris and the Withoutniks, a local band, were just finishing up their first set. His beer was set in front of him as the last strains of "Crowded Off the Dance Floor," a tune that Kring recognized as one of the band's originals, melted away in a shimmer of feedback. There was some applause. Two guys whistled. Kring spun around on his stool and noticed that Lloyd Hubris was once again absent. The singing duties had fallen to the keyboard player, Peejunk, who gave the sound man a nasty look as he left the stage.

Kring turned back to the bar and took a sip of his beer, more out of

20

reflex than thirst. He looked up as an arguing couple pushed their way through the door. His gaze drifted out that open door, into the wash of an unhurried night. The sounds of that night were unremarkable but pleasing in an odd sort of way and drifted in without a breeze, mingled with the quiet bustle of the stage and scattered barroom conversation.

The jukebox began playing all of a sudden, as jukeboxes will when they're in the mood.

Outside, the traffic light changed to red as the other lights along the street glowed a constant white. A beautiful woman in a Mercedes convertible pulled up at the intersection and waited there for the signal to go. At least she looks beautiful from here, Kring thought. And if she isn't beautiful in truth, it's better if I can imagine she is.

He was startled by a hand slapped down on the bar next to him. It was one of the ugliest hands he'd ever seen: bony, thick-veined, scarred and discolored. Kring calmly took a sip of his beer. He knew this hand.

"What's the score, Ricky?" he asked without moving his lips from the bottlemouth.

"It's evil, man, evil and uncompromising, that's what the score is." Ricky Van Floyd was the drummer for the Withoutniks and he wrote most of their better lyrics. This surprised many people, because Ricky said little, usually grunting at people he didn't know, and he had a terrible singing voice and so never sang. While not as ugly as his hands, his face was generally sullen and unexpressive, as if he were perpetually stoned and starting to get tired of it. Still, he was in a band and so had a good-looking girlfriend. A quick look around confirmed that she was not here tonight.

"I see Lloyd's not up there today. What's the story?" Kring asked, wasting no time in getting the latest Lloyd Hubris chapter.

"Ah, he's in New York for laser surgery."

"Oh." Kring nodded. He had been following the band only since the end of last summer and had seen them play no more than four or five times, but each time Lloyd was away on an errand of some sort. Always running someplace for some goofy reason, it seemed. Kring knew most of the band members but had never met Lloyd. Ricky assured him that this was not unusual, not when it came to Lloyd, anyway. Kring thought he hinted at some greater mystery when he said it. The last time Kring had seen the band, in April in Asbury Park, Lloyd had been in Georgia fighting a speeding ticket.

"Laser surgery? I didn't know Lloyd had cataracts."

"He doesn't, really. He's just doing it for the free transportation they offer. Lloyd's never been in a limo before."

"That's cool," Kring replied, without meaning anything.

They talked some more about the band; when Ricky told him the band was going to record an album in the fall, it seemed so far away to Kring. The fall.

He bought the drummer a beer and Ricky left it half full on the bar when he got up to join the band for the second set. Kring sat alone again in the crowded bar, and he thought about Spill and Crank going to meet Lotion in Beach Haven. Kring would have loved to see Lotion, but he didn't want to go all the way to Beach Haven and have to find his way back to Ship Bottom when Crank got drunk and split. Also, there was the chance that Denis would show up there.

Denis wasn't that bad, he just annoyed Kring sometimes, especially over the winter, when no one else was around. At the Terrace Tavern in the off-season, Denis always bought his share of rounds and then some, and was always willing to drive to Philadelphia for concerts. Kring just had little patience with his insincerity and his need to impress others.

In Brighton Beach, a small section of the long island halfway between Ship Bottom and Beach Haven, Denis was probably at that moment putting the finishing touches on his look for the evening and was about to plunge into the warm, dark, unknowable night. Kring had witnessed this ritual and suspected that Denis saw this plunge as heroic, taken like a figure on a beer commercial with no past and no future. This image, Kring knew, appealed to Denis. He would not know why, nor would he stop to think about it. He would be adjusting his collar, folding it up, then down, then up again. He would make a face in the mirror. Denis almost never looked at a full-face reflection of himself. To his MTV-influenced mind, the bathroom mirror became the camera that recorded his features and thoughts as though they were important, and he believed himself too on-the-move to be caught full-face by that camera. The face he made was meant to be full of cool, full of confidence and the secrets that the rest of America wanted. These things couldn't be faked by Denis, but he satisfied himself with his approximation of current style.

Kring could see him driving down the Boulevard, cruising the spinal column of island traffic, a guy caught up in the world of personality through style. It was a world attractive to him, Kring suspected, even intoxicating because continuity had no place in it. It was all about a first impression. Nothing else was as important, nothing else even mattered because the first impression had become the definition. And Denis figured that all he had to do was look cool and a little incongruous. Be-

22

cause if he looked cool enough, then the incongruity could be blamed on his having someplace better to be, that he was just looking in here on his way to something more exciting and offbeat. Denis was pleased with the impression that he was a man-on-the-move, and he assumed others admired it in him. He had told Kring that. Kring believed him.

So this man was on the move down Long Beach Boulevard, preparing to meet friends at Touché. It would be too early in the season for him to have gotten the traffic lights timed, and he would find himself sitting at a few reds that he would be able to escape later in the summer. He'd park on Centre Street, and his feet would clip along the pavement, up the ramp and in the door of his favorite nightspot. He always flashed his brightly colored Touché Ambassador card at the doorman, who already knew Denis and would let him in anyway. And the evening would begin. There were people here, young people, carefree, drinking, yelling at each other, having fun. Some of them were his friends.

When Denis walked into the club, Spill saw him first. His casual remark to Crank caught Lotion's attention across the table. "Shit. Denis is here," he murmured.

Crank said hopefully, "Maybe he won't see us."

"Maybe. I hope not," Spill replied. "Probably not. He's wearing shades."

Lotion looked at the two of them and shook her head. Spill noticed that her face glowed with an early sunburn. Her brown eyes he saw were bright with secrets, as always. Spill had long ago given up trying to discover those secrets, but Crank gave it a shot now and then.

When Denis walked in, the three of them had been hanging out already for a half hour or so, and Lotion was beginning to get bored. As Crank and Spill got more drunk together, she surveyed the room, looking for other friends.

Denis scoped out the place with a smile while behind his Buccis, his eyes adjusted to the diminished light. He finally spotted his friends and wormed his way through the crowd as the music pounded. He mounted the couple of steps and arrived with a posture that implied his journey to them had been an arduous one. He sighed heavily when he reached the table, blowing a cocktail napkin to the floor. No one picked it up.

"How's it going, dudes?" he shouted. Spill and Crank mumbled meaningless responses to the meaningless question. The dance music overpowering the place seemed to have gotten a little louder, and the waitresses had climbed onto platforms throughout the club, and now danced to mild cheering from the patrons.

Spill took a sip of his beer. He shrugged, for no apparent reason. Denis admired things like that.

In a second attempt to communicate, he shouted something at the table surface and looked around. Lotion said, "WHAT?" and bent her ear down to him but Denis said nothing. Crank and Spill both looked abstractedly past him and shook their heads. Crank made a halfhearted attempt at dancing by himself at the table, and soon gave it up. Denis repeated the question and Lotion shook her head. She lifted her gaze and scanned the room once more.

When the music faded and the waitresses had climbed down to the floor again, Denis said, "So, nobody's seen him, huh?" There was no reply. None of them really knew what Denis meant, but his question required no answer.

"Is the Cafe open yet?" he then asked.

"The Cafe's been open for like six weeks. Where've you been? Wait — you were there last Thursday, dude," Crank told him.

"Oh yeah, I forgot. So, how's it been, any babes there or what?"

"It's been pretty cool. There was a crowd last Friday but everyone was gone by ten. Some lifeguard had a party."

Lotion interjected, "You guys ought to try to stop by there for sunsets. It's a great spot for it, right on the bay, and they get some beautiful colors. There's a small group that gathers almost every day, some interesting people."

Denis jumped in. "Women?" he asked.

Lotion nodded. "And women too. Plenty of chicks, dude."

"Who's been hanging out there?" Denis asked of Spill.

"We been there most nights," Crank said, "Kring shows up once in a while, Joanna Plutarch, Irrelevant Roger's working there ... um, who else? You know Tony, the guy who owns the place? His daughter's working there this year. She's sort of cute. Someone said Lloyd Hubris was there on Monday. It's been crazy as usual."

"Lloyd was there? I thought he was in that badminton tournament in Algiers."

"No, Ricky told me he got disqualified in the second round. Tried to smuggle in some underweight shuttlecocks or something. But I heard that he was in Chihuahua looking for this Mexican chick he may have married last fall."

"Cool. I'll have to stop by the place tomorrow," Denis said as he pushed himself away from the table and went to find someone who might dance with him.

A half hour later Denis returned to the table, breathless and excited.
"Who is that incredible woman behind the bar?" he demanded.
All three looked toward the closest bar. Spill craned his neck and said, "You mean that one? The one serving cans of beer to those button-downs with bad sunburns? I don't know, dude. Never seen her before." He paused. "Wow. She's gorgeous."
Crank couldn't say he recognized her, neither could Lotion, but both agreed that she was uniquely beautiful, even for a Touché girl. Lotion mentioned how the girl smiled at her customers at the bar and moved easily, gracefully in the small space behind it. She didn't tell the guys, but she saw how the girl's eyes seemed to shed their own light on men's faces, so universal were their reactions to her. She had jet-black hair and thin expressive eyebrows, and shockingly light, almost white eyes. With her strong and dark features, she looked like an Afghani gypsy princess, one whose destiny is to taunt the dreams of all who fall under the power of her charms, who fall because there is no other choice. She was no ordinary barmaid. Lotion could see that.
Denis obviously wanted her body, wanted her to smile on him.
Spill pondered aloud where she'd come from.
Crank wondered where she lived now and if she had a phone.
Lotion admired her near-perfect grace and beauty.
Denis just continued to stand, transfixed, and of course wanted her. The ice melted in his drink.
After a minute or two of wanting her to the exclusion of all else, Denis began shifting his weight from foot to foot. "I hafta pee real bad," he announced. A moment later he was gone, and Lotion was the only one who noticed he was gone. Crank and Spill discussed the surf movie and the people they had seen there. The repetitive noise of the drum machine grew louder, or more insistent, and Lotion spotted a Beach Haven local she had gone out with once and wanted now to avoid. "Let's go, guys," she said. "Let's go to the Cafe." Spill and Crank quickly agreed with what they saw as a plan to abandon Denis. They left their table, then the humid confines of the nightclub and went to see if they could catch anyone this late at the Cafe, their waterfront hamburger hangout in Brant Beach. Denis emerged from the men's room a second later and couldn't find his friends. The bar goddess was no longer at her station. He asked a bartender where she had gone. She had left, he was told. The guy didn't know anything else. "Sorry, dude," the bartender called after him.

Denis returned home and turned on the TV. He punched up MTV on his remote, with no sound, and played the *White Album* on his stereo. He went to sleep, with the girl from Touché taunting his dreams.

Kring hung out at the Gateway for another hour, drinking with Ricky and Peejunk in between sets. While they played, a hard-core group of fans danced on the floor in front of them, pleased with their intimate friendships with the guys onstage. Kring's attention was drawn to the window when a couple of cars rocketed down the street outside. He stared at the empty road they left in their wake, and he remembered when that road, leading to the Causeway bridge, meant that his summer was over, that he and his parents and sister were leaving the island behind for another school year. His mind swam a backstroke through the years, to those summers, those summers he knew on Long Beach Island when it all was magic.

He saw himself, at ten years old, saving quarters, sometimes stealing them and running to the Hand Store to buy baseball cards. He could hear the music that was always playing, the songs that seemed to define those days and could still bring them back with vivid precision. He recalled the day he met Spill on the beach when they were both twelve, and the adventure of bodysurfing every day until long after the lifeguards left their stands, until the beach was deserted and growing dark. How cool they were then, he and Spill. And there was a girl named Molly that he met later that same summer; he recalled the sheer terror of the first time he kissed her, the first kiss, the first real kiss in his life, on the beach at night and the pungent smell of cedar and coconut and resin in the surf shop when he got his first surfboard the next summer. Looking back now, it seemed that aroma was everywhere in those days. How that surfboard changed everything for him. Everything. These images floated by and were real, and the streets and beaches too, the way he saw it all a decade earlier, as a little kid, when these months on the island were magic, when even the boredom was special, something to be savored.

It was a different place that he knew today, and he wondered where the difference lay, what had caused the magic to erode. He still felt something like it in big waves, or when he fell in love, but outside of those brief extraordinary moments, there was nothing of what he remembered. Just his job, laid back, but common and necessary, just his uninspired friends bullshitting each other. No vast and heroic ocean, no mystery to the adult world, no bridge back home. Yeah, even the bridge back home had lost its power, lost its meaning, since Kring claimed this island as his home after graduation. Maybe that's what growing up meant, he thought.

Still staring out the window, Kring brought his bottle to his lips and tasted beer. A Jeep sped past outside.

As the Withoutniks took another break, Kring drained his fifth. Before the jukebox could begin to supply a soundtrack, he left a single dollar bill on the bar and slipped out the door.

He crossed the street, passed Ron Jon Surf Shop and walked along Central Avenue on his way home. The night air was delicious as he walked and Kring was almost glad that he didn't have a driver's license. Losing it a month and a half ago led him to walks like this, strolls through the quiet neighborhoods around his apartment. He was almost seduced by the peace, seduced into his memories again. It would have been easy, it was all so much like it used to be. He was faintly aware of a small sound carried on the air; it was the irregular delicate hiss of surf on the beach, two hundred yards away, invisible in the night. The air had fallen dead calm. There was no more breeze.

Kring felt a surge of excitement through his body. Waves! A good spring swell was on its way. It would probably be the last before the summer flat spell set in, he thought with a touch of cynicism. The sound from the ocean, he knew, meant little; that was just beach break. But it made him think; the weather service said there was a low off the coast. Today's waves sucked, they were inconsistent and small, but there had been energy there. And now the wind had died, probably glassing it off under the waning moon. Maybe even a light offshore would pick up around sunrise, he thought. It should be good, Kring thought. He was sure of it, ignoring the lessons of so many other nights of anticipation that led to mornings of disappointing sunlit ripples.

He hurried back to his garage, shed his clothes, and fell half-drunkenly to sleep on his couch. He didn't need an alarm. He'd be up by four-thirty, in his wetsuit and out his door in minutes, in the water before five o'clock.

Chapter 3

Four-Foot Rule

The morning sun burned vividly above them as Kring and Buddy walked down the orange gravel driveway that led from the boulevard to the burger shack on the bay. Their hair was still wet and plastered to their heads, their wetsuits peeled to their waists, surfboards under arm. The residue of a great morning of surfing, five hours of absolute overhead fun, rode on their shoulders. The day was beautiful June, late in the morning, and the swell was as good as Kring had suspected the night before. Maybe better. And Kring and Buddy were high. They were high on adrenaline and the ecstasy that great waves can generate in those who love them. As they walked, Buddy kicked a stone along the hard, dusty surface and, not wanting to disturb a mood that approached perfection, quietly said, "Every day should be like this."

Their bare feet crunched along the gravel carefully, often on tiptoe because their summer calluses were not yet fully developed. On their left a stand of phragmites, reeds seven feet tall, bowed slightly with the breeze as the morning surfers passed. On their right, a thin strip of grass and weeds and tiny cedar trees bounded the backyards of clone houses of various pale, chalky colors, built together in a rush thirty years before. Most of them had stones spread in the yards which enhanced their ugliness, Kring thought.

The wide blue bay spread out in front of them as they approached the shack. It was a small wooden building hidden to their left, nestled between the reeds and the salt water. Its sign identified it as "Summer Breeze Burgers" but no one called it anything but the Cafe. Even the phone was answered with a quick "CA-fe" barked into the receiver. Lotion's white Subaru was parked in the lot, Kring noticed. He smiled.

When they got to the planked deck, Kring leaned his board against the side of the building and used his right foot to wipe the sand off his other foot. Buddy stood at the wooden counter and called for the cook, an ex-surfer named Willy, who was only a few years older than Kring. But surfing didn't mean anything special to Willy, so he found it easy to give up when he felt too old for it.

"Yo, Willy, what ya got for breakfast?"

"For you, dirt bag, stale corn flakes and curdled milk. HAHAHAHA." Willy had the same line waiting every time they surfed. Buddy only asked him because he knew how much Willy enjoyed the joke.

"Yeah, well I want a bowl of clam chowder and a slice o' corn bread. And some coffee."

"Ya can't have chowder for breakfast. Yer goddamn weird." Willy also responded this way to Buddy's favorite post-surf breakfast all the time. He looked at Kring. "What do you want, dooooood?"

"What's there to have?" Kring asked. Then, before Willy could seize the opportunity, he added, "Besides the stale flakes."

"Ah, just soup and burgers and dogs right now. It's almost lunch, ya know."

"It's only ten. Even McDonald's doesn't serve lunch this early."

"So go to McDonald's."

"Got any pizza from last night?"

"One slice."

"Heat it up for me. And I'll have some orange juice."

Kring got his pizza and carried it over to where Buddy had joined Spill. Lotion sat with them and she was laughing. Kring liked her face lit up with the sunlight and laughter. It made her brown eyes seem almost golden. Spill was telling one of his stories, an exaggeration of the night before, probably. Lotion reached her hand to Kring in greeting and a silent "Hi" formed on her lips. He smiled back at her, grabbed a chair from the next table and sat on it with its back against his chest. He looked around. Without a breeze, the surface of the water alongside them looked like nineteenth-century window glass.

"This is great," Kring said between mouthfuls of pizza, "what a good day."

His story done, Spill sat now, eyes closed, faced turned to the sun, occasionally complaining about a wicked hangover. Looking at his friend, Kring suspected that the hangover didn't really exist. "Hey," he said, "you on the beach today?" Spill didn't even open his eyes when he replied, "Nah. But I have to work at Shellfish at four."

"How long you been working there?"

"Two weeks. I'm just bussing tables, like three nights a week. It's pretty cool." Spill's eyes lifted open and focused on Kring. "Speaking of work," he said suspiciously, "don't you have to be at Sportswater by now?"

Buddy looked up too. "Yeah, you're late, aren't you, Mr. Corporate Man?" he said mockingly.

"I told Martin I'd be late today. Had an interview lined up for a real job this morning."

"A real interview? So what happened with that?" Spill asked.

Kring's smile burst into laughter. "I blew it off, man, just bagged it and went surfing. Did you see the waves? Priorities, dude."

Spill nodded agreement as Irrelevant Roger arrived for work and started a Bon Jovi tape playing on a crude stereo. Roger yelled from behind the counter, "I can't believe you guys went in the water. There's a shark out there, like a big one. Two guys got bit yesterday. One of them lost his leg, I heard."

Spill rolled his eyes and laughed with Kring. Then he asked, "How were the waves?"

Lotion interrupted a sip of her Diet Coke to exclaim, "Can't you tell? Just look at those expressions." Kring and Buddy exchanged big unfakeable grins. "Those faces are the signs of awesome surf," she declared. "I've seen it before on these guys." The spirits of the two surfers were still higher than specialty kites on a whipping south wind, and Buddy excitedly began to relate their experience in the waves to their companions. It was impossible. Spill was just a boogie boarder and pretended to get as stoked as the surfers, but Kring knew that he was utterly unaware of what it meant to dance with a wave. His enthusiasm was an imitation, a pale shadow of theirs. Kring knew it. Lotion freely admitted that she had never felt the narcotic effect that gripped Kring and Buddy, but Kring believed that she knew its kin, and besides, he knew she enjoyed seeing them work themselves into a lather trying to explain it. As he listened to Buddy frustrate himself trying to describe something that cannot be communicated, and as he tried just as desperately to help him, Lotion just shook her head and chuckled. Kring noticed this and thought Lotion had a sexy way of chuckling. Most girls he knew would have giggled.

Spill broke into their tirade to ask, "Hey, how about that surf movie in Harvey Cedars last night? It was pretty hot." Kring stopped and looked at Spill. His remark made Kring realize the futility of his efforts, as he did every time he tried to talk about surfing to nonsurfers, and said without conviction, "Yeah, it was hot, dude."

Behind them, Denis rolled into the parking lot in his black and gold IROC, power windows down, car stereo pounding bass which effortlessly drowned the small sound from the Cafe speakers. Irrelevant Roger took the opportunity to change the tape as Denis swiftly braked to a stop. A thin curtain of dust rose around the Camaro, and when he shut off the car, his music yielded to the tinny sound of sixties Motown from the building.

Denis jumped out of the car and rushed up to the table, demanding to know if anyone knew anything about the barmaid that he'd fallen in love with on sight at Touché last night. "Anybody hear anything?" he implored them. "Talk to anyone? You guys gotta help me find out who this girl is!" He seemed to have not yet caught his breath from the night before, simply obsessed with a vision, desperate to find out her name, her story, her phone number, if she was seeing anyone, if he, Denis, might have a chance with her.

Kring was baffled by Denis's raving. Lotion seemed to understand and looked amused, but Spill did not try to hide his boredom.

Buddy slapped down his Styrofoam coffee cup. "What the hell are you so hyper about, Denis?" he screamed, his annoyance intensified by his surf-charged emotions.

"Oh, man, this girl I saw bartending last night ... she was UNREAL. I've never seen anyone like her. She was like, um ... Marilyn Monroe, or the chick in that one beer commercial, only, ya know, she had dark hair. Dude, I have got to get to this girl, gotta find out what her name is."

Spill said sarcastically "So, you want us to do your legwork, huh? Like LBI Investigations or what?" He and Buddy laughed.

"Dude, nothing like that, just if you hear any word on a really out-standing girl who bartends at Touch-ees, like let me know, all right?" Denis appealed as the music tapped out its subtle metronomic language behind the group. Then he turned to Buddy, looking ready to interrogate him about his suspicious identity, or lack of one, as he did whenever they met. Denis was the only one of this loose band of summer locals who could not accept Buddy's mysterious nature, could not let it lie without trying to probe its secrets.

"Hey, you got a driver's license yet?" he asked.

"Nope," Buddy said casually, trying to get at the last of his chowder with his plastic spoon.

"You still got that Volkswagen Bug?"

"Yeah."

"Is it registered? Insured?"

"No."

"And you drive it."

"Sure."

"Man, you are out of your mind. No license, no registration, Alabama plates — in this police state of New Jersey, man. Crazy. What if you got pulled over?"

"I don't."

"Whaddaya mean 'you don't'? You could."

"I don't."

"Suppose someone else, some idiot in a fog from New York who is trying to turn left from the right lane just crunches you in the process?"

"Denis, look," Buddy said patiently, looking Denis in the eye for the first time, "I'm a good driver. I have to be. A lot depends on it, more than you can guess. I can't afford to take the intelligence of anyone else on the road for granted, you know? One accident would really mess up my life, blow my whole identity. I can't afford it. I can't afford to get pulled over, so I don't."

"What, you mean you drive without breaking any laws, like do everything by the book, or what?"

"That's part of it. I don't necessarily drive by the book but I don't give cops an excuse to pull me over."

"Too bad Kring didn't feel that way. Maybe he'd still have a license now." Denis laughed, then turned again to Buddy. "What's the rest of it?"

"I don't know. It's just that I can't get pulled over, so I don't. It's that simple, dude."

Denis didn't believe that it could be that simple. He kept complicating Buddy's clear truth with all sorts of possibilities, but soon he kept them to himself. He didn't understand what Buddy meant by having so much at stake, and Buddy seemed to have a will in his voice, a force that intimidated him. At last Denis simply said, "You're weird, man. I don't understand you."

Kring was about to say something in Buddy's defense, until he realized that Buddy needed no defending. Besides, he was suddenly entranced by Lotion. She was only tapping her feet to the music as she sat at the table, but she was a beautiful woman, and beautiful women, he realized not for the first time, had that power, to effortlessly turn attention their way. And Lotion drew attention like a magnet as she sat in the sun, surrounded by young men, absorbing the song in the air that began so slowly and mournfully. Buddy, Denis and Spill one by one became aware of her trancelike energy and they watched her.

The tempo of the song gathered itself and began to hop like exploding popcorn. Lotion responded by springing to her feet, grabbing Kring's
arm, demanding that everybody dance with her. "Come on, you guys,
dance! Dance to the music, dance-dance-dance with me!" she yelled.

Her spirit caught the others like a gust catches fallen leaves, and
while Spill and Denis began whirling with Lotion in an unconscious pop-
soul-driven careless frenzy, spinning and kicking with wild, music-fed
abandon, Buddy approached a pair of sunbathing young girls and coaxed
them into dancing with him and Kring. The girls laughed self-consciously
and joined the party.

Irrelevant Roger turned up the volume on the small box to the point
of distortion, then lowered it just enough to keep the speakers from shred-
ding. He tried to coolly dance alone behind the counter. On the deck
before him, everyone was bouncing and spinning and throwing their arms
around with the beat. Their energy came from the sun and the water, it
came from the music. They were young and it came to them so easily.

Kring saw, out on the water, an old man fishing in a small outboard
boat. He imagined what the old man must be seeing when he turned his
head toward the loud music. He probably saw figures ricocheting about
on the deck of the Cafe, a scene that might remind him of a Charlie Brown
holiday special, with all the characters dancing their peculiar dances while
Schroeder played his jazz piano. As he danced on the wooden platform
Kring glanced at the man a couple of times. He saw the old man turn away
and go back to fishing, probably wishing the music would be turned down.

The song faded, as songs always do and the dancers slowed, then
stopped. Buddy and Kring bowed to their partners. Buddy asked the
girls' names and offered to call them with promises of parties. Denis and
Spill sat down, trying not to breathe hard and Lotion walked over to the
bulkhead. She crouched down and looked at the eelgrass floating on the
water, against the wall, then she lifted her gaze to the clear blue hazeless
sky. A calm smile rode on her lips. Kring studied her at the water's edge.
He heard Denis call him, "Hey, dude, need a ride to Sportswater? I'm
heading that way."

"Sure. You leaving right now?"

"Yeah."

"Cool. Let me get my wetsuit off and I'll stuff my board in your
sunroof."

Lotion said over her shoulder to them as Kring got up to leave, "Don't
forget, guys, sunset here tonight. It'll be great."

33

Kring walked out on the floating dock to guide a speeding jet skier back into the beach. "Slow down!" he yelled. "No wake! Lie down on the ski and go slow!"

The big clock at the end of the dock, visible to the skiers on the water, read twelve-thirty. I've been here only two hours, he thought in disbelief. Work dragged on days like this, when he knew that every minute, just two hundred yards away across the dunes, energy pulsed in as clean, head-high waves rolled from the wide ocean and washed up on the sand, one after another, lining up like furrows ready to be planted.

"Man, I can't stand this. I can't concentrate," he said to Greg Martin, his boss at the jet ski rentals, when he returned to the blue metal building.

"What's up?" Greg asked. "Hey, how did your interview go?"

Kring stumbled for a second, but recovered quickly. "Ah, it was okay. I don't think I'll get the job, though. I don't think the guy liked me."

"What was it for?"

"Some P. R. position, I guess, in Philly."

"Philly, huh?" Greg said as he looked suspiciously at his watch. "You got back pretty quick."

"Yeah, well, I got up early and all," Kring said as he looked toward the water. "It was a short interview." He sensed that Greg had doubts about the appointment. He realized his wet hair didn't help his credibility. But without warning his mind was ambushed by the memory of one wave that he'd had that morning, a long, clean wall that spoke to his subconscious, told him how to ride and where to go. He felt again in a wash of vision the fun, the rhythmic perfection, the watery sense of magic. And he smiled. "Hey, there's not much happening today, how about giving me the rest of the day off to surf?" he said eagerly. "You know, the old four-foot rule?"

"What the hell is the four-foot rule?"

"A variation on the Hawaiian custom among employers who hire surfers. On this coast, when the surf hits four feet, the employee hits the surf."

"No way," Greg said. "Can't do it. It's too busy. There's too many people around. I can't let guys off just because there are waves. You were late again today already. That's bullshit."

"I told you about that yesterday; you said it was okay."

"Yeah, sure I did. *Job interview.* Yeah."

"Come on, man, this place is dead today. Jimmy can handle things," he said hopefully. "Why can't you be a kindly old boss instead of you?"

"Because I've got a goddamn business to run!" Greg's voice rose. "This isn't kindergarten."

He knew Martin was right in his own way, but Kring was under the pull of other forces. He knew the call of those swells rolling in at that moment was not to be ignored. Didn't happen often. He looked around furtively and grabbed his surfboard leaning by the door. "Okay, then, I'm taking lunch. See ya after a bit, Greggy," he called over his shoulder.

"Be back here by one-thirty. Surf all afternoon and you can start looking for another job," Greg yelled after him across the gravel lot. "I mean it!"

Kring heard his boss's threat but paid little attention. He knew it was legitimate to surf on lunch break; that was understood. And if he stretched it to two or two-thirty, Greg would still be cool, he figured. He'd have to. This was Long Beach Island. And this swell demanded it. That is stretching it, though, Kring thought as he jogged across the Boulevard between the widely spaced rushing cars. Maybe he would fire me, the bastard. I better head back at one-thirty, to be safe.

On his way across the Boulevard, Kring decided he'd borrow a spring suit from his buddy F. Scott, who lived in the beach house up the street. Scott's short-sleeved wetsuit would be enough today. The water wasn't that cold and Kring's full suit had kept him too warm and constricted that morning. No one was around when he reached the first-floor deck of Scott's house, but Kring could see that rare LBI sight of clean, head-high surf on a summer day. The active seascape was fairly littered with floating bodies perched on surfboards, hunched over, solemn as Druids. There were a few boogie boarders too, but only one flopped about in the thick of the surfers. The rest skirted the edges of the crowd, sensibly, Kring thought, as they looked wounded and weak, lying on their bellies kicking their swim fins. Though he had surfed this same swell all morning, Kring was still overcome with stoke at a glimpse of it after three land-bound hours. He didn't even bother to go inside and change, just grabbed the rubber suit that was drying on the rail, let fall his canvas shorts and stepped out of them in the open air. He pulled the suit up over his dark, naked legs, his white butt and torso. He heard a girlish whoop from two houses down and acknowledged it with a sheepish grin and a wave, then he scrambled down the steps, grabbed his board and trudged up the dune. He spotted a cake of wax someone had left on the bench by the beach entrance. Someone was always leaving wax on those benches. Kring rubbed it on the deck of his board and then placed it back on the bench to further melt in the sun.

The beach was crowded, but there were no lifeguards, not until the following weekend when the summer season officially began. That meant no designated surfing beach yet, no flags to pay attention to, surf anywhere you want. Kring practically sprinted into the water and vigorously paddled out. He wanted to shout at the very sight of the best of these waves, smoothly curving, a deep dark green rising out of the blue ocean which grew warmer each day, all around him. It was a beautiful sight, entrancing, the different color that fell on the wave as it prepared to break. It was a deeper color, no longer reflecting sky or sunlight, only the light of the surfer's own imagination and the secrets the ocean held beneath her surface, deep and liquid and magic. That spell always ended, however, and this one collapsed in a wash of the fragile green on Kring's head. The whitewater dragged him backwards in its rush to the beach.

He surfaced, shook his head, and matter-of-factly crawled through one wave and over two more. He made it out to the lineup beyond the breakers where he sat up alertly and caught his breath.

There were a few familiar faces among the crowd in the water, and he waved when they greeted him. Kring wasn't one to talk much or tell stories in the lineup, but he listened to others tell about how good it had been earlier, and he remembered and smiled.

Kring was in position for two good waves, but each time he started to dig for the drop, another surfer hopped up before him and he had to kick out of his push. When at last he was in a good spot and plunged into the cup of the wave, he rushed, drove the nose of his board under and pitched forward into the soup.

"Man, you kooked good on that one," he heard someone laugh as he surfaced. "You ate it big time." Kring recognized a guy he knew slightly. His name was Brian, and Kring had to admit Brian was right.

"I'm just so anxious to ride these babies," he said. "I spazzed on the hop-up."

"Dude, isn't this something!" Brian exclaimed. "Isn't this great?" Kring turned to watch a hot-shot manic surfer slash his way across a wave face with an undirected explosion of energy. "That dude will be in the Contest," Brian declared, referring to the island's surfing championship, held in August each year. "Probably win a trophy or something. Knows what they want. Knows the routine. But he's a pussy."

Kring nodded in agreement. He knew the type of guy Brian described: one who knew all the moves, perfected the ones that won contests, whether they fit the wave he was on or not. It seemed like a waste of a wave to Kring.

On the next wave Kring was able to catch, a ten-year-old kid, a pre-pubescent surf Nazi, ignored his calls of "Up!" and dropped in front of him after he was already riding, and the two surfers nearly collided. Kring wasn't able to get close enough to slap him, though he swung at him before he got dumped by the white water. He went under with a muffled curse.

"That little asshole pulls that kind of shit all the time," Brian told Kring on his return to the waiting spot. "He's gonna get his ass handed to him by somebody before this weekend when the lifeguards show up."

"Think it'll help?" Kring asked.

"He'll learn sooner or later, dude. That's just uncool."

When at last, after waiting out two more sets, he was able to slip through the crowds into a wave with no one in his way, Kring rode it with joy and a sense of dancing. The ride lasted maybe twelve seconds, but it was smooth and fast and beautiful and of a different order than any feeling he'd ever known on land. It was like the force of gravity was suspended, or altered. Just like every other really good wave felt, he thought while he tumbled along the sea floor after he lost the track of the swell and sank.

When he pushed his head through the white frothy soup into the air, the beach was half as far away as it had been when he last noticed it, and it was colorful with crowds. He jumped up and scrambled with his board out for more waves like the last one.

"I love surfing in front of lots of people," he told Brian when he got back out to the lineup. "You know, how the beach feels like an arena when there are waves as good as this, and the crowds can't help but watch."

"Yeah, I know what you mean, dude," Brian said. "It's like they're all here to watch me, and they're all jealous."

"And if they're not, they should be."

Kring noticed a watch on the wrist of a paddling longboarder. He asked him if he knew what time it was. The longboarder stopped paddling, looked at his watch and said "Yep." Kring looked at him expectantly, then when he realized that he had heard the sum total of the longboarder's answer, asked, "Could you share it with me?"

"Sure," came the reply from a beard spreading in a grin, "it's ten after two." Kring rolled his head back to face the sky, his eyes closed. Work entered his mind for the first time since before he stood naked in the sun on F. Scott's porch. Should I go back? he wondered. By reflex came the quick answer, *Fuck it.* Greg won't fire me, he said to himself, and even if he does, a swell like this is worth the price you gotta pay. It seemed such an easy decision to make.

Chapter 4

Sunset at the Cafe

Irrelevant Roger's left hand rubbed his right eyebrow as he took the coins offered him by the fourteen-year-old boy. Roger knew that a dollar ninety-five was an outrageous price to charge for an Italian ice. But people kept paying it, and they asked for more. So Irrelevant Roger kept serving it, and kept changing the tapes in Willy's paint-splattered cassette player on the shelf above his shoulder.

The weather had pampered the island all day. Now, at five-thirty, the air temperature was still eighty degrees. The grill sizzled away behind Roger. It magnified the heat, and the sun reflected off the bay in front in dazzling flashes, forcing him to squint. Music surrounded the place, music from a homemade tape that one of the kids brought in. It wasn't a great mix, Roger thought, too much bubblegum metal, but he needed music while he worked, and he'd listened to all the tapes behind the counter ten times apiece, except for Willy's Fabulous Fifties collections. He didn't like to bring his own tapes in because he got Spin Doctors and the Alarm stolen just two days before.

He sighed in teenaged despair. "God, days are so long this time of year," he said to himself, "and I have to like work them all." He flipped a hamburger and looked at his watch, and consoled himself with the prospect of joining Spill and Crank and the crowd for a few beers at sunset.

"Kring ought to be showing up soon," he said to no one in particular, who turned out to be Victoria Tanner, a girl with long brown hair and smooth shoulders who sometimes worked with Roger. Her father owned the Cafe.

"Do you have to play that so loud?" she asked Roger. He shrugged. Victoria reminded him of a girl he had a crush on a year ago, in tenth grade. Victoria was not a stunner, not like — what was her name? Tracy! — but she had the same shape nose and she cocked her head the same way sometimes and that was why Roger decided that he liked her. Nothing special, he just liked to see her and look at her when she was around. It wasn't her personality, because she wasn't really friendly and never paid him much attention. She was a couple of years older than he was, she was in college and didn't take him seriously. Roger had learned to live with that. But it wasn't that she was stuck up, just preoccupied or something. That's the way it seemed to Roger. Others, he knew, thought she was stuck-up.

Victoria wasn't impressed by Roger's news of Kring's impending arrival as she was just a little bit suspicious of that surfer. She told Roger that Kring seemed a little rootless, unconnected, like he was without a world of his own, and that, she distrusted. Roger didn't understand. Kring seemed to be on the periphery of any group he was around, like the group that hung out here. Even among the surfers he seemed on his own, never accepting full membership in their little club. Victoria had never had friends like that, and she didn't know what to make of Kring. She was more interested in Spill — thought he had a cute smile — but only if he showed interest in her. "They're not my crowd anyway," she insisted to her friends from Villanova, who had rented a place in Spray Beach. "Their parties can be fun, but surf talk just isn't my thing. Sounds pretty dumb." Still, she was friendly to those guys, they hung out at her dad's Cafe, and she saw them sometimes in the bars. She had never seen them anywhere else. They were as much a part of summers on the island now as the Causeway, soft ice cream or the planes flying banners over the beaches. "That would be so weird, though," she said to herself, "to see one of these summer faces, like Spill or Denis, in Philadelphia. It would be so out-of-place."

Victoria turned to rearrange the potato chip rack while Roger flipped the tape over to side B. As the first song began Kring appeared at the bulkhead in a one-man boat with a tiny outboard motor. It looked like it came from a bumper boat ride. He set a twelve-pack of Black Label on the deck and reached to tie up.

"Hey, you bozo. You gonna leave that boat there overnight?" Irrelevant Roger greeted Kring. Kring gave Roger a look and tossed him a beer. Roger declared himself off work.

After dropping the line around a piling, Kring said casually, "What's the big deal? I'll take it back after the sunset."

"What's the big deal?" Roger choked. "Man, that's gotta be two or three miles and you don't have any running lights. Are you high?"

"It's less than a mile. The sky's clear, it's like a half moon tonight. Look, it's already out." He pointed toward the ocean, where a pale white fingerprint hung in the bright sky above the horizon. "That'll be plenty of light."

"What about the marine police?"

"Fuck them. I don't worry about the cops, dude."

"Maybe that's why you don't have your driver's license," Roger joked as Kring strode over to the counter. The late sun warmed his shoulders as Roger cracked open his beer. Kring leaned on his forearms on the countertop and smoothly eased himself onto a stool. He waited for Roger to ask about the waves or how his day was. When he saw that Roger wasn't going to ask, Kring said casually, "Well, I'm unemployed."

Roger looked up. "You got fired, dude?"

"Yeah, got fired for surfing. I'm a martyr, man."

"What do you mean?" Roger asked.

"Ah, I blew off work after lunch and surfed until like a half hour ago, after Greg told me I couldn't have the afternoon off."

"Wow. That's not cool. Were the waves good?"

"It was really good, dude. Water got cold, and the undertow was a bitch, but it was a sweet swell, like head high and clean all day. It's dying now, though," he said in a rush. "Flattening right out. And I'm beat. I am dead tired." Kring took a swallow of his beer and said, "Oh, anyway, Greg was pissed off, but he knew I was going. Told me if I surfed all afternoon that was it. Hi, Vick," he said waving, "you want a beer?" Victoria silently declined his offer and Kring shrugged and said to Roger, "Greg was gone by the time I got back. But Jimmy told me that Greg said I was history. I just took the boat." He paused to lift the can to his lips. "But in a way it's cool to lose your job for surfing. It's a statement in these weary times, in this weary world." He scratched some wax off his knee. "We having any entertainment tonight besides Teddy's bad mix tapes?"

"Some guy, friend of Willy's, is gonna play his guitar and sing a few songs. That's what he said anyway."

"What kind of music? Like Simon and Garfunkel, I'll bet."

"No, he does a lot of Buffett. He's played here before, like two weeks ago. He's pretty good."

"That's cool," Kring said as he took another sip of his beer then glanced up suspiciously. "He's not gonna play 'Margaritaville,' is he?" he asked. Kring watched Victoria pack some diced tomatoes in a small plastic container. He watched her for a quiet minute. He admired her looks, her blue eyes and her tight, tanned body, but she seemed remote, as if unwilling to share something with the world. He wondered what it was. She never looked up as she snapped the lid in place and turned her back to him to open the refrigerator.

Kring sat up and turned to one side and contemplated the bay that spread out before him. He smiled at the warmth, at the sun on his shoulder and the air around him. He could see the bridge, arching subtly and sensually above the water a couple of miles away. The job that he had just lost was no more to him now than the unnoticed breeze that barely lifted a strand of salt-soaked hair from his forehead. The sedge island in front of the Cafe, just marsh and grass, was green and full. A ski boat cut smoothly through the water in front of it, a skier dragging behind in a bright bathing suit and vest.

Kring tried to imagine this view in wintertime and could not. It was too removed from this reality. He tried to conjure up in his mind the grey and brown world, the oppressive cold, the biting wind. It was futile. Nothing fit, none of the images would stay before him. That was a world that few summer people ever saw, and now, in June's bright promise, it seemed to be of a different place entirely, even to a year-rounder like Kring. In that distant, dark, isolated winter, in the midst of deserted houses and empty washed streets, it was still easy to believe in the summer ahead, or the summer just past. It made no difference, it was all the same. All summers were the same, whether they had happened yet or not. Because even in that deprivation of winter, surrounded by dormant pizza restaurants, you always knew that it would happen again. The gift shops whose windows said "See You Next Summer" and the tarp-covered boats sleeping on cinder blocks just told you that the summer day in your mind might be a memory or it might be a dream, but it would happen again when the days grew long and the sun moved out of the low southern sky, when even mornings were warm and the rain, when it fell, didn't sting, just refreshed.

And he was right, for here it was happening again, just as it always had, just as it always would.

Spill startled him when he grabbed a beer from between Kring's feet. "What's up, dude?" he said as Crank appeared behind him with a thermos which Kring soon found out was filled with vodka and orange juice. Kring gave them the news of his dismissal. "No way!" they shouted in unison.

"Yeah," Kring laughed, "I went surfing and got fired for it."

"So what does this mean, brah?" Spill asked.

"Dude, it means I can surf all day. I can jump on a swell like today — "

"Good swell, dude?"

Kring focused his eyes on the undeserving Spill and confirmed, *"It was fucking great.* Size, shape, weather, everything was perfect. No life-guards. Just a classic early summer swell."

"You going out tomorrow?" Spill asked. " 'Cause I'll go out, if you go."

Kring looked at him gravely. "If there are waves, I'm surfing," he said, "that's all there is to it. No job now, so I'm free to surf anytime I want. I'm in total control of my life."

Lotion's voice rang out from a group of people near where the guitar player was setting up. "Think you can handle all that freedom, beach child?"

Kring looked over and finally saw her grinning at him. "Hey, Lo," he yelled. As he got up and went over to see her, he could feel his sore muscles complain. He and Lotion took a table and shared a beer, lis-tened to the guitar player and kept tabs on the declining sun. "So, what'll you do for money now?" Lotion asked.

"I don't know. I have a little saved, couple hundred bucks, and rent's no big deal. My apartment's illegal anyway, so I don't figure Mr. Cox will rush to kick me out. It's summer, Lo. I'll go as long as I can, just surf-ing and hanging out. Being cool," he added in a put-on voice.

"That sounds pretty ideal. I hope you can work it, boy."

"You sound skeptical, Lo."

"No, not skeptical — but we'll see."

Spill and Crank and Roger soon joined them, and they drank screw-drivers and admired aloud the colors in the sky. An orange stain bled into the muted blues, growing imperceptibly deeper, redder. The clouds turned purplish.

"Those colors are incredible," Kring said. "So unearthly, huh, Lo? So *out there.*"

"It's like a daily miracle," Lotion said quietly. "Sunrise, too. Same thing. Whenever I'm up that early, or that late, I love to watch the sun come up."

"Why do you suppose a sunset looks so different from a sunrise? It should give you the same kind of colors, shouldn't it? The spread and the effect should be the same."

"What makes you think it's any different?"

"Look at it. The colors are deeper. The light. Even the sun itself looks different. You can just see it. I don't know why."

"Every sunset is different, you know. Not all of them look like this. I think it's in the way you look at them. You could see a sunrise there if you tried."

"Maybe, but I'd always know it was just my imagination. You can just tell."

Just then Denis rushed up to the Cafe from the rest of the island, the same way he had that morning. This time the reflection of the western sky blazed on the surface of his shades. He stopped, looked around, then buzzed quickly over to the table where the gang sat.

"Anyone got anything on the barmaid from Touché yet?" he asked. Lotion smiled again as she had that morning, amused by the predictable question. It had held the same urgency ten hours earlier. She turned her smile to Kring and said nothing. But this afternoon Spill, for one, grew annoyed. "How the fuck should we know anything, man?" he barked. "Why don't you find out for yourself?" Denis was taken aback. His eyebrows raised slowly above the red rims of his Buccis as he looked at Spill. He said nothing, and everyone else settled back to watch the distracting beauty of the sky.

The guitar player stopped singing and just softly strummed the music as all attention focused on the sun's descent. It was deliciously, agonizingly slow, a trail marked in imaginary intervals, then it was gone. Behind it remained only a pale orange wake and a few pink-stained clouds.

After a few scattered "Wows" and one "That was beautiful," conversation returned. Denis was savvy enough to keep from mentioning his vision woman again.

Ten minutes later Buddy showed up with a burlap sack half-filled with clams. "I missed it, huh?" he said, almost out of breath. "I saw some of it from the Boulevard. It was a great one." He lifted the sack onto the counter. The blues of the evening stained the atmosphere, settled and mellow. Victoria's older brother Ben was working the counter and had not yet turned the lights on, but no one minded. The mood had settled itself into mute darkening, and everyone was content with it for a time.

Buddy called Ben over and sold him three hundred clams. He told Denis that the girl he sought was named Mimi Dresden and that she had just gotten a job at the Seashell Club. Then he melted into the advancing evening.

Denis finished the beer Spill had given him and immediately headed for Beach Haven, for the Seashell. He had to stop for the first red light and he cursed it.

The guitarist played a Simon and Garfunkel song, and so Kring set out in the tiny boat across the darkening water.

Lotion sat a while longer with Irrelevant Roger, Crank and Spill.

43

Roger wanted her eagerly. Around ten-thirty she left to meet a girl who worked with her and they headed for Joe Pops Shore Bar. There Lotion met a guy named Mercantile O'Boyd. She liked his name, and let him buy her drinks all night. She was surprised when he disappeared around one o'clock. No great loss, she figured.

Under the cover of night, Kring made it back to Sportswater with no problems and from there walked the twelve or so blocks to his apartment.

Crank, Spill and Roger left the Cafe soon after Lotion. They went to Roger's place in Surf City to smoke a bowl. They eventually found themselves watching Letterman, stoned and giggling.

Denis didn't find Mimi Dresden at the Shell that night. It was crowded, and he ran into some people that he knew. It's like that sometimes. Besides, with his shades on, his vision in the club was poor.

The next morning Kring awoke with no job to tie him down. The waves were still up, and he surfed all morning. He took a nap on the beach and surfed again until the tide came in. It was a good day.

Chapter 5

Three Summer Sunsets

The waves stayed up. They weren't as big the second day as they had been the first, when Kring lost his job, but they were still good. They had enough size. Their shape held up. Kring was out of bed early each morning, eating cereal in the dark, preparing to ride the waves as if under a moral obligation.

On the third morning he noticed a yellow lifeguard stand that hadn't been there the evening before. It was lying on its side in the sand, boxy and out of place, and the sight stirred up the corn flakes digesting in his stomach. The discomfort did not last, washed away with the next waist-high, glassy wave face.

A day later Kring was again out in the water alone when, about midmorning, two figures in red trunks and grey sweatshirts appeared on the beach and busied themselves with erecting the yellow chair and planting their gear in the sand. When they were done, the shorter of the two climbed the stand and blew his whistle loudly. Kring ignored it. Half a minute later the whistle blew again, and when Kring looked up, the guy on the stand waved at him and pointed north, up the beach. The realization hit him that, yes, Saturday had finally arrived and, with it, the lifeguards, symbols of order on the beach, traditional antagonists of surfers. He sat on his board and looked around. There was no one else in the water. No surfers, no swimmers, and no one on the beach but the guys in sweatshirts. He again ignored the hailing.

The next time he heard the shrill, insistent screech, he thought with disdain, It's ten o'clock, the water's sixty-three degrees, there's no one on the beach yet, and this hard-on is trying to move me out of his area. It was a petty power trip. That was clear. Kring's feet dangled in the chilly water as

45

he wondered what to do. This guy must be a rookie, he thought. I should explain to him how things work. Maybe save some hassles on the surfing beach. *Surfing beach.* Kring almost shuddered at the thought, at such an ugly concept, bureaucracy invading the ocean. Still he turned and paddled in, caught a wave too small to be ridden except on his belly.

"What's the problem, dude?" Kring asked the guard who had whistled him in. The kid looked sixteen.

"Can't surf here," the guard replied with a proud air of authority. "You'll have to move beyond the flags to the designated surfing beach."

"What flags?" Kring asked, looking around.

"Oh shit, we forgot the flags, Chris. Radio someone. We forgot the flags." He turned back to the dripping Kring. "You'll see when the flags get here. You have to surf outside the flags on that side. This area is just for swimmers."

"Dude, there are no swimmers. The water's too cold for swimmers. There's no break by the jetty, all the waves are here."

"But this is the swimming area," the lifeguard insisted.

"How can you have a swimming area if there aren't any swimmers?" Kring blurted in irritation. He stared at the guard, who blinked and turned his gaze out to sea, prepared to enforce the rules to the letter. Chris got off the radio. "Flags will be here in a few," he said. "Louie's bringing them down. I *told* you not to forget them. I knew you would." He turned to Kring and sighed. "Surf where you want for now. Robbie here is a little *conservative.* First day. He's scared of the boss. I'll whistle you if our lieutenant shows up; then you gotta move till he leaves."

"I can live with that, I guess. All I want is to surf, dude," he said to the rookie.

Kring returned to the water, pleased with the diplomatic success. The older guard was obviously somewhat of a kindred spirit, a fellow waterman with values set right. All surfers should owe me a debt of thanks, he figured, for playing ball and loosening up the fuzz. He chuckled as he stroked smoothly out to the waves. He was amused by references to lifeguards in archaic slang for cops.

But it wasn't enough, he soon realized, it didn't mean enough. The virginal beach was violated for another year, a part of his home was defiled. The lifeguards were still there, would be every day unless it rained, and he only surfed this spot through the grace of their whistle. They had the power to order him down the beach if they wanted. They could have him arrested. It still sucked, and he knew it.

As he reached for more and deeper ocean, he felt the first stings of armpit rash beneath his wetsuit. Armpit rash. That sucked too. And the waves were definitely dying.

But Kring stayed out there another hour, despite the feeble surf and his burning armpits, because he felt he had to, he felt it was important. He had to show the pigs. When a crowd started to form in the water around ten-thirty, Saturday surfers just arriving from inland, Kring pushed off and paddled in. He felt his point was made.

The summer slipped into July in the next few days, with hardly anyone paying attention. The swell disappeared and Kring amused himself by repairing surfboards for his buddies in front of his garage. It was fun work for him, it was restorative, and it brought in a few extra bucks. When Denis called Kring around noon to invite him water-skiing, saying, "We need a third, dude," Kring declined the offer. He didn't want to think he had to chip in for gas money. So, while Denis went skiing, Kring continued his fiberglass work in the shade of his driveway, his bare feet cushioned by a bed of orange pine needles. He mixed the resin in paper cups and wiped it off his hands on his shorts. Yeah, he told himself, the swell was gone. But the primitive heat of July was here, his needs were few, and there was always the possibility of waves if you looked at it right, maybe tomorrow, maybe with a good weather system. Regardless, Kring had always sensed that the wide ocean infused this whole place with an energy, and it was what he loved about the island. And he loved how the summer weather allowed people to walk about nearly naked. And those people, on vacation, relaxed and free of responsibility, kept that energy level at a constant, inaudible buzz. Everyone there felt it; it affected them all. It would do so until Labor Day, Kring knew, when those who weren't leaving went to bed with it buzzing in their ears and awoke the next morning to the abrupt, relative silence of sudden autumn.

That was weeks away, though. It was still the first days of July and no one *really* thought about the buzzing not going on forever. Certainly Denis didn't think about it. Kring knew that. He saw it all the time in his friend's attitude, in that endlessly misguided optimism. Kring chuckled thinking about it as he collected his materials and put them away. Denis stopped by again, on his way to Beach Haven this time, in singleminded pursuit of Mimi Dresden. "You wanna go along?" he asked, and Kring shook his head, could see that Denis was blindly immersed in the humid cycles of this season, the lusts and the energy, his own unmeasured hopeful source of hope. Appetites expanded in this heat, hunger for fun, for sex, for youthful action. The only one who couldn't feel the snap and sizzle of summer, as far as Kring could tell, was the fat, bald guy who had been lying face down on his chaise lounge across the lagoon for nearly a week. Kring didn't know if he stayed there all night, if in fact he ever moved at all. Occasionally, Kring noticed, a glass of iced tea would appear on the table next to him. Occasionally he would notice the glass empty. Kring didn't take this for evidence that the man was alive, however. He didn't like to jump to such conclusions. The only change that Kring had seen was the color of the guy's skin, which had gone from a painful shiny pink to progressively deeper shades of bright red, like the shell of a boiled crustacean. This might be an indication, Kring thought, of whether or not the guy was still alive. Kring wasn't sure if dead people could get a tan.

When Lotion swung by in late afternoon to tell him about a party in Harvey Cedars, the figure was no longer in the chaise lounge. "I didn't see him leave," he told Lotion, "so I don't know if he got up under his own power or finally left on a stretcher with a sheet over his face."

"You need to get laid," said Lotion.

Kring sadly agreed with this unexpected advice. "It's been too long," he said. "And the waves have been lame too. I'll meet you at the party. It's on Spinnaker? I guess if I get close I'll hear the music." Lotion nodded, and left when some friends picked her up in a big old pale yellow convertible. She was thinking about her friend Kring as she rode in the open car through the delicious air.

Kring is definitely different. I've always thought so. Not weird or bizarre, really, I like him because most of the things he thinks about, like whether dead people can tan, he doesn't take seriously. He just thinks about them to amuse himself. That's why I told him he ought to get laid. Because it's summer. Because he wouldn't take it too seriously. And because Kring is just getting too wrapped up in his own world. He ought to mingle it with someone else's once in a while. Yeah, someone else's ...

At least he's got his own world, even if he's not sure yet what to do with it. Most of the people around here have no idea even how to be themselves. No imagination, no courage. Kring's got it, but it's like he doesn't trust it yet. I just wish he'd have more fun with it.

God, I love the summer! This convertible of Sean's is the greatest. He calls it the Attitude. "Hey, Sean, you bringing the Attitude down this weekend?" Yeah! It's so great because it's the whole idea of freedom, of the wind in your hair and rock and roll all summer .... like Spill says, in a convertible every stoplight is a social situation, and a chance to impose your musical tastes on others.

"Hey, Sean, turn the tape up louder. I love Robert Palmer.... Whose party is this? At whose house?... I don't know him. Yeah, well I don't hang around your yacht club much.... Hey, Jimmy, there are girls — I said THERE ARE GIRLS — turn the stupid stereo down for a minute. There are women who hate to ride in convertibles because it messes up their hair. Isn't that pathetic?"

I feel a little hyper tonight. I don't know why. I guess because I don't have many nights off this summer and it's nice to be able to party before midnight once in a while. I hate waitressing sometimes. I mean the money's good where I work, but God, I hate having to choose between either taking a shower after work or getting out while everybody else is still coherent. It sucks. But not tonight. There's a party and I have all night if I want. And maybe I'll meet someone really cool. Maybe I'll have some fun. I know I'll have some fun.

"Sean, the song's over. What other tapes have you got?... Lonnie, hand me that tape box over there. No, I'm not going to climb over you to get it. You're a pig. All you guys are pigs. Ha-HA!"

Wow, this is great. There's music coming from that house over there and the way it's echoing off all the other houses around makes it seem like it's coming from everywhere, like all the world is alive with music. I love this song, too. What's so funny 'bout.... With the sun setting across the bay, God, the reflection makes all the windows that face it burst into flames almost — just bright, shimmering iridescent orange. Wow. The whole island is spitting out music and setting itself on fire. It is bursting with life in front of me. It's partying. This is magical, I hope this traffic light never turns green. And I'm not going to pick a tape until this song out there is over. Peace Love and Understanding.... Yeah!

Kring sat down on the bulkhead as the daylight slowly and unmistakably passed its vital prime. The same sky that ignited itself before Lotion at a traffic light was, only a few blocks back, burning leisurely down to the horizon. As he watched its mutating colors, Kring tried to gauge the evening. Was he now in the calm ebbing of daylight, its parting gestures of light and warmth, he asked himself, or was he in the groundswell of the evening, so fresh and, yes, full of promise? Or was he in that vague transition, neither late afternoon nor early evening, a dividing point of the kind that went by unnoticed three or four times a day? Fuck it, he thought. Why did he have to place himself in a specific point in the day, a particular day in the calendar? Perspective destroys magic, he decided. It drags an experience down to reality. This would not be one of those degraded, somehow lesser moments. It would be touched with magic. It would glow with its own superreality.

He would take this moment out of context. He would not destroy it by assigning it a time on a log chart: *8:43 pm: contemplated perspective and reality. Came to no conclusions.* None of that, he thought, for these few minutes of delicious air and tranquility. They would be savored. He took another mouthful of his dark beer and settled his back against the piling, letting the beer drown his tongue, letting the twilight drown its own context. Why not have a moment of generic reality?

Before he had even finished his beer, however, Kring had to admit that the magic moment, if it ever existed at all, had passed and he was now unquestionably in the evening, newborn and fresh. There was no mistaking that. It was definitely a sunset.

"The nighttime is upon us," he sighed. He emptied his beer and rose from the bulkhead to go inside. He had a party to go to. Buddy would be by soon to give him a ride.

Denis parked his car next to the baseball field in front of the Bay Village mini mall, climbed out and muttered about the heat. He heard reggae music thumping through the windows upstairs at the Tide Dancebar. He couldn't see if it was crowded because the sun was low in the west and reflected wildly off the glass. He adjusted his Buccis and made sure his car door was locked.

Upstairs in the bar there was a Happy Hour "beach party" going on. Casual, tanned people dressed in Hawaiian shirts and spandex biking shorts drank frosted fruit drinks and laughed with friends. They told stories. They didn't dance. The DJ was playing "Kokomo" by the Beach Boys when Denis mounted the top step.

He was at the Tide because earlier, at lunchtime, Crank caught him at the Cafe with news that Mimi Dresden had been seen tending bar there the night before. "I thought she got a job at Crane's this week," Denis said. But Crank insisted, "Nah, that was just a joke, dude. Just a rumor. Can you imagine her at *Crane's*? But she was at the Tide *last night*, man."

So Denis was at the Tide's afternoon beach party trying to track down a summer spectre. He recognized a few people, but Mimi Dresden was not behind the bar. He talked to a guy he knew and tried to start a conversation with a Hispanic-looking girl who wasn't interested. He ordered a Corona and when it arrived he stole fruit from behind the bar and stuffed it down the neck while scanning the room, as was his habit. He leaned back and rested his elbow against the polished wood surface of the bar and took another look around. The room was uncrowded. Mimi Dresden should be easy to spot, he figured.

He lifted the bottle to his mouth and took a sip. Immediately his face contorted in disgust, and he spat out a coarse spray of white foam. He stared at the bottle in his hand, then reached a finger in to pry a maraschino cherry from its long neck. Luckily, he thought, no one noticed his foolishness. Denis didn't realize the impossibility of extracting the cherry from the neck until he had inadvertently pushed it into a slow free-fall to the floor of the bottle, contaminating what remained of an expensive twelve fluid ounces. For just a moment he was aware what a fluke it had been that the cherry had lodged in the neck in the first place.

He placed the bottle on a bar napkin and pushed it to one side of him. He ordered another, making sure to be served by a different bartender than the first. Denis turned his back on his waste. It was a tragic error in a clear glass bottle that he would simply ignore. He'd let the bartender dispose of it.

He had his back against the bar rail when a bouncer named Joe, whom Denis knew, walked by. Denis asked him if Mimi Dresden was working.

"That dark-haired girl, you mean? The one they just hired? No, she's not working tonight," he said. "Get this, dude. She works one night and wants the whole weekend off to go home. They said, fine, babe, you can take the rest of the summer off, how's that? Yeah, they fired her, just about an hour ago."

"She was here an hour ago?" Denis asked in disbelief. "Hey, where does she live?"

"I don't know where she lives on the island. I think she's from ... y'know, I don't know that, either. She just got the job, only worked here one night, *one night*, man, and wants to take the weekend off." Joe walked away shaking his head.

Denis turned back to the bar, a little depressed now. He stole an orange slice and ate it, leaving the peel half-circling the ruined beer next to him. An insidious pink tinge was seeping upward in little rivulets, slowly and thoroughly trashing what had been in some people's estimation a smooth and finely drinkable Mexican brew. He finished his good beer and turned from the bar. The sun was already down but it wasn't dark out yet. The dance floor was still empty. The DJ, in an inspired move, Denis thought, played "Twistin' by the Pool." Still no one danced.

Denis left the bar. He estimated that it was too early yet to go to the party in Cedars, so he stopped at the store where Crank worked just to bug him for a while.

Two girls that Denis knew but hadn't seen came up to the bar after he had gone. There they saw the toxic dump of a beer that he had left anonymously. Or so he thought. The girls hadn't seen Denis, either, but the blond one immediately concluded that it must have been his. "He always leaves orange rinds around his bottles," she said. The other nodded knowingly and they both giggled at this image of Denis. The bartender soon came and cleared away the refuse of Denis's early evening. He served the girls their drinks and they wandered off to talk about stuff.

Chapter 6

Kring Gets Laid

Kring lifted his head off the pillow and moved his arm to support it, elbow on the bed. With his free hand he lightly stroked the back of the girl who slept beside him. It was early yet. Kring could tell that by the angle of the sunlight on the wall across the unfamiliar room and by its somber orange shade. He didn't want to awaken Rebecca, partly out of concern for her comfort, but as much from a desire for solitude.

He studied the skin stretched over the joints of Rebecca's shoulder and the lightness of her hair. She was a girl he had met before and liked. She had that charming quizzical look, and an imagination, and most of all she was attracted to him. That was one of Kring's standards; he had never gone to bed with a woman who wasn't attracted to him. It made the party worthwhile, that Rebecca had been there and made an effort to pay attention to him. The night, as he remembered it, had swirled around them like a soft dream when she laughed at a joke he made, and teased him about his uncombed hair, and, late in the night, kissed him, there on the balcony of Kim's house, pressing him against the emptied keg. And when Buddy said he was leaving, Kring told him, "Go ahead, I've got a ride," and a half hour later climbed into Rebecca's MG and the two of them whipped through the open air of the night, dark and still in Loveladies at 3 A.M., to her father's summer house, which was as dark as the night outside, and as still.

Now in the morning, lying between new sheets in an unfamiliar bed, the smell of the home's cedar interior, sweet and woody, filled his senses as it had the night before. He could practically taste it.

It was warm, he remembered, their time together last night. The moments were sweet because Kring and Rebecca did care for each other, or were beginning to, and it was exciting because it was the first time and unexpected. Kring did not want to let go of it but he couldn't help dropping off to sleep sometime in early morning.

He lay awake now in her bed, thoughts of the night before drifting through his awakening brain, moments that seemed special. They had been getting happily drunk together, trading sips from a beer cup. Music carried the party on the air. Summer friends filled the house. Rebecca's fingers rapped on her own knee, tapping percussion, tapping rhythm as he watched. Gently they struck, one after another on the stretched, brown skin of her leg, as if they were striking notes on a piano, and he watched as they almost kept time with the music that interfered with their conversation. She knew the song by heart, he could tell by the way she shifted seamlessly from the cadence of the drum to the guitar. He watched in a trance while she talked of things he didn't hear. And when he closed his eyes he could almost see, he wanted to see, those fingers tap this same tune as gently on his bare chest. He wanted the words to the song she now mouthed to be blown at his face, like an airborne kiss. He wanted to feel her warm breath, freshly perfumed by the summer, on his cheek, on his throat, as they lay in someone's bed.

He thought this as he opened his eyes again to watch her drum the music unconsciously on her thigh, but all he could do was want it. He hadn't been able, he thought now in the morning warmth, to *feel* the taps on his ribs, to feel the heat of her breath, while he watched her. He just wanted it to happen. And he tried, oh he tried, to see it. The thing was, in the hours that followed, this scene had nearly played itself out, nearly true. They had lain, just like he'd hoped, in her bed, one on top of the other, she on top of him, both drained and drugged in the early morning's privacy. It was great.

But she didn't gently drum on his chest, an unconscious touch, and she didn't sing in a whisper to him like he had wanted her to when they were getting drunk from the same beer cup. Maybe, he thought, if I could have seen it really happen, instead of just wanting it to, that little fantasy would have come true too. Maybe she would have tapped out a hollow little song on my rib cage. Maybe it would have happened. Kring rolled over onto his back. Maybe, he thought, I'm just a freak.

Now, in the morning's stolen gaze, Kring again sat up and he moved his hand from her back to her dark hair, and he was the only one who felt it there. He stroked her hair softly, alone. She said she liked to feel my fingers through her hair, he thought. It might make her feel good if she wakes up while I'm stroking it.

But she didn't wake up.

I wonder why Lotion told me I ought to get laid, he wondered. Like sex is some magic cure-all or something, the prelude to a soft-drink commercial, the secret source of whatever happens to be missing.

Movement caught his eye outside the window by the bed. A sparrow flitted among the branches of a tree on the other side of the screen. I wonder if Lotion ever feels alone when she wakes up with someone, when she wakes up first. I wonder if she feels as alone as I do now. She always seems so together, he thought, like she's got some secret ... like she knows what it means.... He trusted Lotion, her wisdom and her instincts, but sometimes she confused him.

His elbow grew tired from supporting his head and he lay back down. He extended his arm above Rebecca's head, still turned away from him in her sleep.

Here he was, he realized, and his own form, tanned and bare, was lying beside a woman, in her bed. Just hours before in darkness he had known her body as closely as a man is able and had offered his own to her. And that communication, that night's adventure had changed the way they would look at each other, forever. They could never go back and hide behind certain mysteries. Those curtains were pulled apart and Kring would always have slept with Rebecca, at least this once. Such a thing was rare with him. But still, in this early morning bedroom, with orange sunlight streaming silently above their heads, cut into ribbons by the blinds in the window, with the voice of the sparrow talking to itself outside, Kring was caressing, not a friend, not a lover, but a back. Just a woman's tanned, taut back and a length of her long dark hair.

Kring wondered if he should leave, maybe slip out of bed to see if there were waves, before Rebecca woke up. He stared at the ceiling and considered. But he didn't leave. He rolled gently to her, so that he would be there when she awoke, so that she wouldn't wake up alone.

He lay there and watched the sunlight through the window for a while, and when he finally looked back over his shoulder there was Rebecca, watching him with a self-conscious smile. She whispered a puffy-eyed "good morning" and reached to rub his neck. He felt her fingers trace lines under his hair. This is nice, Kring thought, as he closed his eyes. Maybe it is worth it after all.

But when she was in the shower and getting ready for work, he again felt alone, just as if she were still sleeping. He pulled on his shorts and shrugged his shirt over his back and collarbone. He didn't bother to button it. "Hey, could you give me a ride down the island? You work in Surf

City, right?" he yelled through the bathroom door.

"Sure" she said cheerfully from under the water's spray. "I'll even treat you to breakfast."

"Great. That'll be cool. At Subbogies?"

"Of course."

"You're really something, you know?"

"You better believe it."

At Subbogies Kring ordered the breakfast special, and Rebecca, an omelette. When they were finished Rebecca went off to work and Kring headed up to the beach, where he walked along the waterline, gradually making his way south. Tiny waves crumbled on his feet and the morning beach looked freshly scrubbed, although the sun was already hot. When he got to the line of motels and condos along the dunes in Ship Bottom, Kring was beginning to trickle sweat. He knelt to pick up a scallop shell lying in the sand, then on impulse sprang up, threw off his shirt and dove into the water. He splashed around a little. It felt good. He tasted the salt water, rinsed his mouth with it and squeezed it through his hair when he surfaced.

"Nothing like a morning swim after some good sex," he would have said to Buddy. And Buddy would certainly agree. "Nothing like your sex buying you breakfast," Buddy might even reply.

But Buddy wasn't there. The only ones who shared the beach with Kring this morning, as he wiped his face and chest with his once-dry shirt, were a family early for the day's fun, two joggers, a free-ranging dog, and an old man with a metal detector. And the damn lifeguards would show up any minute, he thought as he looked at the sun above him. Uh-huh, there's one now, he said to himself when he spotted a figure setting up a stand a few hundred yards across the sand. So he left the beach to the families, to the joggers and the lifeguards, and moved down to the Boulevard, heading toward home along the busy road with his thumb extended.

Lotion was there in her car at the curb before he knew it. "You're all wet!" she yelled at him from the driver's seat. "How can you expect to get a ride in a decent person's car when you're dripping all over the place!"

"Hey, gorgeous," Kring teased her back through the open window. "Where ya headed?"

"Don't you 'gorgeous' me. Where did you and Rebecca disappear to last night?" she asked as Kring climbed into the car, spreading a beach towel on the seat beneath him.

"Went back to her place."

"Oh yeah? How was that?"

"Fun."

"Good. Let's go to the Cafe. You hungry?"

"No, but I'll go with you. Got nothing else I gotta do."

At the Summer Breeze, their Cafe, Lotion had a bagel and coffee, and Kring just had coffee. They sat by the water, they sipped their coffee, they listened to the music squeaking from the shack. At last Lotion said, "So who put the moves on who?"

"Ah, it was kind of mutual consent."

Lotion smiled knowingly. "That means she seduced you," she said.

"She did not," Kring protested. "You don't know, babe."

Lotion just smiled.

Kring looked around him. He watched Irrelevant Roger behind the counter, staring at Lotion's legs whenever he saw the chance. Next door to the shack, workers were putting a roof on a huge, new bayfront house. Kring drew Lotion's attention to them and smiled a self-satisfied smile. "All these poor working slobs who have to earn a living, out in the hot sun," he said dramatically. "I'd spend more time feeling sorry for them, if I didn't have to take a nap later." He leaned back with his hands laced together behind his head and laughed. "I may not be rich," he said, "but I'm blessed with leisure, you got to admit that. I'm smart enough to take advantage of it."

"You are blessed with leisure, dear boy. Another way to look at unemployment. And you're happy with it now, are you? Yeah, I thought you might be."

"For now, Lo."

She took a last bite of her bagel and tossed the remaining chunk to a gull perched on a nearby piling. The gull made a big show of his wingspan before dropping lightly to the deck and swallowing the piece of bagel whole.

"You going to call her tonight?" Lotion asked casually.

"Yeah, probably," Kring replied, matching her nonchalance. "After my nap," he added with a smile.

"Well, I've got to work lunch shift today," Lotion said as she rose from her seat. "Have a good nap, *gorgeous*. I'll talk to you later."

"What time is it, Lo?"

She laughed. "It's any time you want it to be, isn't it?" She picked up her bagel wrapper and cup. "You don't have to be anywhere."

After Lotion left, Kring sat at the table, reliving Rebecca's voice and the way her hair smelled. "Any time I want it to be," he repeated to himself as he settled into a sun-drenched nap, there on the deck at the Cafe.

Kring knew the guy, or thought he looked familiar, otherwise he probably wouldn't have pulled over to pick him up. But maybe he would have, after all, it was beginning to rain and just about dark, and Kring had a fellow hiker's sympathy whenever he drove. The guy seemed grateful for the ride, but Kring didn't remember asking him where he was going. They just started off from the graveled shoulder and headed down the road. The hitchhiker shook some rain out of his hair and reached into his backpack. He pulled out a gun and very casually pointed it at Kring. He asked if he could change the station on the radio. Kring said nothing. The hiker turned the selector knob until he found a generic Top Forty station with an overexcited disc jockey. It was the worst kind of radio, for Kring. "You hate this music, don't you?" the guy asked insultingly. The voice was familiar, something about his looks haunted Kring's memory, but he couldn't place him.

"It sucks," he answered.

The passenger laughed, then cracked, "Too fucking bad," from behind the barrel of the handgun.

Kring felt fear like a stone in his belly. He didn't know what this madman wanted to prove, or why he'd pulled this weapon on him. Did he want money? Did he want the car? Did he want to hurt someone he didn't know? Did he simply want to insure that he wouldn't have to listen to heavy metal when he got a ride? Kring did not know, and the guy didn't say. He just sat there, in the passenger seat, in the darkness. Kring couldn't even see if he was smiling or not.

"Um, I don't have much money on me. Only like five dollars," Kring said uncertainly. "Uh-huh." the hitchhiker replied distractedly, as if it were a strange thing for the driver to think about saying. Kring felt confused and helpless. He had never before been confronted with an armed assailant, and with this one he didn't even know the purpose, or the ground rules. It was clearly in this hitchhiker's powers to set the ground rules if he liked. He had already taken control of the radio. This was a frustrating, helpless emotion for Kring to face, this submission. Physically the dude was about the same size as Kring, maybe a little skinnier, though it was hard to tell. Kring would probably be quicker than the dude. But there was that weapon, that simple over-equalizer. Kring was at his mercy, and that scared him. It made him angry too. His foot pressed on the accelerator pedal a little. Then a little more. The car was traveling at seventy-five, eighty miles an hour before the hitchhiker noticed their speed.

"Hey, what are you doing?" the dude cried. "You'd better slow down." He made a vague threatening motion with the pistol. Instead of following his instructions, Kring stepped a little harder. The car rocketed down the highway at ninety, ninety-five, a hundred miles an hour. It was exhilarating. In the drizzle, the queer darkness, lighted signs whipped by them in blurs of scattered brightness — some white, some blue, traffic lights yellow and green, all scattered on the wet road in front of them and on the windshield in each drop that exploded on the glass. The highway sang and hummed beneath them, the baked pavement now oily and slick from the summer rain. The car was really out of control — just a blur of headlights and taillights and nothing in between — exploding past intersections with insane speed. Only the straightness of the road they were on allowed Kring to maintain even an appearance of control over the vehicle. And this, he realized, gave him control over the weapon pointed at his side. The radio was saying something about chance of showers tonight but was all but drowned out by the car going too fast. Drowned out too was a dance diva trying to sing over the road noise. Kring recognized the song, he thought, but he couldn't be sure. The hitchhiker said nothing but Kring could tell he was terrified. He could almost smell the fear. Kring was charged with electricity. He was wild with quiet excitement and he floored it, taking the last little bit the throttle had to give him. Kring felt the car go a little faster and to him it seemed like a great surge, and it probably felt as great to the hitchhiker. The dude hadn't yet peeked at the speedometer but he knew, had to know they were going dangerously fast. They were four hundred, five hundred yards from the traffic light when it turned yellow. Kring made no move to slow down. They were still a hundred yards away seconds later when it turned red. He made no attempt to do anything other than speed through the stoplight like a bullet. Kring could imagine the guy's face going white as a sheet, and this gave him a secret joy. They were well past the light, which was still red, before either of them realized that there had been no one waiting at the intersection. Then Kring noticed that there were no other cars on the road, and there were no more lights along the highway, just trees on one side, a fence on the other, and another traffic signal a mile away. It had stopped raining and they were through the next light, and then they were on a bridge and Kring ordered the gunman to open his window and toss his piece over the side. This the frightened hijacker did with little hesitation. Kring saw that the wind through the open window at that speed forced the hitchhiker's eyes almost shut and nearly tore off his arm when he extended it out on the next, bigger bridge. Kring began to ease off the gas pedal slowly when the guy pulled his empty hand back into the car. "And put MMR back on," he ordered.

They were still racing when they crested the big bridge moving at ninety-five miles an hour. Below them, two hundred yards ahead, Kring saw the cars from an earlier accident, figures moving in the flashing orange lights. Kring saw one of the figures in the headlight turn its head to them in surprise, but he could see no face.

It was the first time, as far as he could remember, that Kring had ever awakened in a cold sweat. He remembered screaming at the hitchhiker, "IT'S ALL YOUR FAULT!" before bursting awake.

He was startled to be suddenly on the deck of the Cafe, and he was sure he jumped in his seat just then. He glanced around to see if anyone was staring at him, but he was alone in the sun. Victoria, he noticed, had come in to work during his nap, but she had her back turned to him and he hoped he hadn't yelled before he woke. He shook his head to try to clear it, and his racing heartbeat began to slow, but his neck ached from the awkward position in which he had slept.

He strained to pick up his Styrofoam cup that had blown to the ground beneath his chair, and he deposited it in the trash can as he headed for the beach to check the swell. He knew the ocean was flat that morning, but thought it couldn't hurt to check it again anyway. Just to be sure.

Chapter 7

An Evening Session

Kring bobbed chest deep in the Atlantic Ocean, straddling his surf board, weighing it down until just the sharp white tip protruded from the water as the sky drained of brightness around him. Water dripped from his hair into his left eye. A T-shirt clung to his chest, soaked and heavy. He sat patiently, thinking of other things and hoping that Mother Ocean would provide one last wave for him. The island's ten-day flat spell had been broken in weak fashion by two- to three-foot surf. The waves were crumbly and littered with stinging jellyfish, but Kring surfed them anyway. It was a typical summer swell, and now the tide was slowly rising to swallow what was left of the break. Buddy was already on shore. Kring could see him leaning coolly against his board and chatting to a couple of girls. They looked good from where Kring sat, but he was suspicious. They were probably teenagers.

The sky above him was clear. It was the kind of sky he always pictured when he thought of unrushed summer evenings. The moon was already high in the still-blue east, but haze on the western horizon smothered any sunset and the beach grew dark all by itself, it seemed. The houses gradually surrendered their windows and decks to shadows and then became dark grey silhouettes, and Buddy was visible only when he moved. The girls were gone now.

Kring gave up waiting and started to paddle in, but Mother Ocean was generous with him this time and he found himself stroking into a nice little peak. He felt the board gather speed and when he hopped to his feet it dropped down a short slope. He made a quick adjustment and cut into the wall as it formed in front of him. His hips and legs gyrated as if dancing and he waved the board up and down on the face, generated speed, and then punched the lip and snapped down the wall again. The wave disintegrated, as if it were unhappy with the surfer's violence, and Kring dropped to his belly and paddled the last fifty yards.

Buddy greeted him on the sand and Kring asked about the girls. "High school" he was told. "They said you were really good," Buddy added. Kring laughed and shook his head. He knew that to a twenty-three-year-old, high-school girls were dangerous. They were attractive at first glance, and several glances afterwards, and they were everywhere in the summer, but they just got you in trouble. Looking at Buddy's reaction to them, Kring could tell that he had learned that lesson, too, somewhere.

The surfers walked silently up the dune and back through the streets to Kring's garage, where Buddy laid his board on his car racks and strapped it in. He climbed into his Beetle and left without another word. It was Buddy's way. In his apartment Kring threw on some dry clothes and ran his fingers through his wet hair. He went to the refrigerator and pulled out half a hoagie, still wrapped in its oil-stained paper from lunch. He took a monstrous bite and chewed it thoughtlessly, then took another. It took him several seconds to finish it. A few strings of lettuce and a limp onion strip were all that remained. His soul had been fed by a summer swell, unspectacular but satisfying. His hunger was stilled by the sandwich. If he had money, he would be ready to go out and party. But the five dollars he had splurged on the hoagie meant that he couldn't afford to go out. Poverty, it seemed, dictated another night of television. Poverty sucked when there were no waves. He switched on his nine-inch TV set, then ignored it.

Instead he sat on the couch and looked through a surfing magazine. He read the letters from grommets, studied the pictures from Hawaii, glanced at the surfwear ads. He thought again about Rebecca. "How long are you going to live like this?" she had asked him at the party before they spent the night together. *Live like this.* She had made it sound like a bad thing.

"Live like what?" he had asked her.

"Like you live. Devoting your life to surfing."

He had shrugged and never answered her.

Maybe that was the reason he hadn't called her in the weeks since, he thought. Back then waves were plentiful, and she wanted him, and that was enough. The flat spell that followed had done little to change his attitude. *A jobless, poverty-stricken surf bum* she had called him. She was a poetic one, he thought. Well, surfing was full of jobless, poverty-stricken figures. The subculture glorified them; in the magazines, in the movies, surf gypsies were icons. Other surfers aspired to the position Kring now occupied. It's not a big deal, he wanted to tell her. It happens all the time, on many coasts.

But he didn't call her and tell her, and he couldn't explain why he didn't. There was a vague uneasiness there, and it had nothing to do with the way they looked at each other, or the way they had made love, or the way they said goodbye after breakfast. It was something else, something Kring couldn't define, and all he could think of to blame was the slightly disapproving tone he heard in the question, *How long are you going to live like this?* "I'm young," he wanted to say. "There will be waves. I can afford it." That wasn't the answer either. Maybe because, he thought, he had the question wrong.

There was a knock on his door and Kring looked up from the magazine. Lotion pressed her face to the screen from out of the darkness, chasing away a moth and three mosquitoes that had settled there in the light. "You ready to go out, beach child?" she asked playfully as she pulled open the door. Kring put the magazine down and stood to greet her. "I can't afford to go out, Lo," he said. "I'm broke."

"But Lloyd Hubris and the Withoutniks are playing at the Shell," Lotion pleaded. "I need someone to go out with me tonight. I'll pay your cover. Come onnnn."

It was an offer he couldn't pass by. "Hang on while I find a clean shirt."

Lotion stepped into the room and rubbed a mosquito bite on her smooth shoulder. Kring looked up from his search and saw her examine the cold, murky saucepan on the stove that had been last night's dinner. "Just a second," he mumbled as he flipped clothing in the air.

"Have you called Rebecca lately?" Lotion wondered distractedly.

Kring straightened with an orange T-shirt in his hand. "Um, no, not yet. I haven't gotten around to it."

"Been busy, huh?" she suggested in a mildly mocking tone.

"I don't know, I just — it's like, what am I going to say? I can't ask her out, not without any money. She thinks I'm a bum because I don't have a job, and she's got all these rich friends, you know?"

"Bullshit." Lotion looked squarely at him. "Excuses," she said. "I know you, Key. If you were really into this girl, none of this would bother you. You'd be calling her and having her pick you up, take you out, or you'd just go to the beach or something. What's with all this thinking? That's not you."

Kring shrugged. "I don't know. It's not the same as it used to be."

"So you say it was a good night, huh, and pretty good sex?"

"Yeah, it was real good, as a matter of fact."

Lotion hesitated a second, then asked, "But then, what, you felt a letdown in the morning, or what? Like your stomach ached a little?"

"Well, yeah, like I said. And it had nothing to do with how much I drank, or with Rebecca. I mean she was great. Beautiful smile, bought me breakfast, I mean what more could I want, Lo?"

"I don't know, but you do want something more."

Kring nodded.

"Maybe a connection that you didn't try to make," Lotion suggested. "You know, guys always think there is some standard of 'good' that they have to be able to reach in bed. Like it's a competition, like there are certain things you have to be able to do to be proclaimed an official Good Lover. Wrong. Totally wrong."

Kring paid attention even while he shed his T-shirt like a peeling flake of sunburn and made sure that the sleeves of the shirt he'd chosen were right side in. He knew from other conversations they'd had that Lotion knew what she was talking about.

"So you say it was good sex — no, let me correct — 'really good sex.' " she continued, "then in the morning you felt depressed. I think the thing is you shouldn't separate the morning from the night before. They're all part of the same time with her. It's not a performance, it's not like it's just a series of techniques applied properly to the right spot."

"Well, what is it then?" he asked, trying to see what she was getting at as he slipped the shirt on over his arms and head. "You're pretty good on what it isn't."

"Oh, you think if you do this and make her feel something then you deserve praise, you deserve to be bought breakfast or something. But it's not like that. It's nothing that athletic. It's emotions and feelings and the whole experience. You, her, the night, the bed — everything you notice, everything you say. It's all blended together. It's like, I don't know," she said, glancing again at the mess on the stove, "like a warm broth, like a soup — "

"A soup, Lo? You mean, like warm and wet?" Kring interrupted.

"I could get in trouble with this metaphor," Lotion said with a sheepish smile, "but yeah, warm and wet and delicious and murky. Sure. And all the details, the tricks and techniques, they all just flavor it. And the important thing is how the broth tastes when it's done. Do you understand? If it's not real, or at least if it's not good, you'll know it."

Sitting at his kitchen table, Kring stared sideways at his beautiful friend. He turned his smile to the dull surface of the table, shook his head and sighed. "Okay, so, how do you do that blending that turns an ordinary encounter into a wonderful flavorful soup, Lo?"

"That, my dear, is a secret that takes years, and lots of practice, to learn."

"Of course."

"But it begins with how you see. You can either see just the sex, just the body parts and the sweat, or you can see the sparkle, the magnetic field that surrounds two people. That's where it starts."

"Lotion, you romantic chick you."

She laughed. "But it's more than romance, boy. Because when you can see the magnetic field, when you are aware of the magic, you can shape it. You can change it. That's when it gets really fun. You don't know what I'm talking about, do you?"

"Magnetic field, huh?"

"Kind of. Yeah. Exactly right."

"Hmm ... so that's the secret, you say." Kring absently reached to grab his wallet from the table and opened it. "Well, I got five bucks," he said. "I can afford a beer at the Shell tonight. Tomorrow will take care of itself." He stood and wedged the wallet into his shorts pocket. "I got friends. I got options. I got change hidden deep in the folds of my couch."

"Sure you do," Lotion said. "Let's go."

Kring followed Lotion out to her car and climbed in with a groan, his surfing muscles, sore from unaccustomed use. Lotion backed the car out onto Bay Terrace and punched a button on her tape player. Out popped a cassette. "Hey, could you dig *Jimmy Buffett's Greatest Hits* out of my tape box? So when was the last time you saw Lloyd and the band?" Lotion asked as Kring searched through her tapes in the dim flashes of light from the street lamps.

"Maybe three or four weeks ago," he said. "At the Gateway. Lloyd wasn't there, though. I don't think he'll be there tonight, either. Ricky told me they busted Lloyd for making an unauthorized copy of some CD. I think it was Guns N' Roses. Anyway, he's trying to claim entrapment, like some undercover cop gave him a blank and asked him to make the tape for him. He's in Baltimore talking to a lawyer who specializes in these cases."

"That Lloyd is a character, isn't he? Always in some kind of fix. It's a wonder that he can keep his band together."

"Yeah."

"So how were the waves today?"

"Pretty small. Buddy was out with me and I got a couple of decent rides. But it wasn't anything great."

They were silent for a few minutes until Lotion asked, "Why doesn't he ever go out with us? Buddy, I mean."

"He doesn't have ID."

"He's of age, isn't he? I mean, he's over twenty-one."

"Yeah, I think so. I think he's like twenty-three. But he has no ID to prove it. You know he doesn't have a driver's license, but he doesn't have anything else, either."

"Not even a birth certificate?"

"No. He told me his parents a few years ago were put into that federal witness protection program, you know, given new identities and all. During the transition Buddy just split. Took off. He couldn't use his old name, and he wasn't around long enough for them to give him a new one. Not many people know that, Lo."

"Wow. That's kind of strange."

"Yeah, it's weird. I don't really know what his game is. He never talks about it. Never talks about anything. But I don't know whether he's like rejecting the government's attempt to redefine him, or if he just wants to create his own story, you know?" Kring fell silent for a minute. "I think that's cool, to live that way," he said finally.

Eight minutes later they arrived at the Seashell Club. They were a little early for the first set. Lotion paid their cover and Kring had finished the only drink he could afford before the band came on. Lotion bought him another. And Kring was right, when the Withoutniks took the stage, Lloyd Hubris was absent.

Chapter 8

Tropical Storm Way Offshore

Kring stirred the next morning before sunrise as if an alarm had signaled the hour and minute. He had been asleep less than four hours, but the possibility of waves flashed in his mind as it always did, and he wasted little time in his surface into alertness. He swung his legs off the sofa and pulled a pair of boardshorts over them. When he stood and stretched, he noticed a sleeping figure on the floor, blocking the door to the closet-sized bathroom in the back of the small garage. Kring checked the figure. It was Spill. Probably passed out after a night at Joe Pops or the Gateway, couldn't make it home, Kring figured. He left him there, with a wetsuit for a pillow, and climbed in Spill's old Volkswagen camper bus parked outside. He drove it to check the waves two and a half blocks away.

This was the first motor vehicle he had driven since his court date in April when they suspended his license, and it gave him a little thrill to be behind the wheel again, and illegally. The morning felt alive to him, vibrant and fresh. As he rolled off in the little bus toward the ocean, Kring pushed in the tape that was sitting in the player and music, manic and nearly tuneless, filled the space of the van and drifted out its open windows. "What the hell is this?" he wondered aloud, and he punched the eject button as the vehicle stumbled up the street with its characteristic wheeze. The cassette slid out into his fingers and the label said "Red Hot Chili Peppers." Why not? he figured and shoved the tape back in the slot. Music flooded the atmosphere again.

Kring braked the van when he came to the empty Boulevard, casually guided the vehicle across it, and turned down the access lane. Up Twentieth Street he went, alongside Joe Pops Shore Bar to check the waves from the end of the street.

"Oh yesss," Kring whispered when he rolled the bus up to the vehicle access at the top of the dune and saw the waves. Clean, chest-high waves gathered toward him from beneath the cloud-choked sky. The sun was just peeking over the horizon, waves breaking all up and down the beach, offering smooth walls and gentle drops. This is a very good swell, he thought. And it may be here for a couple of days.

As long as I've got a vehicle, he figured, feeling a rebellious power in his hands, I might as well check out other spots before I paddle out. Some place else might be breaking bigger. The Chili Peppers accompanied him on his journey as he made stops at Thirty-first, Forty-sixth and Seventy-ninth streets, anywhere there was a vehicle access to the beach, before swinging north again to check behind the Fishery. All of the breaks looked inviting; none stood out from the others. So he headed down the Boulevard to pick up his board, set to paddle out at Joe Pops.

When he turned down the sidestreet, Kring noticed a looseness in the van's ride, a wobble that he had to correct with the wheel. The van dragged when he tried to accelerate and Kring felt like he had to persuade the little vehicle to move. Halfway down the block, when he swerved to avoid a darting cat, the van didn't recover like Kring expected and he sideswiped a plastic garbage can that was sitting mostly in the street. Clamshells scattered on the pavement. When Kring stopped the van and got out to pick up the spilled garbage, he noticed the vehicle's right rear tire was soft, almost flat. "Bummer," he said. "I hope I didn't do that." He climbed back in the driver's seat and guided the wounded little bus back to his driveway, where it rolled to a peaceful stop.

As he was getting out of the van, Buddy's little Bug, wearing a surfboard like a baseball cap, whipped around the street corner and came scooting toward him. It slid on the sand in the street when Buddy braked hard. "You see the waves?" came the yell from the driver's seat.

"Yeah. I'm heading up right here. You ready?"

"No, no, man. Not here. Load your board up and let's go to Cedars. It's twice as big as here. I was just up there. There's hardly anyone out. It's sweet-sweet-sweet."

Kring's urgency cracked his voice as he burst out, "Yes! Let's go! Let me grab my board and I'm with you."

He shoved through the door of the garage, banging it against his dented refrigerator, and he slapped the van keys on the table. He grabbed his board from the corner of the vaguely sunlit room and looked with pity at Spill, passed out in the same position as Kring had left him. He went over to the body and rolled it slightly with his foot. "Dude," he said toward Spill's ear. "Dude, your van has a flat tire. It's up the street. Keys are on the table. Gotta run, there's a swell."

Spill didn't really groan in reply, but he did make some sort of noise, muffled and unconscious, and that was enough to satisfy Kring as he headed out the door, pulse racing, impatient to greet the overhead waves that were rolling in that very minute — and had been all morning! — up the island in Harvey Cedars.

The empty lineup that Buddy promised had long vanished. With the sunlight came the first of the morning surfers, and by the time Kring and his partner arrived at the beach, familiar water-bug figures were sprinkled across the surface of the water. But Buddy had been right about the waves. The oceanscape was spectacular — everywhere creased and folded over by the best Kring had seen all year. He watched one figure in the water paddle for an approaching swell. The distant surfer dropped down the face into it as it exploded behind him and he rode and carved and slashed with white water for sixty, seventy yards. The surfer's whoop just before he was swallowed told Kring all he needed to know. Goose bumps raised all over his flesh. Must be the morning chill, he thought as he glanced at his bare arms. But he knew it was the thrill, the anticipation of riding great waves, waves that rolled in right now at his feet. The swells charged, one on top of another, and then the next right behind, charged as if concerned that they would not have enough time for all to reach shore.

"Man, even if I hadn't lost my job, I'd have to quit it for this swell anyway," he said to Buddy as they jogged to the water.

"Anyone who wouldn't is an asshole," Buddy declared with the certainty of the self-employed clammer.

For an early weekday morning the water was crowded, but this wasn't an ordinary weekday. There was a spirit Kring sensed among the crowd, a drunken, generous spirit that floated like mist in the sunlight, passed from surfer to surfer. He could feel it as he paddled out through advancing lines of whitewater. Kring and Buddy were provisional locals, having spent a winter here, but they didn't surf Harvey Cedars often. Maybe once or twice a month at most, and they knew only a handful of guys who were out there. But there were no hassles for waves, no sharp remarks. As far as Kring could see, everyone was respecting wave rights, and he heard three different hoots of approval when he dropped into his first thrilling, blue-green wave. The abundance of the ocean today was a long-dreamt-of wealth these waveriders were willing to squander, that they could not keep for themselves. Kring could taste it when he surfaced after his first wave, it was the combustible mixture of adrenaline and seawater, and it coursed through his veins, flooded him more quickly, more powerfully than any emotion, any drug, even orgasm. He felt the ride over again as he floated head out of water and drew his board back to him, pulling on its leash. The second time it wasn't his mind that was reliving the rush and rhythm. It was the muscles of his back, where its image was burned into the tissue by the forces of speed and gravity and the pulse of some far-off Atlantic storm. The fibers of muscle would not let go the delicious tension, the floating, flying momentum, the lyrical up-and-down glide of speed. His paddling motion had merged with the wave and dropped him down its face. He'd popped to his feet and cut a path to his right, so that his back was against a wall rushing and forming and smoothly curving. It was a rocket-fast ride, it was fluent and long, and over his shoulder Kring could see the lip of the wave spit above his head. When he guided his board to a path higher on the face, near the lip, he stood triumphantly over it and felt like he had hit a bubble of pure oxygen in the atmosphere and carried it with him for an instant. Then the ski down the short green slope invested him with so much speed that it seemed like his ears were pinned back against his skull by the force of the wind. He thought that maybe he let out an involuntary "Yeeooou!" just before the lip dumped him, but he wasn't sure.

He paddled back outside furiously, not so much to avoid getting caught under a succession of rollers; it was mostly because he had so much energy that he had to vent it through some channel. His arms seemed most convenient, paddling the best means.

He met Buddy, paddling from the other direction, outside the breakers. "What a wave! Buddy yelled breathlessly.

"Which wave was that?"

"The same one you took right, I went left and it was just intense. Big and fast. Really tasty. I didn't know Jersey could get like this!"

A blond guy with a brown beard floated by on his board and said, "Don't happen often. Live it up while you can, dude." He sat up just beyond them and stared out to sea.

All around them the ocean rose and fell in restless, watery hills that moved toward shore as if drawn by some powerful magnet — mounds of seawater, huge and insistent, that lifted Kring and Buddy and everyone out there higher than a third-floor deck and dropped them gently seconds later, mounts that pulsed like the slowed bloodstream of a sleeping giant. Kring was used to the feeling and sight of waves all around him, but this was beyond ordinary. Behind the waves as they swept past him to the beach the surface was calm. The backs of these swells were glassy and lulling, not fearsome, not threatening. But they were five, six, sometimes seven feet higher than the surface they passed through and left behind. The faces as the waves gathered themselves up to break were bigger still. Nothing had changed, really, except the scale. Kring suddenly felt very small, and the world was different now than when he had stepped from the sand into the ankle-deep swirling water a little after sunrise. He was different. He felt grateful to be here, in this extraordinary place, this extraordinary moment, so unlike standing on solid earth. He was feeding on this energy, feeding on the pure stoke. He smiled, not because he was happy exactly, just because there was nothing else for his body to do. He caught another wave, a swift one with a face taller than he was and he rode it beautifully, like he always dreamed he would ride it. Positioning. Direction. It felt right. He knew just what to do, just when to do it and how to make it happen. He felt plugged into the ocean like never before.

"Dude, you're hoggin it! You're insane!" Buddy yelled at him after another wave that he had ridden almost to the beach and another paddle back out that left him exhausted. Kring took the compliment with a weary smile.

"It's so easy to ride these waves, man," he said between waves. "So easy to ride *good* waves. Some days you're just on it, you know?"

Buddy nodded and grinned.

Between their rides the surfers were occupied with a struggle against the current to maintain position, and an occasional scramble to escape a threatening wall. It was those moments that gave Kring the most vivid perception of these waves. For it was then, as he clawed for the precarious lip above him, and reached it, and looked back, that he saw the full sweep and geometry of the breaking wave, just for an instant as it rolled on past him. The power he saw there scared him.

Thirty yards away Kring recognized a surfer paddling for a wave like a furious, buzzing winged insect. It was Kelly, who owned the surf shop Kring used. The guy dropped into a steep, dark cavern wall, and Buddy and Kring both hooted as he made his bottom turn and straightened out along the line.

As the wave swept past them and Kelly disappeared from their sight, Buddy squinted at the sun and said, "Let's take the next wave in and get something to eat. It's almost eleven."

The introduction of clock time gave Kring's head a spin. It came out of nowhere and lent some perspective to this day. It turned it back into morning, the morning that they had driven up here and paddled out, and framed the experience in a sad way. Until now Kring had been surfing in another day, listed on no calendar, with no clock, a day fragile and of unspeakable beauty. Now that beauty, while not destroyed, was no longer infinite, not the same transcendent moment he had just lived. That moment was gone. Now he was hungry. Maybe breakfast would be good. "Okay, next wave."

"Did you see those couple of guys taking pictures on the beach?" Kring asked Buddy as they worked on their sandwiches and cokes at Cafe Mundo's, a block from the beach in Harvey Cedars.

"Yeah, some dude told me there were a couple of pros in the water. I think he said Dale Allewegen was one of 'em, guys who are on the island, like just for this swell."

"Yeah, right," Kring snorted.

A guy with shoulder-length hair and a scab on his chin leaned over from the counter and said, "No, dude, it's true. I was at a party that he was at last night. Allewegen is here, man. He's friends with one of the Aussies who guard for the Township. Last night he was *wasted*."

"So what's he doing on LBI?"

"He's crashing at this pad in Surf City where the Aussies are staying. He was on some promo tour for RedNightSky Surfwear or something, I don't know."

"Was he out there this morning?"

"I didn't see him. They probably went out in North Beach. They don't have to worry about the pigs there."

"Why not? Aren't there guards in North Beach?" Kring asked.

"They're pretty laid back about surfing, especially on days like this. And his friend guards there. They do what they want on that beach."

"But he didn't come here to surf, did he? I mean, who woulda thought we'd get a swell like this?"

"Musta been tracking that tropical storm as it came up. It's now like four hundred miles straight off, and stalled, dude. We're gonna have these waves for a while, brah."

Buddy nodded. "Tropical storm. I knew it had to be something like that."

Kring just chewed his cheese steak and nodded with Buddy.

"So," Buddy continued, "If these pros are in North Beach, why are the photogs here in Cedars?"

"Shit. Those guys, they're locals, man. Out here every swell. They don't care about pros or shots for the magazine, they just wanna shoot their friends. By the way, brah," he said to Kring, "I saw you out there.

You were rippin' it up. I bet they got some outrageous shots of you."

Kring looked surprised. "Me?" he said. "Ah, I had a couple of really good waves, but everyone was getting good waves today. It was so easy."

"Yeah, dude, but you were all over, carvin' and stylin'. I heard one guy on the beach talkin' about that frontside off-the-lip you cut on that one overhead screamer. Outrageous."

"I told you, dude," Buddy said, his attention drawn to his bare feet, shuffling on the checkered tile floor, "you were owning those waves. All those days of nothing to do but surf have made a difference, I guess."

Kring laughed. "Hey, here's to unemployment." They touched paper cups and drank their toast of Pepsi. "Where do you wanna go out? Up here again?"

"I don't know how the guards are here in Cedars. They were cool this morning, but let's go to the surfing beach in Ship Bottom."

Kring expected the lineup at the end of Thirtieth Street to be crowded, but only seven guys had been able to make it out through the big surf for the midday session. They were all surfers Kring knew, guys who either lived on the island and surfed all year, or who would drive down in February for a good swell. The sand, in contrast, was covered with bodies and surfboards that would not find their way out among the big ones today. The whole scene was perfumed by the mock-tropical smell of sunscreen. As he and Buddy trudged across the sand, Kring greeted a couple of grommets that he knew, P. J. and Rich, both about sixteen, both real surfriders, not just window surfers. "Couldn't make it out or what?" he asked.

"Aw, it's a killer paddle, brah," P. J. said, shaking his head. "We tried twice already."

"Gonna give it another shot? You gotta. Look at those waves."

"Yeah, I'll get out there, I just gotta get my strength back," P. J. said. Kring saw him hiding his fear behind determination.

"See ya out there, dude," Kring said as he and Buddy entered the swirling shorebreak. They paddled through it and tasted the struggle that had defeated P. J. and Rich and so many others who were on the beach now, watching. The swell was unrelenting and stronger now than it had been earlier, and Kring felt they only made progress when the ocean ignored them for a minute here and there. It took them twenty-five minutes to get outside, and when they made it they sat up with relief and rested for fifteen more.

"Seems bigger than this morning," Buddy said as they sat in the churning water, panting.

"Tough paddle," was all Kring replied.

But they were out there again, and again Kring rode the waves with his new-found mastery. Three or four waves, big ones, beautiful waves Kring rode without putting a foot wrong and Buddy insisted, "You're the best one out here, dude. You're better than Jersey Jack. I want to know what the hell happened to you. You on some good drugs? Make a deal with Huey the wave god? You got it wired."

"Jersey Jack? Dorner? Isn't he the guy who took fourth in the East Coast last year?"

"Yeah, but he's still riding like he's on small waves. He backs off if it's too big a drop. He never woulda taken the one that you just scored."

"Which one?'

"That last one, the double overhead that had you screaming. You got barreled on that, didn't you?"

Kring instantly relived the ride. "Yeah," he said as a smile took over his face. "This is so much FUN!" he yelled to the sky.

As in the morning, Kring lost himself in the self-contained world of the waves almost as soon as he entered it, and by the time his physical exhaustion began to fray the edges of that world, to unsettle his footwork on his board, the lifeguards had left the beach and the other seven surfers had gone home. Three more had at last made it out, including P. J. and Rich. Kring was proud of them. He knew it was important to them to make it out and surf on a day like today, at least sample these waves. He knew they would stay until dark.

Buddy was already on his way in. Kring watched him paddle toward the beach and decided to follow. "Ten hours is enough for me. It's all yours, dudes. Treat it right," he said as he pushed off to catch an inside wave to the sand.

"Catch ya later. Rip it up, Kring," P. J. yelled after him.

Buddy and Kring arrived at the garage a little before sunset. They struggled out of the little car and plodded inside to crack open a couple of beers. The pop ring of the can seemed especially stubborn to Kring's pruned, water-softened fingers. He collapsed on his couch, Buddy on a ratty easy chair. Kring barely noted that Spill was no longer passed out on the floor from the morning.

Kring lay there in the silent, dim glow from his tiny television set and bathed himself in the adrenaline high, the warmth of sore muscles. The waves he had seen and the places he had put himself rushed through his mind again, and he was there. He blinked and was back in the room, darker now. Buddy was hidden, just a part of the chair in which he sat.

"Do you really think that the number twelve pro surfer was on the same waves as we were?" he asked Buddy.

"Shit, that's just one of those rumors that no one realizes is too stupid to be true. So they just wonder about it. I mean, what would a pro surfer be doing on LBI in the summer?"

"Yeah," Kring agreed, "but it would be cool to surf with him on our home break, wouldn't it? To see how good he really is. To see how good we really are."

A muffled sound emerged from the slumping Buddy, just an indistinct grunt, nothing more, and Kring wondered some more what it would be like to surf with one of the top pros on the planet. To surf flawless waves alongside such talent, then just walk home afterwards. He closed his eyes while he imagined it.

Chapter 9

The Beach Minstrel Arrives

A 7-Eleven store sat where the lone bridge to the island emptied itself of arriving cars. The convenience store's parking lot swallowed up the overflow, and the brick-and-glass structure spat out convenience customers every couple of minutes. A clutch of young surfers huddled near the side of the building, eating chili dogs and sucking down Slurpees. Just off the bridge, a red Dodge pickup rolled into the parking lot under a midday sun and bounced as it met the curb in front of the store. Out of the passenger door dropped two Reeboked feet, a nickel and two dimes. The twenty-five-year-old man who belonged to the feet ignored the coins as they rang out in a pathetic little chorus on the pavement. He bent to grab his backpack from the floor of the cab. An empty wine bottle with his spittle still drying on the neck rolled out and fell with a clink at his feet. He stared blankly for a second at the delicate green bottle, then grinned and leaned over to pick it up as he swung closed the door of the truck. "Thanks for the ride, Ray," he yelled as he lifted his duffel bag and guitar case from the truck bed.

"No problem, son," the driver replied. "Hope ya find your friend here. What'd you say your name was? Morrie? I ever tell you I had a cat named Morrie once? Got run over by a truck."

Maury, squinting in the heat of the parking lot, thought, Only told me seven times, dude. Instead he replied simply, "Yeah, I think you did tell me, Ray," as he surveyed the beach town in which he found himself, a place so different from what he was used to. He felt maybe he really was changing things like he hoped. "Well, I better try to find my buddy. Thanks again, man, and take care."

Ray nodded. The red truck coughed out a cloud of exhaust and backed away from the sidewalk. It rolled with an unsteady growl toward the Boulevard with Ray's hand hung in parting salute, framed in the rear window. Maury spun around to face the store as a barefoot surfer leaned his board against the wall, then pushed his way through the glass doors. Maury stood alone in front of the window and stared at the alien surfboard. He felt the weight of his big olive-green bag slung over one shoulder, his guitar case and empty wine bottle in the other hand. His backpack sat at his feet. He was half-drunk and confused and sweating in the Jersey shore humidity. Beginning a new life. Scared of the unknown. Startled when the surfer burst violently out of the store almost as soon as he entered it. "Need shoes," the surfer spat. "You got it wrong, dude. I don't need shoes, assholes, I don't NEED to go in your store!" The group of younger surfers had migrated to the plastic garbage can and they buzzed among themselves in their strange tongue when the other picked up his board and strode past them. Maury tried to pick up what they were saying.

"Hey, brah, that was that guy Kring. He's really hot. Saw him ripping up that big swell yesterday at Thirty-first Street. I was out there with him. He was like in hyperdrive, man. Like way out of control."

"Yeah, I hear he's gonna go pro. Quiksilver might get him to ride. Exclusive package, that's the word."

"Cool. Like, out-of-the-boat, yah?"

Maury quit eavesdropping when he realized that their talk was making his head spin faster than the wine and the heat had, and he felt a flush of loneliness settle in his gut, a sense of loss that pissed him off.

Ray Tolbin's red pickup had been Maury's passage out of his uninspired and too conventional life in the city and the suburbs. It carried him away from Peabody and Droog Advertising, away from his sleek, new American car and its payments, his apartment with the insufferable blood-red carpeting — the suffocating sameness of his life and the other lives lived out around him in the Cherry Hill apartment complex and the Philadelphia office. He told the whole story to Ray on the ride down, as they passed through the pygmy pines of Burlington County, across the flat, hot coastal plain of New Jersey. He slugged wine at intervals for courage, from a bottle he found unopened in his empty apartment that morning. "My fiancée left me two months ago, Ray," he said as they wheeled around one of the traffic circles that lay between them and the coast. "Left me for a drummer, man. A fucking drummer in a jazz band. Not even rock and roll. Can you believe that?"

"That's rough, that is," Ray said in shallow sympathy over the talk radio mumbling from the dashboard. He seized the chance to tell a story of his own. "Let me tell ya, when my wife left me when I got back from Nam...." He paused to spit some tobacco juice out the window. Maury soothed his dry throat with a sip of the wine, turned to the woods they were passing, and forgot to listen to Ray's story.

When he heard Ray's voice pattern indicate that the story was over, Maury resumed his own tale of woe, knowing full well that Ray wasn't listening to him, either. "Yeah, so I figure I'll go down to the shore, hang out for a while, try to write some songs, you know. Live in some artists colony or something. I got a buddy down there, on Ninth Street in Beach Haven. Fuck all this button-down shit, I say. I'll live on bread and water like a sea gull and sleep in the sand," Maury rhapsodized, making a mental note to use the words as lyrics someday. At the same time he edited out the soundtrack of his epic trip, for in Ray Tolbin's truck, the background music was the drone of an excitable talk show host with deliberately incorrect political views.

Maury had seen this trip many times in his mind in the past two months, and always playing in the background he heard "Born To Be Wild." Oh, sometimes it was "Hand Me Down World" or "Backstreets" by Springsteen, or some other anthem of youth, hope and rebellion. Talk radio didn't fit the script Maury was writing. Not a phlegmatic voice preaching distrust and firearms. That would be edited out when Maury went to recall the legend that he was creating right now. The rest of this story would fit as is, he decided. Catching a ride to freedom with a Vietnam vet ... each telling his story ... getting drunk on the way to the beach ... the way his spirit soared as the truck crested the big bridge to the island and he saw spread out like a long buffet table, the landscape of open sky, rippling blue and silver bay, and thin, stubbled island sandwiched in between. All of that would fit his screenplay. The music, of course, he would write that, that would come later, the songs that would change his generation.

And now, standing alone in a convenience store parking lot, surrounded by day-trippers and surf stars, this, too, belonged, he decided. He still felt the ache of alienation in his belly, but it had gained a flavor, the flavor of something that took the edge off the pain: an excitement, an adrenal rush of adventure that must carry him through, he realized, until he got settled here, until he found his niche. At least until he found his buddy. George was somewhere on Ninth Street, which looked like it must be right near here. The 7-Eleven was on Twelfth.

It looked like the beach was pretty near here, too, and Maury decided finding George could wait. It was the beach, after all, that had drawn him here, the ocean and the freedom it represented. Bare feet, no clock, horizon far distant across the water — these things Maury wanted to make parts of his life. At twenty-five, he believed he had learned a thing or two about making his life work, and telling himself stories was not the way to go. "I have to live my life for real," he had decided late one lonely night two weeks ago. "I've got to follow my heart."

He picked his backpack off the cement and dropped the bottle in the trash. Across his path strode a summer girl who looked like she was wearing nothing but a long T-shirt. He followed her to the beach and admired that teenage body as he struggled up the block with his life's accumulation of stuff. His burden wore him out by the time he was half-way up the street, and, breathing hard, he dropped his bags, sat on his guitar case and watched the shapely little vision, long shiny hair and beautiful ass, disappear over the top of the dune.

He rested and checked out his situation. Just ahead of him, between where he sat and where the girl had vanished, was an abandoned Volkswagen camper van. The right rear tire was flat. The back window glass was gone, and the curtains hung out of the opening, waiting for a breeze to stir them. The adventurous surge flashed over Maury again and he hopped to his feet, grabbed the damp handles of his baggage with his sweating hands and humped it up to the side door of the van. The door was stiff but yielded with a groan when Maury put most of his weight behind it. He lifted his gear and set it on the floor of the camper, on a carpet of yellowed newspaper. He took off his shirt and draped it over the pile, and when he tossed his shoes on top they rolled over to the other side.

Maury felt much lighter as he forced the door shut again, and he almost flew the remaining yards to the sand. At the top of the dune he stopped and drank in the scene: dozens of people scattered across the sand, the screams and motion of children in the rough water, the shrill whistle of the lifeguard. The hazy sky stretched out over what looked to him like huge waves, with surfers riding them. It all stretched out for-ever before him.

Maury raced down the sand and charged into the ocean and washed the sweat and the stink of his journey off his body. He splashed like a sparrow in a puddle and laughed to the sky with the two little children playing near him in the hip-deep water. He strolled contentedly from the surf and sat down on the warm, soft sand. Maybe I'll work on a tan, he thought.

His chest was dry and he was almost asleep when from behind him he heard a deep voice ask, "Can I see your beach badge, please?" It hurt to open his eyes and face the sun, but there he saw a slender boy, maybe college age, poised over him with a small satchel in his hand. "My what?" Maury asked.

"Your beach badge. You must have a badge in Ship Bottom."

"What about Beach Haven?"

"I think you need one there too, but this is Ship Bottom, sir, and you need a Ship Bottom badge."

"I thought I was in Beach Haven. You mean this isn't Ninth Street here?"

"Yeah, it's Ninth Street."

"Then isn't this Beach Haven?"

"No, that's a completely different town, like seven miles south of here. Um, I'm afraid you'll either have to buy a Ship Bottom beach badge or leave the beach, sir. You don't have any weapons on you, do you?"

Maury looked at the guy and shook his head in disgust. "What a weirdo," he said under his breath. The weirdo didn't hear him. Maury stood up and wiped off the sand that clung to his legs and his still-wet shorts. The weirdo impatiently reviewed his daily sales figures while he waited for Maury to move. "I'm going," Maury said. "Shit. Seven fucking miles." He made his way up the beach, defeated. His dreams of raw freedom and the land as his home were trashed. "Jesus, you have to pay to go on the beach," he fumed. "They probably have fucking vagrancy laws too."

He reached the top of the dune and saw immediately that the abandoned van with all his stuff was gone.

"Oh shit," Maury said aloud.

He walked slowly toward and stared at the empty parking space where the van had been. The sand was sculpted where the flat tire had sat, sculpted into an odd-shaped bowl. A small blue Honda rolled up to take the spot. Maury still stared. The couple who got out of the Honda saw Maury staring, and they glanced nervously around them. "Oh shit," he said again. The couple got back in their car and left.

Kring strode across the white sand with a big paper cup in his hand, to where Buddy shared a blanket with Bev, a happy blond girl from North Bergen. Bev's friend Maria, darker and more sullen, sat in a beach chair with her nose buried in a thick paperback. Buddy had met Bev and Maria just two hours earlier after surfing dawn patrol with Kring. They had been walking the beach when he emerged from the water.

Bev smiled brightly as Kring approached. "Hi, King," she bubbled.

"What took you so long?" Buddy called. From her chair, Maria said nothing, just sighed loudly. She had a boyfriend in Lodi, Kring had learned, and he was pretty sure that was the source of her attitude.

"Assholes at 7-Eleven wouldn't serve me unless I wore shoes," Kring grumbled. "I had to walk like five blocks to that drive-in that has all those little chicklets working there, just to get a Coke."

Bev said, "Can I have a sip?"

Kring looked down at his cup. "Yeah, well I figured since I was at this drive-in, I'd get a milkshake instead. Here. You can finish it. Chocolate." He handed it to Bev with a smile. "Where's Spill?" he asked.

"He left," Buddy said. "Said he was going to go boogie boarding in Spray."

"He won't."

"Why not, King?"

"He's just talk when it comes to surf, especially surf like this. You'd think a lifeguard would ... no, maybe you wouldn't."

Buddy gave Bev a little shove. "Hey, why you call him 'King'? I told you that's not his name."

"It's short for 'Surf King.' " She looked at Kring. "Your real name is weird. It's too hard to pronounce."

Buddy kidded her, "Your mouth is used to that 'Nawth Jaerzy' accent. You can't get your lips to make the proper sounds."

Bev let out an unconvincing gasp. "And I bet you'd just love to help me get my lips around it, wouldn't you?" She pounded him lightly with her fists.

Buddy grabbed Bev's shoulders and ducked his head to avoid her pretend punches. Kring laughed. Maria read her novel on the other side of the blanket, barely glancing up through her sunglasses. Kring was aware that Bev was more attracted to him than to Buddy, and she was cute. But even while he kneeled in the sand and watched the waves, Buddy was drawing her to himself. Big deal, Kring thought with a mental shrug. For some reason it didn't matter. He wasn't going to chase a disposable summer chick, wasn't going to get in a tug-of-war over her. Especially in the middle of an all-time swell.

He picked up his board and headed for the water. "Keep an eye on these girls, dude," he shouted over his shoulder, "I'm going surfing."

Buddy looked up from wrestling with Bev and said with a laugh, "I'll be out there in a bit."

Maury stood in the sun, repeating "shit" six or seven times at two minute intervals. At last he woke up. Hey, he said to himself. That van has a flat tire. It can't make it far. Maybe I can hunt it down. He marched down the Boulevard, to a One Way sign pointing north. He looked that way, then the other. Maury thought, was sure he saw, at a stoplight a few blocks down, a brown VW bus limp from a side street on one flat tire and disappear into the Boulevard's flowing sea of traffic. He set off in that direction.

He hiked down the Boulevard amid the scattered collage of music from cars with open windows. His sense of alienation grew deeper with each Chinese restaurant he passed, each pizza place. Bike riders whipped past him, surfers crossed his path. Boats rumbled by on trailers. Then the street widened in front of him, to twice its size. He followed the bending beach town sidewalk, and the whole time he tried to realize that he was no more than a hundred yards from the Atlantic. As he stumbled and searched, he worked on imagining that he could turn this adventure into a song someday, but he was too panicked, too hot, too disoriented to hear any song in his head just now.

Then he saw the van.

It was parked against the curb on a corner in front of a grocery store. It faced the wrong way, against the traffic. As Maury got closer, he could see the flat tire. The curtains still hung out the broken back window.

Maury peered in the window behind the driver's seat. His pile of possessions was still there on the yellowed, newspaper floor. He braved the traffic to slink around to the other side of the van, tried to jerk the side door open. It would not budge. He jerked on it twice more. No effect. He moved to the passenger door, stuck his head in the window to check things out. A face intent and covered with lots of hair and sunglasses glared back at him from the opposite window.

"Dude, you better be ready to make an offer on this fine machine," the face said as a hand slowly brushed aside much of the hair. "'Cause otherwise what the fuck are you doing trying to break into my van?"

Maury moved back a step or two, his hands up. "I- I'm —" he began. A Jeep roared by within inches of his back, blaring its horn as it passed. He ducked and hurried around to the front of the van.

"I'm sorry," he began. "This is gonna sound weird but I just hitchhiked down here from Philly and I went up to the beach and I dumped all my stuff, my guitar case and clothes, in this van because I thought it was abandoned on the street and you must've left while I was at the beach and so all my stuff's in here and I was just gonna get it back and that's all, you know?"

The owner held up his hand. "You're full of shit," he said.

"No really, my stuff's in here. I can identify it and everything."

The owner cast a glance behind the seats. "Holy shit, you may be

82

right, dude. There is an unfamiliar lump of stuff on my floor. But what makes you think it's yours? And what made you think this vehicle was abandoned?"

"Well, the window was broken and there's so much rust and the flat tire and all."

"What flat tire?"

"You didn't know your tire was flat? This one back here. How the hell did you drive it over here?" Maury said as he dragged the owner to the rear of the van.

"It's been driving like shit for the last two days. I thought my transmission was going or something. Holy shit," he said when he saw the tire. He looked right at Maury. "Hey, dude, you can have your stuff back if you help me change this."

"I'll help you if you give me a ride to Beach Haven."

"Cool," the driver said as he lifted the rear hatch and dug for the spare tire. He dragged the wheel out and flopped it on the ground. "Now you gotta take this down to that gas station down there and get some air in it." He pointed down the Boulevard to a station Maury couldn't see.

"Are you serious?"

"Hey, you want your stuff back. You want a ride."

The station was only five or six blocks back the way he came, but Maury felt ridiculous carrying a Volkswagen wheel down the street in the sun, and he felt foolish rolling it back when it had been pumped up hard. Sweat dampened his hair, and the other guy had the flat off the hub when Maury returned. He suggested that Maury make the same trip with the other tire. He backed off when Maury firmly replied, "Fuck you."

The job done, they climbed in the van and as they sat waiting for a break in the traffic so they could spring from the wrong curb, cross three lanes and head south to Beach Haven, the other guy looked over from the driver's seat and said, "By the way, what's your name, dude?"

"Maury."

"You're not a local."

"You can tell?"

The driver nodded.

"You're right, I'm not a local. I came down here to get away. Start a new life, man. I want to join an artists colony and write songs."

"Cool. My name's Spill." He held out his hand toward Maury but before they could grasp and greet each other, their break came and Spill let the clutch out with a jerk. The little engine almost stalled and Spill had to gun it to avoid being plowed into by a phone company truck.

"Yeah, she's riding a whole lot better now than she did this morning. That tire change did the trick," Spill said as the van buzzed its way down the island's main strip. "Where you going in Beach Haven?"

"This guy I know is renting a place for the summer with a bunch of his friends. I figure I'll stay with him for a day or two until I can decide which artists colony I want to join."

"Artists colony? What artists colonies do you know of?"

"Well, none really in particular. I'll just check 'em all out. There must be a bunch here — I mean, it's an island, right? There's always artists colonies in places like this."

"I know of this place up in Loveladies that has ceramics classes and piano recitals and stuff, but I don't know of anything else. I don't hang out in the art scene. Hey, how much does it cost to live in one of those places? You don't look like you've got a ton of cash."

"They're usually like communal and you just pitch in like your share of the rent and groceries and do dishes and cook dinner like once a week and chop wood for the fireplace and the rest of the time just work on your art. You know, write songs. Or paint or sculpt or write poetry. It's pretty cool, pretty anti-establishment. And the parties — really cool," Maury concluded with a knowing nod.

Spill's face broke into a devilish grin. "Cause I've been thinking of moving out of my house while my parents are down. You know what?" he said. "Maybe I'll join with ya. Sounds like a blast."

"That be cool," Maury said uneasily. He didn't want to encourage this beach bum but he needed the ride. Maybe if he just played along this guy would forget about it once they got to where Maury was going. He could just picture showing up at an established retreat house for a bunch of serious, committed artists with this beachnik alongside him.

They found the house that Maury sought. The renters, Maury's friends, had been kicked out a week ago. Too goddamn rowdy, the new tenants reported.

"Shit," Maury said as they climbed back into the van. "This is a great start to my new life. What the hell do I do now?"

"Let's go to my place. You can dump your stuff and crash there until we find a colony to join. Or until my parents come down next weekend."

There was a skinny guy with a blond buzz-cut, about Spill's age, helping himself to a ham sandwich in the kitchen of Spill's house when they got there. "Hey, Marty, this is Crank," Spill said. "Crank, Marty."

"Maury," he corrected.

"Want a sandwich?" Crank offered.

"Mighty goddamn hospitable of you, in my house," Spill retorted.

Crank took a bite of his sandwich. "So, what's up?" he asked.

Maury held his breath. Spill barked, "Get this, dude," and proceeded to tell him of their plans, now assumed to be mutual, to join an artists colony. He made a big deal of Maury's music and especially the easy communal living Maury had described, the parties. Maury nodded weakly. Crank laughed at them.

"Artists colony? What, like on Cape Cod or Key West, that kind of shit? There's nothing like that on this island. This place is too uptight to let anything like that go on," he asserted. Then a thought struck him. "But hey, we could start our own goddamn artists colony. Find a place, set up a commune with babes, live the life, man. What do you think?"

Maury bit his lip. Spill thought a minute. "What kind of money we talking?" he asked.

"Shit, it won't cost anything at all hardly. We get a few of our friends, like Denis, maybe Kring would want to join, and we rent some tiny place real cheap — " He snapped his fingers. "I've got an idea. I know this guy who has a shack in Holgate that he can't sell and he can't rent 'cause it's in terrible shape, like falling down. Maybe I can talk him into letting us live there if we fix it up for him. I bet he'd go for it. He doesn't give a shit. Ah, this is gonna be cool."

Maury's silence continued. He just sat there at Spill's mom's kitchen table, wondering what kind of inspiration could be found in this mutation of his original dream.

Surf Stardom

K ring made his way slowly from the beach through the streets of Ship Bottom with his surfboard under his arm. He walked in a trance, barefoot and alone. Buddy had left the beach before him, with Bev and Maria. It was the second day of the swell, and tropical storm Annie was still spinning four hundred miles off the coast. The fatigue in the surfer's muscles had a familiar pattern; the same muscles hurt that had ached yesterday. He knew which arm movements would be abruptly shortened by dull pain, and how delicious the pain would be. Delicious because it came from surfing, from hours and hours of paddling through the magic surroundings of big powerful waves, from being pummeled by those waves, from arching his back and craning his neck lying on his board, stroking furiously to catch swells about to break. The waves, the ocean, they fed his soul on days like this, days so rare, with food pure and rich and ready to be absorbed into the bloodstream. The fatigue was a consequence of his gluttony.

As he walked he thought of waves, and of how Spill had once tried to defend surfing to some girl at a party by citing some "valuable lessons" he got "out there." Kring knew it was bullshit, but then Spill never really had a clue about waves anyway. If there were lessons to be learned out there they were small ones, and anyway, Kring did not surf to be tutored. He went to be sustained. The rest of his life, land-bound and unsettled, was rendered irrelevant when there were waves breaking on the beach. He underwent a change of state then, and found a meaning in that ocean that lasted only as long as the waves did. It was profound and it was abstract, but no one who knew of it had to puzzle over his purpose then. It was obvious. And he felt its effect now as he walked home through the neighborhood in the muted pinkish light of a late sun swallowed by the haze.

When he reached his garage Kring lovingly laid his board on the ground, out of the way underneath a Japanese pine. He stripped off his wet T-shirt and hung it on a branch of the same tree. Inside the door, he grabbed the only beer in his fridge, then stretched out on the couch. He just lay there in the silence, glowing from the bloodflow through his body. No music floated in the air. No breeze rustled the bushes outside. No cars swept by. The damp spot on the couch beneath his buttocks spread slowly.

Kring must have fallen asleep, because he didn't hear any vehicle pull up. He was startled when Spill burst through the door. "Dude! 'Sup! You see the waves? Awesome, huh?"

"Hey, dude," Kring replied sluggishly.

"Two things," Spill said hurriedly. "One, did you check out the new *Surfer*? There's a picture of you in it, dude, from Mexico. When were you in Mexico, dude?"

"What the hell are you talking about? I've never been to Mexico."

Spill showed him a copy of the magazine, open to the middle. "Right here. There you are coming out of that tube, brah. It's you. Don't deny it."

Kring knew Spill was kidding, that he didn't believe that it really was him in the magazine. But goddamn, he thought, that picture does look a lot like me. It displayed an unidentified goofyfooter, like Kring, just breaking out of a clean Baja barrel, wet hair the same color as Kring's, right hand gripping the rail of the board like Kring had a habit of doing in tight spots. The face wasn't clear, but that, too, could be his own. It had an intent look he had seen in other pictures of himself.

"Does the article say who this guy is?"

"No, uh-uh," Spill said, shaking his head. "It's about this bunch of pros who headed down to Baja, and they camp and surf with a couple of photographers. It says this guy was there surfing when the group first got there. Says he surfed as good as any of the pros, then split before they found out who he was or where he was from. Mystery man. Sounds like something you would do, brah."

Kring snorted. "Sounds more like Buddy to me," he said, still staring at the picture.

"Yeah, but it doesn't look like Buddy. It looks like you. It is you. It's Kring."

"That's bizarre. Maybe I'll hang it up and tell high school girls it's me. You know, make up a story." He laughed. "So what else did you want?" he said as he reached up to hand the magazine back to Spill.

"Oh yeah, get this, dude. While I was at the beach with you guys, this guy, today, he dumps all his shit in my van, like a guitar and clothes and shit, and I drive away with it, right? And he catches up with me at Foodtown and says I've got his stuff. So I give him a ride to Beach Haven. But get this — he wants to join an artists colony here on the island and he wants to write music. So me and him and Crank are gonna form our own artists colony. Dude, we already got a place lined up in Holgate. Gonna move in this weekend. Won't cost anything, just like fifty bucks a month if we get a couple more people, and we gotta fix up the place, do some work on the house. It's gonna be so cool. You interested?"

"I don't think so, dude."

"Dude, how can you say no? Come on, it'll be great. Really cheap, think of the money you'll save living there that you can spend on beer. Chicks will be all over it. I figured you'd be into it cause you're unemployed. Need to save money on rent, don't you? And we need a couple more people. It'll be great. Come on."

Kring shook his head firmly. "I'll come to your parties, sure, but why would I want to leave this place? I don't pay Mr. Cox much more rent on this than you'll probably pay. Plus he's been really cool to me. I don't want to leave him hanging. He might not be able to get another illegal tenant he could trust."

"But dude, you don't have income."

"I got enough in the bank to see me through the summer, to pay the rent I owe him from last month and this month. I'm set. And maybe I'll even get a job after this swell. It's a lot easier to get a job in Ship Bottom than Holgate, if it comes to that." He picked his beer can off the floor. It was half full and warm by now and he set it back down. "Besides," he finished, "when I meet some summer girl, this place is a little more private to bring her back to than some commune."

"Dude — "

Kring stopped him. "No, man. I'm settled here. No reason to leave. Just let me know when your first party is."

Spill's face betrayed disappointment as he turned and flopped the magazine on the floor at Kring's feet. "Here, you can keep this. You at least got a beer for me?" he asked as he pulled the refrigerator door open. "Shit!" followed when Spill saw no beer and shut the door. "All right, dude, I'll catch you later," he said on his way out.

The solitude returned to the room. Kring picked up the magazine and flipped through it for a minute before he found the page with his picture. That's weird, he said to himself as he examined the page. Really weird. It looks just like me. I wasn't in Baja last year, was I? Kring shook his head no to reassure himself and twisted around to push Play on the tape deck behind him. The music of Midnight Oil corrupted the silence Spill had left behind, forced it out the open windows and screen door. Kring reached around again and turned up the volume on the black plastic box.

The cascading guitar sound of the Aussie band sounded just about right to Kring's wearied ears. As the vibrations sank into his shoulders, and through his weary body, he settled back on the couch to look at the picture again.

But his post-surf meditation was interrupted once again by another voice, this one outside the building calling, "Yo, dude! You home? Hey surf star! You in there?" It was Denis. His round, white face appeared framed in the screen door. "Dude. You're here. I thought maybe you were surfing," he said as he pulled open the screen and stepped in.

"Hey, Denis," Kring said, "what's up? Haven't seen you in a while. How goes your search for your karmic barmaid?"

"I've almost caught up with her. I'm like half a step behind now. I heard she was working up in Barnegat Light, at Kubel's. I'll get her, dude. It's like my mission," he said. "But how about you? I hear you're big-time surfer now, picture in the mag and everything."

"You heard?"

"Yeah, Crank told me. Haven't seen it yet, though. Is that it? Let me see." Denis examined the page that Kring handed him. "Dude, that's you!" he fairly screamed. "That's you! How did you get in the magazine? When were you in Baja?"

Kring considered, for an instant, going along with the story. It would be fun, he thought, to watch it spread and see how people would react. And Denis would spread it like the flu. He thought about this as Denis stared at the page.

"Ah, that's not me, dude," Kring instead confessed. "I was here all last winter, you know that."

"No way, dude," Denis said as he shook his head in disbelief. "This is you. And even if it isn't, you should play it up, go along with it. They'll eat it up. Chicks and grommets will worship you, man. No one from this island has ever had a picture in the magazine before, have they?"

"Not that I know of. Unless you count that Aussie lifeguard a couple years ago. And he wasn't in the water."

"Aw, dude, think about it, man. You should play the surf celeb. I would. It would be cool when you enter the LBI contest."

"I'm not entering any contest," Kring grumbled but Denis didn't seem to hear him as he handed the folded periodical back to Kring.

"Hey, you hear about Spill's deal he's got going? His painters commune or something? He said you were gonna join."

"He was just here. I told him I'm not gonna join. I'll party with him, though."

"You and me both. That'll be cool. Well, I'm heading north to track down Mimi Dresden. Catch ya later, dude."

"Later." The departure of Denis seemed to leave a bigger wake in the silence than Spill's had, Kring noted, maybe because Denis displaced more of it with his presence. But the solitude seemed to wash up against the walls in little waves for a minute or so, until it settled down to its calm surface and Midnight Oil played a somber, plodding tune over it from the tape. Kring relaxed again, a little light-headed, and flipped through the pages of *Surfer*, checking out the other articles, pictures, the letters. The delicate crinkle sound of each page as it turned mingled awkwardly with the music.

A girl's voice rang outside his door and the shadow of a head darkened the doorway. "See, I told you he'd be looking at it," she said to her companions yet unseen.

After a moment's confusion he recognized the voice. "Bev from the beach," he said in greeting. "Where's Buddy?"

"Right here," she said brightly.

Buddy shoved his way past the summer girl and laughed out loud when he saw Kring with the magazine in his hands. "Hey, you saw it!" he yelled. Buddy showed him another copy as Bev followed him in.

"Where's, ah, what's her name ... um, Maria?" Kring asked.

"We blew her off," Buddy said conspiratorially as he reached to turn on a lamp. "She had to call her boyfriend."

The lamp's sudden light shocked Kring's eyes and he recoiled behind the glossy pages he held in his hand. "Didn't realize it was getting so dark," he mumbled.

"I can't believe that's really you with your picture in that surfing magazine," Bev gushed. "I knew you were the surf king, but I didn't know you were famous."

Kring looked at Buddy and winked. "Yeah, well, I like to keep a low profile, you know. That's why I wouldn't tell the photographer my name or anything. That's why they only got one picture of me."

"That's why you're on LBI," Buddy said, grinning, "and not on Oahu."

"Exactly," Kring said. "So what are you two crazy kids up to tonight?"

"We're going to the movies," Bev told him. "We wanted to see if you wanted to go."

"Ah, I don't think so."

"Oh, come on, surf king, it's not like we're on a date or anything. It'll be fun. Maria was going to come but she decided not to."

"I'm kinda tired and I wanna get some sleep so I can surf tomorrow early." He looked at Buddy. "You going out on dawn patrol, dude?"

Buddy's face grew earnest. "Yeah, man, I'll be there. If I'm not here when you get up, just head to the beach and I'll meet you. You going up here by the Bath House?"

"Yeah. I wanna hit North Beach for lunch, though."

"Cool. Think it'll still be good tomorrow?"

"Oh yeah. At least one more day. Hey, you guys enjoy the movie."

"You should come," Bev pleaded with pouting lips. Buddy stood behind her and made a face and vigorously shook his head no at Kring.

"Maybe next time," Kring said as he settled back on his sofa. "See ya."

"Sure," Buddy added, "surf star's gotta get his rest. Heh heh." He escorted Bev out the door into the night, and the Midnight Oil tape played itself out.

Thus the music no longer disturbed the silence that the darkness seemed to intensify. Kring could vaguely hear — although it could have been his imagination — that faint seashell sound, the far-off crash of waves that sounded more like the violent crash of earth or solid matter than of water. He could only hear this sound when there was an onshore breeze or the air was dead still. And it would only be the beachbreak making noise, unless the surf was very big. This time, Kring knew, it was very big. But the rumble was distant and intermittent, and he had to concentrate to hear it. It was probably his imagination. At last, he fell asleep.

Kring slept right through the dawn patrol, his internal alarm failing under the weight of so much fatigue. It was after eleven before he got to the beach at the boundary between Surf City and North Beach, and when he did he entered a scene that was much the same as the day before. The waves still rolled in unabated and broke into white, churning froth yards off-shore. They weren't as big as yesterday but were still head high. The crowd up here was small, but Kring could see that the surfers were good. Their movements on the waves were precise and in tune with something. "Yeah, these guys are good, but I got my picture in the magazine," he joked to himself as he stripped off his T-shirt and tossed it on the sand. There were two girls nearby, fifteen or sixteen years old, gazing at him, whispering and giggling to each other. He gave them a smile before he strolled to the water with his board, casually entered it and waded out.

He paddled to where the surfers sat. A few faces that he recognized came into focus, and he picked out an Australian accent among the group, one of the guards the Township imported every summer.

A set rose and loomed outside and Kring dug hard for the horizon, his face almost level with the surface of the water, a few impassioned strokes toward safety. He lifted his head to gauge his progress and saw the first wave gathering itself to break before him. Instinct told him he wouldn't even have time to duck-dive into its belly. The wave would be a torrent of white water when it reached him. He lowered his head and grabbed another few handfuls of ocean anyway, just for momentum, and the wave fooled him, held up and didn't break on him as he thought. But when he looked up again, there he saw, perched on the peak of the wave directly in front of him, a surfer about to drop on him. Where did he come from? darted through Kring's brain, then, Shit. I'm in his way. In the flash of the surfer's bright orange vest, the guy was standing and plunging straight down on the helpless Kring, who had no time to duck. The next instant the surfer was gone, as if he had passed right through Kring like a ghost. Wow, Kring thought just before the white water hit him and he was swallowed by the wet mouth of the sea, that guy's *good*.

He surfaced after a struggle and was able to beat the following two waves before they collapsed. He sat up beyond the breakers and watched the horizon. Minutes later the guy in orange appeared in the water near him, paddling out.

"Sorry about that," Kring said when the guy got closer.

"No worries, mate," the surfer replied with an Aussie syrup in his voice and a self-possessed smile. He was muscled and good-looking and carried a rigid air of familiarity about his face that made him look to Kring like stone perhaps, or plaster. One of the guards that Kring hadn't met, maybe. The guy sat up and looked around. "Nice swell, this," he said. "Didn't expect it."

"I didn't even see you when I was trying to beat that wave you took," Kring added, more making conversation than apologizing.

"That's 'cause I wasn't there then. I'm quick," the guy returned matter-of-factly. "Anyway, Oy missed ya. No worries."

Kring saw the guy's head rise from his shoulders, mechanically, like a robot's, and he followed his gaze to the horizon where a wave appeared, a dark line in the water. Both began scratching for it as it approached, alongside each other stroke for stroke. "Mine!" the Aussie yelled, and he hopped to his feet a little too early it seemed to Kring, but he made the downward plunge gracefully into a pitching eight-foot wave. Kring pulled back on his board as if reining in a steed eager to charge down a hillside, and the Aussie sailed past, beneath him, triumphantly.

Haughty bastard, Kring thought as he watched him, even though the Aussie had had wave position on him on that one. Kring watched him disappear as the wave rolled off toward shore. A few minutes later there he was, farther down the beach, on another big wave. The guy moved on the face, Kring thought, as if to music he himself had written. It was a remarkable performance, without a flaw, yes, but more than that: artistic, almost inspired, unlike anything else Kring had ever seen on Long Beach Island. Then it struck him — why this guy's face had that glow of familiarity to it — he had seen it in the magazine. That surfer was Dale Allewegen, the pro who was rumored to be staying in Surf City. There was no doubt. It was him. No wonder the guy was such a dick, he thought.

Man, he said to himself, I'm glad I kicked out of that wave. I would have dropped in on one of the Top Sixteen in the world. He chuckled and looked around him. Most of the other surfers were watching Allewegen too. It wasn't often a celebrity came to surf LBI, and it was incredible fortune that he found waves to ride. Maybe this guy Allewegen was charmed.

A small wave presented itself and Kring took it and hopped off before riding too far inside. That made it an easy paddle back out for his sore muscles.

"That was a pussy wave," Buddy barked to him as he came gliding outside.

"Just a warmup. Where'd you come from?"

"Bev's. I just got here a minute ago, dude. She dropped me off."

"Ah, you did her, huh?"

"No, man, she wouldn't let me."

"You spent the night with her?"

"Sure did."

"Then what did you do all night?"

"Everything but." Buddy laughed and hid his dark eyes and splashed some water on the nose of his board. He picked at some sand embedded in the wax. "Besides," he admitted, "all she wanted to talk about was you. You and that stupid picture."

Kring laughed. "She's not my type. Her tits are too big. Just tell her that's not me in the picture."

"I did, but she didn't believe me. She accused me of just trying to get laid."

"Which you were."

"Of course. But it *is* true, isn't it? Anyway, I'm taking her to a party tonight. Springer is having a keg at his house."

Buddy took the next wave and was gone. He didn't return — probably caught inside or surfing down a beach, Kring assumed. He, meanwhile, sat on his board as waves surged beneath him and toppled and peeled all around, none close enough to chase. He drifted until he was in the swimming area, then he turned and paddled back south against the breeze. He passed surfer after surfer, a group of four waiting together, Allewegen among them, talking sporadically. Kring glided past them and took up position to the south of the group. There he waited.

A dark line appeared on the horizon. Kring alertly paddled farther south to line up with the best spot on the approaching swell. No one else beyond him had better position, and he anxiously urged the wave on. "Come to me baby ... that's it, there you go," he murmured, coaxing it steadily toward him. He directed himself slowly to where he wanted to be, then turned to face the beach and paddled with a burst. He knew he was there, in the spot. He knew this was a great wave. He could feel it beneath him.

He made the drop and was on his feet in a reflex and lined up along the trough of a huge, flawless wave. Ahead and above him the tip of a board and swirling arms poked out and a second pair of arms beyond. "UP!" Kring yelled to claim the wave. The first pair of arms backed off, the board disappeared. The second set kept churning and with them a surfer appeared at the lip of the wave. And it was a beautiful wave, the wave of the day. "Up!" Kring yelled again, "I'm up!" The surfer dropped smoothly a few feet in front of Kring. Orange competition vest. Model Earth Sunscreen logo. Allewegen. "You son of a bitch!" Kring screamed. The pro didn't hear, hadn't heard Kring call him off, or else had ignored him.

Kring's shoulders dropped and he was ready to bail out. But something in his gut said NO. No, this is too good a wave. It wants you to ride it. Just outride that bastard. It's your wave. In an instant, without thought, Kring's body tensed again and he crouched low on his board and concentrated on speed. Allewegen was fast but he was dancing and carving, and when he made a sweeping, showy roundhouse cutback, Kring just flew past him, above him, along the top of the wall. He didn't look back, just rode the rest of the wave as it should be ridden, as it wanted to be ridden, but he had seen the look of utter shock on the face of the pro when he passed him. He thought he saw Allewegen fall, and it was incredibly satisfying. He rode until the wave trailed off into nothing, he rode like a victorious quarterback rides a parade. At that moment, he owned this place, this break, this beach, this island. His temples swelled with stoke, and he recognized it as a grin spreading that far on his face.

Then, that quickly, it was over. The wave, the ride, Kring's stunning ambush, it was done and he found himself standing on the sand bar, halfway between the biggest breaking waves and the beach, seawater washing his shoulders. He looked around him, at the surfers in the sun, and no one reacted to him. He almost believed no one had seen him outsurf Dale Allewegen. The Australian was already paddling back out to set up for the next wave. He was fifty yards beyond Kring. His white-bottomed feet trailed behind him. He didn't look back.

Kring collected his board with a big smile on his face. I stuffed him, he said to himself, and he deserved it.

He made his way out to the lineup, and no one shouted to him, or splashed him in celebration, or hailed him as a stud. No one said a word. They sat on their boards as he stroked past, and he felt their eyes on him. Kring was unable to tell if they were mortified by his sacrilege, his profaning of a Top Sixteen deity, or if they were in awe of his stunning triumph. They wouldn't tell him which. They just followed him with tribal stares trained on one suddenly revealed to be no longer one of the tribe.

Kring paddled off to an empty spot in the lineup and sat on his board, alone with his accomplishment. The few familiar faces he had earlier seen had disappeared into the growing crowd that sprawled over the water, and the unfamiliar ones regarded him warily or just faced the open sea. Even Allewegen, his instant rival, had disappeared, melted into the flock, leaving Kring to wonder if he was a prophet or a pariah to this tribe.

That question disappeared like a soap bubble burst in the air when a set revealed itself on the horizon. The first wave was big and it was long, and on both sides of Kring surfers began scratching for the safety of deeper water like ants seeking the high ground. As it arrived, several paddlers hadn't beaten it and were swallowed mercilessly, and two figures that had made it spun around and took off on the wave. The only evidence in its wake were delicate bubble trails on the surface where the bodies had gone down. Everyone else continued to crawl, because the next wave was bigger and would break farther out. A long way down the advancing line of surfers, one figure turned to take this one. Kring recognized it as Allewegen. The distant surfer disappeared behind the breaking wall and an instant later surfed back over the top shaking his head.

The third wave of the set loomed almost immediately, bigger than either of the others, darker, more awesome. But from where Kring was, it looked like it might almost be ridable. He decided against it, although it was the biggest wave of the summer. It was threatening. And Allewegen, number twelve in the current world ratings, had just kicked out of its smaller brother. Too much to handle, Kring figured. He was content to sit and watch it roll toward him; it would be enough to watch it begin its slow, agonizing curl as it passed him, as it toppled down on itself.

He was transfixed by the awesome natural power that approached. A kid alongside him, who looked almost too young to be out here in these waves, exclaimed, "Hey, you're the dude! I saw you. You're the dude who — aren't you?"

Kring regarded him as coolly as he could. "I'm the one," he said.

There it was, decided. I must be the prince. No pariah, no outcast. I'm the prophet, at least to this kid. A reflex in him swung the nose of his board around to face the beach. He paddled slowly, majestically, peering back over his shoulder at the darkening swell as it charged him. He no longer thought of safety, only of the wave of the summer. He was the prince of these people and his obligatory ride to glory had taken hold of him.

Kring's strokes quickened to match the wave's momentum. Its force picked him up and carried him forward and dropped him. It was big. It was real big. He hopped to his feet and guided his board but he was in a free-fall. There was no water beneath him. The panic that flooded him yelled *Mistake!* and he hit the water at the bottom of the trough at the same time that the lip grabbed his head and whipped him furiously forward. The violence crumpled him up in its fist and slammed him on the ocean floor and swept him up again without a pause. It rolled him and tossed him and growled at him, like a puppy shaking a rag doll, and when Kring's lungs told him it was time to breathe, there was nothing he could do about it. He was helpless, caught in it, he had no control over his limbs to swim, didn't even know where the surface was, which way to search. A new panic reached for him and he fought it off. He'd been here before and knew he'd get out. He knew he would breathe soon. But when the storm in which he was caught concentrated all its power on him, and rubbed shells and sand in his hair and in his suit, and still would not let him up, Kring tasted fear. Its cold, metallic taste touched his tongue and it told him he had to breathe *now!* And Kring struggled and flailed and still couldn't find the surface and the force of the wave seemed to reverse itself each second, first pulling one way, then the other. And still he hadn't taken any air, still he hadn't taken any air until at last, by accident, he found his head out of the water and the force had spent itself, the wave was gone toward shore and Kring pulled air into his lungs with all the urgency in his being, gulp after gulp. "Man," he said as he shook his abused head, "that was stupid."

He looked around for his board. He felt it still connected to his leg by its leash. Floating peacefully a few feet behind him he saw the back half of it. "Holy shit," he said to the nose piece that was ten yards away and upside down. It was a clean break and the gleaming white foam grinned back at him. At his first movement toward it, a newly bruised shoulder complained, and an ankle too. "Oh shit," was all he could moan. In pain, he collected the pieces of his board in pain and half limped, half floated in to the beach.

No one on the beach seemed to notice him struggling up the sand. No one looked like they'd seen his wipeout, certainly none of them looked at him as the triumphant hero he had felt a scant minute before. All eyes seemed turned to the sea. Kring glanced over his shoulder in time to see Allewegen send up a spectacular sweep of spray with a cutback. "Did you see that!" he heard someone exclaim.

"My wave was twice that size," he mumbled as he limped up the dune with half a surfboard under each arm. Then through his pain, he remembered his ride, and smiled.

He hitched a ride back to Ship Bottom and limped back to his apartment, and there set the pieces of his board on the pine needles. He grabbed an apple and took stock of his situation as Buddy rolled up at the curb in his Beetle. When he got out of the car, Buddy asked no questions, as if out of respect for the board lying in the shade. He hadn't seen the wipeout but appeared humbled by the destruction.

"You could repair it," he suggested.

"Too much extra weight. Be too slow. Too ugly. Not even worth the trouble." Even as he said this Kring recognized that going without a surfboard for the rest of the summer was no option either.

"Good used board is the answer, probably find one at Toad's shop," Buddy offered. "Maybe at Ron Jon's."

"Yeah, but where do I get the money to pay for it?"

"Get a job?"

Kring shot him a look that reflected the absurdity of the suggestion, but then his face softened as he realized the possibility had to be taken seriously. "I could, I guess, but it would take practically the rest of the summer to make enough. Besides, damn, I like unemployment. I like all this free time. I like surfing all day."

"How much you got in your account?"

"Just enough to cover my rent for the rest of the summer." He paused. "Or to buy a new surfboard."

Kring puzzled for a few minutes. He weighed his options and didn't like any of them. Things had been so good. So finely balanced. This fucked up everything.

At last he stood, walked over to his landlord's mailbox and pulled out the rent check he had put in there just that morning. He looked at it, regarded his broken board, and tore up the check.

"Priorities, man," was all he said to answer Buddy's quizzical look. Buddy nodded.

The Artists Colony

So what do you think of it?" Spill asked as Kring poked his head inside the door of a pale yellow bungalow on a quiet, sand-strewn Holgate street. Kring carried his new surfboard, a shiny white-and-orange piece, under his arm and it swung with him as he looked around the place.

Old cardboard paneling, cheap and dark, lined the walls. The paneling was bubbled, water-stained and split in places all around the room, mostly within three feet of the floor. The floor was almost empty, but clad with thin-worn, faded-blue indoor-outdoor carpeting. There was a small card table, two metal chairs and a threadbare couch that was covered in a fabric that looked to Kring like it would itch. That was all. The scars were plain where a wall had been ripped out to open the main area into one big room. The look of the house said it had been built very cheaply, probably in the island building boom of the early sixties, and had probably never had an owner or tenant who didn't leave it in worse shape than they found it. Suddenly, out of the small, open kitchen that was tucked in the corner of the house, a small projectile shot towards Kring's head. He ducked, and a bottle cap bounced off the window behind him with a sharp, metallic click.

"I can see why the guy couldn't rent it to anybody but you," Kring said admiringly. "This looks just about perfect."

He gingerly set his board against the wall next to the window. The point of the nose he rested in an indentation in the paneling.

Crank, leaning against the counter that separated the kitchen from the rest of the room, swigged from a bottle of cheap beer. "Hey, surf star," he said with a burp, "nice blind shot, huh?" He mimicked his cap-flipping technique. "Did I hit you?"

"Ha!" Kring retorted. "All you did was almost break the window. Not that anyone would notice. Nice place you've got here."

"Hey, dude, this is our place. You're one of us, ain't ya? We're getting cable installed on Monday, in just three days."

Kring looked for a television. He saw none. "But you don't even have a TV," he said.

"Denis is bringing us one on Tuesday. We'll have HBO. Cool, huh?"

Spill pushed his way past Kring and scanned the room, his dark eyes narrowing. "Where's the man?" he asked. "Where's Maury the Man?"

"He's in the can," Crank said, delighted that he had stumbled on a vulgar little rhyme. "Likes to sit in there and write his songs. Says it's the only spot in the place that has any acoustics worth a shit." He stepped toward a door alongside the kitchen and beat a fist on it. The flimsy plywood surface rattled with the force of Crank's pounding. "Hey, dude, we got a new roommate!" he yelled. "Come meet him!"

The door opened and out stepped a dark-haired guy about Kring's age, with a skinny neck, confused squinting eyes and a guitar in his hand. His face broke into a reflexive smile as he moved to greet Kring.

"What was your name again? Drink or something ... Krink? Oh, like in 'ring,' huh? Yeah, well, maybe someday I'll have a roommate here with a real human being name. Just kidding. My name is Maury." He held up the guitar. "I write songs."

Kring looked amused and said simply, "I surf."

"Oh yeah, they told me you're like a big deal around here. Picture in a magazine, and you beat like the world champion surfer, or something. That's cool. Celebrities are good to have around. A good draw." The introduction over, Maury turned around and headed for the bathroom again. He stopped before the door and casually said over his shoulder, "They tell you about the party? We're gonna launch this thing with a party, tomorrow or the next night maybe. Tell your friends. If we get enough people, maybe we can make some grocery money." He disappeared back into his enclave with his instrument.

Kring looked at Spill. "Make some grocery money?" he asked.

Spill shrugged. "Charge a couple bucks at the door, I guess. We get enough people to pay for the keg, the rest is gravy."

This made enough sense to Kring that he could forget about its conceptual absurdity and move on to other matters. He commenced a search for a safe place to keep his surfboard, ducking his head in the two tiny bedrooms, one after the other. Neither had a bed or dresser in it, just mattresses on the floor piled with thin blankets and uncased pillows and mounds of T-shirts and jeans. Neither looked like a very secure place for his fragile, new equipment. He headed back toward the front door, grabbed the board from where it leaned and took it outside to the yard. In front of the house, stones were spread widely across the sand, among isolated pockets of weeds. The stones trailed around the corner of the building, where gravel took over the landscape. His gaze fell on the outdoor shower, a wooden closet tacked against the side of the house. It looked to Kring like it might be an adequate storage place for the six-foot-four piece of foam and fiberglass that eased the heartache of losing his beloved Romantic three-fin. He yanked open the shower's half-door with one hand and held his surfboard at arm's length with the other, admiring one more time its clean lines and slick exterior. He guided the board into a dark corner and with his finger reverently traced over the "Enigma Surfboards" logo on its deck. As he did this the thought occurred to him, Nothing sucks more than getting a new board just after the waves die.

Comfortable with the hiding place he had chosen for his stick, Kring hurried to Spill's vehicle to unload the rest of his things. As suddenly as always, Buddy's car appeared from nowhere and pulled up next to the van. Buddy yelled from the driver's seat, "Dude, I finally found this place. I've been up and down every street in this town looking for you guys. Hey, I didn't know there was a trailer park on this island." Kring heard the door handle click and Buddy unfolded from the seat into the sunlight, dragging a big laundry bag with him.

"What's up?" Kring questioned. "You here to check out the new pad or just think you're gonna do your laundry?"

Buddy's face broke into a grin that belonged on someone else's face. "No, no, dude, I'm joining the Artists Club."

"How come, dude? What happened with your apartment?"

"Artists Colony," Spill corrected from the open doorway. "You two guys get to fight it out for the last mattress."

Buddy turned back to Kring. "Artists Colony, okay. So anyway, I heard what happened when you broke your board. I didn't know that you smoked Allewegen. Number twelve in the world, man. On your wave. And you smoked him. And then some dude told me you took off on a wave that had to be fourteen feet and that's when you trashed your stick. He said you looked good, you almost made it. You're a legend, dude. I said, 'I gotta party with this guy.' Man, I wish I'd seen it."

"Aw, dude, I didn't almost make it. I never had a chance. I almost drowned," Kring said. Then he looked off into the middle distance and mumbled, "But it was an unreal feeling."

"Hey, so let's get moved in and have some lunch."

"Good plan. I'd fight you for the mattress, you know I was here first, but I don't really give a shit. It's yours if you want it. I brought a hammock I had stored away."

"Cool deal."

"Oh, and we're supposed to be having a party, like tomorrow or the next day."

Buddy stared. "Why not tonight?" he exclaimed.

"I don't know. They said tomorrow or the next day. But party tonight sounds good to me."

Buddy marched through the door and announced, "Okay, dudes, we're having an inaugural party tonight, like an open house, right? Tonight, okay?"

From the bathroom came Maury's voice, "Who the hell are you?" and Spill protested, "Shit, we don't have enough time to get a party together tonight. We're not moved in yet even."

"What's to get together?" Buddy insisted, "We get a keg, we tell people we got a keg. Real simple. Let's do it."

Crank yelled from the bedroom he would soon share with Buddy, "I'm up for it."

"But we don't have any stereo or TV and Maury wanted time to write a couple of songs."

Buddy grimaced at Kring and said in an aside, "What is it with these guys? Do they want an artists colony or not?" He turned back to Spill and explained, "Hey, listen to me, all we need for a party is beer and girls. After that, everything falls into place. So we have music next time. We'll have other parties. Right now we gotta spread the word. Get this place rockin'. Summer's not gonna last forever, dudes. It'll be a blast."

Spill shrugged, gave up his argument and fell into line. "Okay, then I guess I better go make some calls to people," he said, and he gathered some scraps of paper from the table and disappeared through the door.

Buddy was pleased. "Yeah, man, we got like eight hours to put something together. Plenty of time. Whaddaya think?"

Kring nodded. "No problem," he said and, looking ahead, wondered where he would sleep that night. Idiot, he thought, you'll probably wind up passing out on the couch or something. And at that moment the prospect seemed inviting to him.

Buddy dumped his bag in the bedroom with a flourish, then followed Spill out the front door with a nod to Kring and a mischievous smile. "Party tonight," was all he said. Kring heard the familiar whirr of the Volkswagen engine and when he looked out the window, there was an empty space where Buddy's car had been.

Spill returned ten minutes later and banged on the bathroom door, halting the wails of Maury's guitar. The singing stopped too, but there was no answer from behind the door. "Come on, man, I gotta go," Spill yelled at the thin barrier. But Maury still said nothing. As he stood at the door Spill seemed to remember something. He looked at Crank and snapped his fingers, and said as he hurried out the door, "I gotta call Molly. And Heidi."

"Where does he go to call these people?" Kring asked Crank.

"Pay phone at the deli down the street. We gotta run down there when we hafta call someone." He sighed. "It's a drag not to have a phone."

Inside the bathroom, Maury's singing resumed.

"He sounds like he's singing with his Walkman on, doesn't he?" Crank observed.

Kring stepped outside into the oppressive, pale heat of an overcast day. The sky was a depressing, featureless white, the color of ever-present, thick summer haze. He jogged the short block to the beach, where he sat and stared at the ocean with a watchful eye. But it was as flat as a mill pond and picked absentmindedly at the shore with tiny white foam fingertips. Kring sat there in the sand for five minutes, just watching. His mind was blank, in retreat from this strange upheaval, the move to the end of the island, to this so-called Artists Colony. He just sat, wishing to be reassured by waves that just weren't there. When he could no longer stand the sight of an ocean so placid, he returned to the house, stopping at his bike to retrieve his bag. He had to step over a pile of debris that blocked the front door. Stumbling to the far corner of the main room, he took a couple of eyehooks out of his bag, and with great effort screwed them into wall studs. Between them he strung a Mayan hammock that had served as his primary piece of furniture the first summer he spent in his garage apartment. He climbed in unsteadily and settled for a nap. Maury's music floated weakly in the air, mercifully muffled by the bathroom walls.

When he awoke, the light in the house had an undefined quality of sunset, a pallor of graying, exhausted daylight. He could tell by looking out the window that the hazy July sky was just letting the evening leak into it like tainted liquid. From his hammock he saw a room now magically transformed, filled with motley pieces of furniture: a green couch leaking its stuffing; an easy chair, junky and worn and only fit for a place such as they were creating; an uneven, soft armchair with a flowered print. Maury and Spill and Crank had evidently carried out the threat made earlier to scavenge the trash piles of Long Beach Island and they had thus remade the shack into a weird parody of a home. An aroma warmed Kring's nose, the starchy airborne flavor of pasta being boiled. Cool, he thought, his disorientation fading, I'm hungry.

A door burst open, slapped against the wall. It was the bathroom door, and Maury burst out exclaiming, "Ha ha! Listen to this." He strummed through a few chords on his guitar with a mediocre hand. "Is this an artists colony or what?"

"Cool," Crank said from the kitchen. "Ya got words too?"

"Yeah, but I'll wait until the party to like debut the whole song, ya know?"

Kring rolled out of his hammock and wandered sleepily over to the kitchen. He slurped down a length of spaghetti from the pot. "Just about done," he said. He leaned over to examine the thin, red sauce bubbling away cheerfully in another smaller pot on another burner. "Hey man, let's eat."

Spill struggled through the door with a quarter keg at his knees as Kring and Crank and Maury were polishing off the last few strings of their meal. "Do me a favor, dude," he said, looking pleadingly at Kring, "get the ice from my van? And the tap and the cups?"

The keg was quickly set up, tapped and iced by experienced hands. All four of them drew cups full of foam and toasted themselves. "Now we're ready to party!" Crank yelled. Maury dropped into the flowered-print chair, spilling some foam in his lap. Kring backed into a seated position in his hammock and swung briskly while they waited for people to arrive.

It grew dark. No one arrived. Crank glared at Spill and challenged him, "Did you call anyone?" Spill responded with a list of names: "Heidi, Derek, Bobo, Mickey, Hope, Guggenheim ... they all said they were coming," he claimed. They waited some more, drank more beers. An hour later Kring saw that the ice cubes on top of the keg had shrunk and were sitting in a thin pool of water. But the foam in the beer had settled down and when they drew a cup, it was liquid like it was supposed to be, golden and pungent and plenty good.

At ten o'clock Buddy burst through the door with Bev and a grouchy-looking Maria. "The party's here!" he announced. Kring wasn't sure whether he was announcing to the girls that the party was here at the Artists Colony or to the colony that he had brought the party with him, but either way, Kring figured, Buddy had overstated things. He filled his cup while Spill and Crank swarmed over Maria with their attentions. He laughed at them when her attitude didn't change, except to maybe take a downturn.

"Hi," Bev said sweetly to Kring as he took over Maury's spot in the soft chair. Behind him, Buddy filled three cups from the valve on the tap hose.

"Hey, Bev." Kring was aware that after waiting an hour and a half for a party to start, he settled quickly into the cushions like a bored king in a deep throne. Bev sat on the arm of his chair anyway, shoving aside his wrist with a swing of her hip and claiming the high ground for her own. "Did you go surfing today?" she asked with a lively cadence in her voice. He looked at her with a half-drunken smile. "You need waves to surf, Bev," he said patiently, a little sarcastically, as if only an idiot wouldn't realize that.

Bev didn't seem to sense the sarcasm and she remained planted on the arm of the chair when Buddy handed her a beer. She stayed there as long as Kring sat under her, in a chair that threatened to swallow him at any minute in the broken folds of its cushions. "Do you surf a lot?" she asked him. "Do you like living here? ... Do you know Buddy very well? ... Do you live here in the winter?" She gave him only time to answer and take one quick breath after each question before she posed another. Kring tried to turn the interview into a conversation, but he didn't struggle very hard. At one point Bev sighed and said, "I thought there'd be more people at this party," and Kring thought they might now have something to talk about, but without pause she came back with more questions. "So where do you work? Or are you rich?"

The evening seemed to slide downhill from there, and not just for Kring, but for the whole group, the whole colony. He kept himself from getting mean with Bev, but as he got more drunk her attention began to bore him, and it annoyed Buddy. Spill and Crank seemed to tire of their jokes bouncing off Maria like hailstones off a window. Maria had had enough of Spill and Crank almost as soon as she came in, and she made no secret of it. Finally she insisted to Bev that they leave. Reluctantly Bev agreed, but not before Maria turned surly. "This party sucks," she spat as Buddy ushered the two of them out the door toward his car.

Kring, Spill, Crank and Maury remained to drink the beer by themselves in their crumbling hovel. They were drunk and alone, but at least they had things to joke about now: Bev's star-struck adoration and Maria's antisocial attitude, just for starters. As they put away beers and took turns stumbling to the toilet, Crank decided that they had to finish the keg.

"Dudes, it's a bad precedent to set, not finishing the keg," he slurred with authority. "We can't be the kind of artists colony that lets a keg get warm. Other artists colonies will laugh at us, man."

They tried. For some reason it seemed important. Kring forced down two cups that he didn't want and the beer tasted more bitter and foul with each sip. When the room began its counter-clockwise spin, all he could say was, "Whoa!" and he concentrated on making it not spin. It worked. The room stopped its rotation and he was relieved that it was just an isolated incident, a warning sign. He stared curiously at the keg, as if he could gauge how much beer remained in it by its appearance. When after a minute of staring he realized that wouldn't work, he rose to his feet and bent to lift the barrel to test its weight. It was heavier than he expected, and the room spun again, clockwise this time, and Kring stopped trying to control his world for the rest of the night.

He dropped back in the hungry soft chair, looked at Spill and Crank and Maury, and wondered what the hell he was doing here. He felt like he was taking charge of his life in a way, by joining with these guys who said they wanted to be artists, but he was only here by accident, and he knew it. It was clear to him, in the new awareness of truth that he had found in that keg, that this adventure, this new chapter was not one he chose. That seemed important, that he just kind of fell into it. It might work out okay, though, he thought as he watched Spill imitate Maria's expression. A slow smile opened Kring's face, and he said again, audibly this time but still to himself, "It might work out okay."

Chapter 12

A Real Party This Time

Kring knew he was awake before he had the courage to open his eyes. He lay wherever he was — it felt like the beat-up couch; smelled like it too — and tried to avoid the morning light by keeping his eyelids shut tight. He told himself he would go back to sleep, but he didn't really believe it. He was hot, and his mouth tasted terrible, dry and sticky, and now he was uncomfortable and more awake than ever, but in desperation he insisted that he would go back to sleep. He stretched his limbs to find a more comfortable spot and his feet pressed against something firm. When it yielded with a creak Kring realized it was the loose arm of the couch.

He rolled onto his side and opened his eyes. Right away he knew that was a mistake, for his head began to throb. Directly opposite him there was a sleeping body splayed out in the stuffed chair. It looked like Crank, with fists stuffed in the front pocket of his poncho, head back, mouth open. The morning light hurt Kring's swollen eyes. The smell of stale beer hung in the air like it was at home there. And we didn't even have fun, he thought with a groan. When his arm dropped off the couch, it knocked over a full cup of flat beer, spilling it onto the carpet. "Shit," he blurted, then decided there was no point in getting anything to clean it up. He raised himself off the couch and lifted one side of the keg, as he'd done last night. It felt just as heavy, but it was almost as warm as the morning's humid air, and it sat in a wide stain on the coarse, faded-blue rug. The carpet rubbed like burlap on the bottoms of his bare feet. He set the keg back in its place and headed outside, on his way to the beach for a symbolic wave check.

Under the glaring midmorning sun there were no waves, but he had expected that. He jogged to the water anyway and dove under. A short swim helped his head and washed some of the stink of a wasted night off his body. He felt better, he felt refreshed.

He was just getting back to the end of the street when Buddy's car rolled up on the front yard. "Hey, man," Kring called, "you checking the waves?"

"No," Buddy replied laconically, "how is it?"

"Nada."

"Figures."

"So where were you? Getting breakfast or something?"

Buddy fixed Kring with a brief glare, then looked away. "No," he said sullenly. "I stayed at Bev's. Her parents aren't down this week. She has the house to herself."

Kring was puzzled. Buddy was obviously pissed off, but what about was not so clear. Maybe Bev wouldn't put out again, Kring thought. He studied his friend's face and just said, "Cool." He let the matter drop as Buddy seemed to wish.

Inside the house, the aroma of coffee had replaced the party stink, and Maury's plaintive singing, more awful than the day before, wafted out of the closed bathroom like one more foul odor. Buddy shook his head with a smile and Kring laughed.

"Good, ain't he?" Kring suggested.

"Is there anything to eat?" was Buddy's reply as he headed for the kitchen.

It was a solid hour before all of the residents were up and functioning, but one by one, through their depressions and headaches they appeared on their feet and consumed coffee. They traded assessments of the night before and laughed at the pathetic event. It was unanimous that they had to get up another party. It would be a real one. This time, they decided, they would give themselves a few days to get the word out.

It didn't take much effort to publicize their plans. A word or two to a few key characters, and the island's "pinecone telegraph" came alive.

Denis brought them a television a day early, and so on Monday the house had fully operational cable TV. Spill's stereo had arrived, and it seemed that the island was abuzz with news of the bash, from their block in Holgate all the way to Barnegat Light at the other end.

It was about five o'clock when Kring, sitting in front of the TV, heard Spill pull up and unload a half keg from his van. He jumped up and hurried out to help. "I had three different people today ask me if I knew about this party," Spill grunted as they wrestled with the cold metal barrel.

Kring nodded.

"Yeah," Spill continued as they struggled through the doorway, "I was spreading the word for two days, and now I'm hearing about it all over, from people I don't even know." He exhaled forcefully as they set the barrel on the floor. "Let's get this baby tapped."

And so it began.

This party, Kring noted, started off the same way as their first attempt, only earlier and with a bigger keg. The Colonists, as Crank had taken to calling the group, poured themselves beers, sat around on their trash-rescued furniture and drank, waiting for people to show up.

Kring was feeling the subtle effects of the beer before the first surfers knocked uncertainly on the doorjamb. "Hey! Terry and Tom!" Spill called out. "Welcome to the Artists Colony!" Terry and Tom greeted Spill with upraised palms and each gave him a couple of dollars, grabbed a cup and made a beeline for the keg. For the next half hour the group grew no larger, and as the seven sat around the quiet room and drank, Kring recalled with chagrin the other pathetic episode.

"Maybe no one will come," he wailed to Crank. "Maybe we're too far away from everybody. Maybe —" His panic attack was arrested when a feminine form darkened the doorway. Then another. He turned a grin to Crank and they shared a silent toast. The newly arriveds were just girls Spill knew from the beach, badge checkers, still in high school, but Crank acknowledged their bodies with a nod and growled, "They'll do."

The party began to creep in from that point, like a tide slowly rising to flood one of the flat islands in the bay. The crumbling house was soon filled with beach kids looking for some drama or romance.

Kring was talking to two of the badge checkers when Lotion walked in with a couple of friends ten minutes later. Her passage through the room distracted him as always. She was as impressive as ever, he thought, her dark eyes alive, shining dark hair draped on her shoulders, an exotic cream-colored shawl over blue jeans. He smiled at her from the arm of the chair where he sat, and she headed towards him. Tina and Sage saw they had lost his attention and as Lotion came up to him, they moved off. She playfully grabbed his hair, pulling his head back, and said, "What's this I hear about you being some underground surf hero? Tell me the story, and it better be good."

The crowd soon swelled to twenty, twenty-five, more and Kring had to divide his attention as cars filled the yard and people poured through the door. Most of the early arrivals had looked hesitant, as if wondering whether this were the right place, but when there were enough cars outside and enough noise inside, the hesitation was gone. Lifeguards, waiters, barmaids, locals and weekenders arrived in bunches. Surfers greeted Kring with stories and challenges to enter the LBI contest. "Dude! You gonna surf the True Classic?" asked one grommet Kring didn't know. "Dude, I'll trash you in the contest if you enter," claimed another that he knew slightly. "Where were these people the other night?" he asked Buddy. "Where'd they come from?"

"Hey, Spill," he yelled, "how many people you figure are here now?"

Leaning on his shoulder against the refrigerator, Spill reached into the pocket of Crank's Baja, which he now wore. "I don't know, maybe thirty, maybe more," he said, pulling out a fistful of bills. "I haven't been counting, dude, but we've got a stash. Enough to pay for this keg, and maybe another half. If we play it right, we can collect for that one too."

Kring heard a yell behind him and swung around to look, but saw nothing except a churning sea of faces. The crowd climbed on the furniture and pushed against walls and spilled out the door into the muggy night. They were loud and they were active and they were getting drunk. This was what this deal was supposed to be like, he decided. This was the reason they got this place. Kring didn't hang out with one group, just spun from one friend to the next in a frenzy of hosting. He spent time with Lotion and he talked to guys he knew from the beach, from the jet ski place, guards he'd met through Spill. He took notice when Victoria walked in with two girlfriends. "Hey, Vic!" he called, "can I get you a beer?" She seemed to take a moment to recognize him, then smiled politely and shook her head no.

From that point, the party became an evening that grew with each beer he poured in his mouth, a collection of isolated moments — conversations and observations and insights that could have occurred in any order. Indeed, he would think as the night wore on, there was less of a sound basis for assuming that they had occurred in the order he remembered them.

The first keg was emptied and replaced before Spill incited a moonlight surfing expedition that charged out the door with tribal whoops. Kring had to charge after them when he realized they intended to christen his virgin surfboard. After rescuing his most treasured possession, Kring returned to the house and got in line for another beer.

In the crowd around the keg he overheard Maury talking to a short girl and her friend, both with pretty smiles and fine, firm bodies beneath their T-shirts. "Why did you guys get Budweiser," the bustier blond girl wanted to know, "when everybody is drinking Coors Light these days?"

Kring heard Maury reply, "Well, I've always been happy with Bud, never seen any reason to switch. It's never let me down."

The girl seemed confused. "What do you mean, 'never let you down'?"

Maury thought a second, then said, smiling, "Whenever I've drunk enough of it, I've gotten fucked up." He and Kring exchanged grins and gave each other thumbs-up.

The music exploded, some techno-dance tune Kring didn't recognize. Someone screamed, "Turn that shit off!" The thumping bass died a quick death and Kring's ears adjusted to the din of conversation. He wasn't even sure where in the room the stereo was. A group of the partiers had gathered to his left, around the flickering images of the television that Denis had donated. Kring sidled over to watch MTV with them. One girl caught his eye; she was a tall, striking thing with short, dark hair, and she seemed absorbed in the ebb and flow of the action on the screen. When a Robert Palmer video came on she jumped and screamed, "I'm in this video!"

"Oh yeah? Which one are you?" asked a blond guy that Kring had seen at the keg earlier. The girl didn't answer, just stood transfixed with her fingernails pinned between the rows of her teeth. When a line of pancake-make-up models appeared, moving to the beat and miming with instruments, she exclaimed, "That's me there!" and pointed to the left side of the screen. Kring couldn't really see a difference between any of the figures in the video, and neither, apparently, could the blond guy because Kring heard him ask sarcastically, "That's you, huh? How can you tell?" But the girl didn't hear him. Seconds later when the video title appeared, the excitement in her face vanished and she said disappointedly, "Oh, that was 'Simply Irresistible.' I was in 'Addicted to Love.' Shoot."

Kring looked her over. He could see she was a little older than most of the crowd, but he liked what he saw. Still, he couldn't help laughing at her pretension, if only gently. Over her shoulder he caught sight of Ricky and Peejunk from the Withoutniks as they slipped in the door. Kring waved and yelled "Yo!" and started threading his way over to them when he felt his brain swerve; he was getting buzzed. Just as quickly as it had set on him, he compensated and was straight again. He felt strong. He was in control. "Hey, man," he greeted the musicians, "how's it going? Is Lloyd going to be here tonight?"

"Na, I don't think so," Ricky said. "He's been up in Vermont for the last week. There's this government-in-exile from some West African nation up there and they been partying it up pretty heavy. I'm not sure when he'll be back. I hope by next weekend because we gotta play a blueberry festival in Chatsworth or something like that —"

Peejunk broke in, "Aw, dude, we got to play that gig? I thought we were just going to like pick berries."

Now definitely, pleasantly drunk, Kring wished them luck with the berries and pointed them toward the keg. He wandered over to the kitchen counter where Crank and Irrelevant Roger were sharing a bottle of tequila with a guy about Kring's age, maybe a little older. He was skinny, with straight, dirty blond hair falling out from under a Colorado Rockies baseball cap.

"Dude!" Crank wailed. "Come join us. We're just doin' shots. And playin' this game. You gotta make a statement before you drink. Like a toast or somethin'. If it's a lame quote, you got to drink another. Join in, man." He held a hand up to indicate the stranger. "Kring, this is Fee Waybill."

Kring's eyes grew wide. "Not THE Fee Waybill," he said.

Fee shook his head. "No, no relation."

Kring played their game, downed a few shots quoting movies and TV commercials. The bottle was getting light when he was assessed a penalty shot. He had quoted the Clash and he believed he'd been treated unjustly, since the round before Crank had gotten a rousing cheer for "I hate fat chicks," and Fee Waybill had snuck through something that Kring was sure he recognized as one of the rules of Parcheesi. He was about to complain when Irrelevant Roger was tagged because no one could understand what he'd said, even when he repeated it. Rog protested vehemently but no one could understand his protests either, and Kring leaned on the counter and considered this in the very fluid character of mind he had just then, a pleasing, unfettered motion of thought, and he discovered something profound about the game they were playing and about the world in general. It was something about trust, and how things were true if enough people believed them, or something like that. The insight was only with him for a second, then it split, leaving ghost images in his mind. But it was clear for that second. It made sense.

He started to explain his revelation to the others, but Roger was still complaining loudly, incoherently over the music, and he finished the bottle with his penalty shot. Then he announced what sounded like his intention to join the Colony. Someone shoved by Kring, bouncing in time to the music. It was a little girl named Kim that he knew hung around the Cafe. She danced over to Roger and exclaimed, "This song is so much like this place, I can't believe it! I love it!" Kring cocked his ear to listen. The song playing was "Love Shack" by the B-52s. That's pretty cool she would think that, he said to himself. But Roger stood up from the stool on which he had been perched, looked at Kim blankly and said, "What

112

song?" before stumbling backwards into the trash. Crank looked at Roger, looked at Kim and said, "Wanna go for a walk?"

Kim looked down at Roger, struggling drunkenly under the kitchen light among food wrappers and milk cartons. She looked at Crank. "No. Well ... maybe," she said, and they disappeared out the side door. Fee Waybill headed for the keg.

Kring slid onto the stool that Roger had just abandoned. It was unsteady but he was relieved to be off his feet. The party swirled around him, chaotic and loud, alien. This was his place, his party, but it didn't feel anything like his own. He saw familiar faces and antics, but he was not yet used to this place, didn't claim it as his. He felt as much of a guest here, as much of a tourist, as Fee Waybill.

Buddy tapped him on the shoulder. "Hey, you know these dudes?"

Kring followed the toss of Buddy's head to the corner of the room. Gathered there were three figures, light-haired and bronze-bodied. They laughed loudly with a bare-chested lifeguard Kring knew as Bose. They were boisterous and had an aggressive, almost jaunty air about them. Their voices floated over the general din of the party to his ears. He picked up accents. Australian accents. "Yeah. Yeah, I know that dude. That's Allewegen."

"That's right. Those other dudes are guards the Township imported for the summer. One's name is Martin. He was here last year. The other I think is like Roderick or something."

Kring made an effort to appear casual, but he felt a tightening in his gut as he remembered how he'd outsurfed the big Aussie. He didn't guess that would go over well with him or his compatriots. But it's a party, he thought. Maybe they'll be cool. Maybe the guy doesn't even care.

He hopped up and walked into the door of the bathroom when it didn't open like he expected it to. It was locked and concealed at least three people, judging from the voices coming from within. He was on his way outside to relieve himself when a gentle hand touched his shoulder.

"Here you are, surf king. I've been looking for you all night."

"Hey, Bev, when did you get here? Where's Maria? Where's Buddy?"

"Oh, I've only been here like a half hour. Did you go surfing today?"

"No waves, Bev. Is Buddy around?"

"I don't know, I guess so," she sighed. "He keeps trying to get me to sleep with him. I haven't, though. But it's kind of annoying. And he won't tell me his real name. He won't tell me anything about himself, you know, like where he's from and stuff? I think that's kind of spooky."

"Yeah, well, that's Buddy." He smiled, then shifted his weight. "Ah, excuse me, Bev, I gotta go outside for a second." He weaved his way through the party to the open side door. There he paused, and watched an Aussie, the one that Buddy had identified as Roderick, chatting with Lotion. She rang out with a great laugh. Kring pushed his way through the crowd blocking the door.

The night air, though muggy, felt refreshing after the mob scene in the house, and it was quiet away from the crowd that had spilled out into the front yard. As he urinated in the bushes, he looked up at the night sky; it seemed as though someone had blown the roof off the atmosphere with dynamite, just blown a gaping hole through what people on earth knew as the sky. He was sure he could feel the cold of outer space rushing through that hole, but it was only a breeze off the bay at the end of the street. He closed his eyes and focused on the sound of his piss cutting through the leaves at his feet.

He heard, from inside the walls, laughter and an Australian accent orchestrating its chorus.

Bev's voice at his side startled him. "I guess you really *did* have to go outside," she said. "I thought you were blowing me off."

Kring sealed up the velcro fly on his surf shorts with his fingertip as he turned to face Bev. "I'd never blow you off, babe," he said jokingly.

"I'm glad," she sighed and moved closer to him. "I'd be sad if you didn't like me." Her perfume imposed itself on him with an overwhelming force. It hung like car exhaust, and he knew it would stick to him wherever she touched him, as sure as a bad reputation.

She leaned forward, up on her toes, and kissed him. Her lipstick tasted waxy, but her tongue felt friendly when it found its way behind his teeth. Who wears lipstick to a party on LBI? flashed through his mind while she enclosed his neck with her arms. When she didn't ease up, he closed his eyes and enjoyed the moment. Things like this didn't happen often to Kring, and even though he felt nothing in particular for this girl, that was no reason to stop her. He did feel an automatic stirring in his loins. Bev probably felt it too, as she rubbed her belly aggressively against him. When she finally pulled away for a breath, Kring murmured, "Well, that was cool."

"I've wanted to kiss you for a while," she said between heavy breaths.

Kring said nothing, just blinked to clear the floating images in his eyes. He suspected her panting was a put-on.

"You know," she continued in a near-whisper, "I wouldn't go to bed with Buddy. I told him that." She gazed at him with a look that Kring figured was meant to be seductive. "But I would with you." She giggled softly with pretend embarrassment as Kring struggled for something to say. Convention demanded something cool and clever and eager, but all he could come up with was "That's good to know." Then, with his hand on her elbow, he guided her back to the house. As they entered the room, he realized that he'd been right about her perfume. It clung to him like an infant chimp abandoned by its mother.

"Oy knoy this guy," Kring heard as soon as he stepped into the lighted room. The words had a strange kind of music to them, directed at him. He turned in their direction and there was the man who had spoken them, larger than life, Dale Allewegen. Kring thought the Aussie looked bigger on dry land. He stood at least three inches taller than Kring, and probably carried thirty pounds more on his paddle-hardened frame. But he had a smile on his face, a face made familiar by the surfing magazines and his Bare Breast Surfwear ads. He had a friendly hand extended toward Kring. "Nice surfing, mate. Like the way you ride."

"Thanks, dude," was all Kring said as the hair settled comfortably back down on his neck and he breathed a silent sigh. The guy was going to be cool.

"Great party, too. Rad place you've got here."

"All right."

Allewegen then swept by him with a majesty that befitted, Kring thought, the man's humility and his position. He was, after all, royalty, surfing royalty, and this was part of his kingdom; it was a beach town, one of the beach towns of the world. These were his subjects, these surfers, grommets and ocean people. His subjects watched as he knocked on the bathroom door with a sonorous "Anybody in there?" The door opened immediately and Allewegen disappeared into his chamber as two grommets scrambled out.

"Whoa, dude, that was really Wegs. It was really him," one of the young surfers blurted to the other.

"Yeah, and he told that dude he likes the way he rides."

Kring gave no indication he had heard, pretended to be interested in the game of quarters that was being played on the table. But he knew he was being talked about.

"Who is that dude?"

"I think he lives here, like in this house. Word is he's like the best surfer on the island."

Kring smiled in spite of himself. This was cool. He knew that the "best surfer" tag was bullshit and he was about to correct that kid, but another voice entered the discussion, an Australian one less sonorous than the pro's. "Oh, yeh," he said loudly, "ennyone can surf if they snake waves from better surfers."

The hairs rose again on Kring's neck. Still he watched the game.

"Ennybody," the Aussie said in a drunken growl, now in Kring's ear, "even pussy American wankers."

Kring resisted the urge to whip his elbow into the guy's shallow eye sockets, but why he resisted, he did not know. The guy certainly deserved it. He was in America, after all, talking like this. Besides, Kring was the snakee on that wave, not the snake. He leveled his gaze at the pale eyes that sat in Roderick's face.

"Is that how Australians get a leg up?"

"I'll show how we get a leg up, ya Yank bastard."

The Aussie leaned in toward Kring. Kring tensed his muscles but did not move. The other Australian grabbed his friend's arm. "No more fights, Roddy," he said. "Come on, let's get a beer. Let's do a kegstand."

"Fuck off. This is the Yank that snaked our boy on that one wave last week. He's a fucking wanker. A fucking wanker."

Kring glared, his stomach in knots. This dude, drunk as he was, looked mean. Stocky and simple, and more than that, an eagerness to scrap made his eyes glow. Kring felt a trembling in his legs. He hadn't been in a fight since seventh grade. Other than stupid words between them, he had no problem with this dude. As calmly as he could, he looked Roddy in the eyes and said evenly, "Why don't you go see about your friend in there? He might need help wiping his ass."

Lightning quick, Roddy was free from his friend's grasp and whipped a fist at Kring's face. It glanced off his cheek and Kring struck back and that quickly they were in the middle of a brawl, a vortex of aggression that sucked in half a dozen people in an instant. Roddy flailed in all directions trying to get at Kring. Spill and Roger were in the tangle and the other Aussie was caught too, trying to settle things and hustle Roddy outside. But the pack closed in on them with more people shoving and swinging and cursing and yelling.

"Fucking Aussies!" someone yelled from the scrum and was answered "Fucking Yanks!" as a huge form landed on the pile with a percussive Whump! It was Allewegen joining in the struggle, punching blindly and shoving people, digging for the center of the fight. Kring's cheekbone was sore and felt puffy, and someone in the tangle elbowed him in the back of the head. From the middle of the swarm, out of his swollen eye, he saw Allewegen swinging blindly and felt an arm close in on his neck. Instinct told him it was Roddy's arm and he squirmed enough to get free.

116

Allewegen worked his way in and trapped Roddy's head. Through the underbrush of bodies Kring saw a big box fly over the crowd. It looked like one of the speakers, launched perhaps by some unseen rioter. Kring ducked and the flat side smacked against Irrelevant Roger's head and bounced to the floor. Like a ringside bell, that missile seemed to signal the end of the round as Allewegen and the other Australian muscled Roddy free of the tangle and toward the door.

"Fucking everywhere we go, mate," Allewegen grumbled as he limped through the crowd with his friend. "Everywhere on the fucking planet, you've got to get in a punch-up." Roddy seemed dazed, but he was grinning like a mad fool.

"Oy, Wegsie, my shirt got torn. Can yeh get me another?" he said, looking down at his Bare Breast clothing.

"Sure, mate, let's just get the fuck out of here."

Kring turned to Spill when they were gone. "What a bunch of assholes, huh?" he said with a grin.

Spill was pumped up. "That was cool!" he yelled. "Not only do we get one of the most famous surfers in the world at our party, but we beat him up! That's awesome!"

After a few minutes Kring went into the kitchen to settle down, searching for something to eat. When he saw no food lying out in the open, his mind went blank and for a second he forgot what he wanted. Someone must have set up the stereo again because the music resumed with some thumping late-night reggae. Kring reached for the door to one of the cabinets and at that same instant Buddy flew across the counter and slammed Kring into the refrigerator with a menacing growl. "You sonuvabitch," Buddy snarled through clenched teeth. Kring was stunned. He wasn't recovered from the last attack and hadn't even put his hands up to defend himself. But now he shoved Buddy back against the doorway, yelling, "What the fuck's the matter with you?"

The crowd right around the kitchen gathered closer. Everyone outside that circle partied on, unaware of the tension. Bunny Wailer played on as if nothing was wrong, the way the music had done all night.

No one held Kring and Buddy apart. They just stood, glaring at each other, separated by an invisible referee.

"You're a scumbag," Buddy spat.

"What's your problem, man? What *is* this?"

Buddy simply turned with a sneer and a cynical laugh and walked away into the party, into the outer circle that had never known there was a fight.

Kring stood in the kitchen, surrounded by people who seemed as confused as he felt. "What the hell was that all about?" someone asked. Kring was silent, watching the spot where Buddy had melted into the crowd.

Maury came up to him through the mob. "He saw you kissing Bev outside," he said. "That was uncool, dude."

Kring looked at Maury with surprise and said, "That's the first time I ever heard you say 'dude.'"

It probably gnawed at Buddy to see him with Bev, but Kring knew that one kiss shouldn't have been enough to provoke such an attack. But he said nothing while Maury shook his head and repeated, "Uncool. Uncool." Kring just ran his fingers through his hair and mumbled, "Shit." This was getting to be one fucked-up night.

Kring stumbled over to the keg and drew a cup mostly full of foam. There was some beer in the bottom of the cup, enough to make it worth drinking, so he drank. Victoria had vanished. Most of the girls were gone. He searched the shrinking crowd for Lotion. She, too, had bailed apparently.

He dropped onto the green couch, into a seam where two of the cushions met, and the couch had never seemed this comfortable before. The little bit of beer in his cup was still cold and he sipped it gratefully for a few peaceful minutes, minutes that were punctuated by random shouts and that reggae beat. When he emptied the cup and looked up, Irrelevant Roger was standing above him with a strange look of fear on his face and a red flush. Then his face was white. Then flushed again. Then white. He glanced in the direction that Roger stared and saw the source of the fear and strangely alternating complexion. A Township police officer stood in the doorway.

"Someone report a disturbance at this address?" he barked.

Everyone was all of a sudden quiet and respectful, and Crank stepped forward to take charge of dealing with the cop. "Um, no, sir," he said. "There was some trouble earlier in the evening, but everything is straightened out now. No problems now. Everything's cool. Thanks for stopping by to check, though. We appreciate it."

Roger timidly concealed his beer cup behind his hip, and Kring saw two heads with baseball caps on backwards flash past the kitchen window in the dark.

"No problems, huh?" the cop confirmed wearily. "There aren't any underage drinkers here, are there?"

"No, sir."

"Well keep the noise down because if I have to come back, I'm writing tickets and checking IDs and busting anyone who's underage and confiscating the keg. Okay?"

"Yes, sir. Thank you. Have a good night."

When the cop had gotten back into his car and shut off the flashing lights, the room seemed to breathe a quiet sigh of relief, and Crank turned to Spill and Roger and said defiantly, "I hate cops."

Spill and Roger agreed. "Cops suck."

A Colony's Drama

They awoke the next morning flushed with success. Their second party had been a huge hit, and most of Long Beach Island knew it, most of Long Beach Island that mattered, anyway. Even the cops knew it. The Colony had cleared forty dollars and cared nothing about the mess they found in the morning.

"This is great," Crank crowed as he sidestepped a battered speaker lying face down in the middle of the floor. "A couple more parties like that and we'll be notorious on LBI. Famous, just like Kring, our resident surf star."

"But what about art?" Maury protested.

"What about it?" Crank shot back. "We'll get to it. Dude, it'll be there, part of our legend and all."

Maury put his palm to his forehead. "Does anyone else have a head-ache?" he quietly asked.

"I feel great," Crank said energetically as he moved toward the kitchen. "Nothing like getting laid to put a little spring in your step."

"You didn't get laid," Spill accused him.

"Whaddaya mean?"

"I watched you try to maneuver that chick into the bedroom, dude. And she gave you the Heisman."

Crank gave a sly smile. "Well, I almost got laid."

Maury was the only one who admitted to a hangover. Even Kring felt clearheaded and spry, which amazed him in the wake of the tequila he'd had. "How many kegs did we go through?" he asked.

"Two halfs," Spill replied, "and a case of Meisterbrau."

"And the rum."

"And the tequila."

"Oh, the tequila," Crank groaned.

"Hey, there were a lot of good-looking women here last night," Spill noted. "And a decent male-female ratio."

"Yeah, where'd they all come from?"

"I met a bunch of them on the beach and invited them," Spill said. "And Lotion brought a few friends. And, of course, Bev." He leered at Kring when he pronounced her name.

Maury shook his head and murmured, "Uncool. Uncool."

Crank glanced around and asked, "Hey, where is Buddy, anyway?"

"I think he's still asleep."

Just then Buddy emerged from his bedroom. He was naked and he gave the group no more than a semiconscious wave on his way to the kitchen.

"Hey, man, there's coffee," Maury called out. Buddy was already pouring himself a cup. He grabbed a second chipped "LBI" mug and filled that with the steaming dark brown liquid. Then he shuffled sleepily back to the room carrying the two cups without acknowledging his roommates.

"You're really ready to wake up, huh?" Maury called again. "Two cups of coffee?"

Buddy stopped at the door and glanced over. "Bev's still in bed," he declared matter-of-factly. He sniffed the steam rising from the cups in his hand. "I just hope the aroma doesn't wake Irrelevant. He's still passed out on the other mattress in here." He laughed and disappeared behind the door.

"Hmmmm," Maury intoned dramatically, "the plot thickens."

They spent the next few minutes discussing the party, trading stories of the night before and assessing the damage to the building and their reputations. A half hour after his first appearance Buddy emerged again, this time wearing Spill's lifeguard shorts and a wrinkled U of Delaware T-shirt, and he walked swiftly out the door. They heard his car engine start. It idled for a few minutes. Then Bev crept uneasily from the room, looking awkward and disheveled. She managed an embarrassed smile toward the guys as she scurried out the door.

"See you, Bev!" Crank called after her.

The parties continued every night for a week, each one a little bit bigger than the last, a little bit louder, the cops arriving earlier in the evening, the crowds dispersing deeper into each morning. The Colony accepted that it had been born to provide these parties, and in turn the parties provided for them. They were pulling in an average of fifty dollars a night.

Each day following, however, Kring found himself bored by lunch-time. There were still no signs of waves on the horizon. The island was in the middle of a summer flat spell so typical for the East Coast. Spill and Crank and Irrelevant Roger all were working most days. Buddy disappeared regularly, but according to a schedule that defied pattern. Kring would just wander around the empty house, halfheartedly cleaning up the debris from the night before. There was no more violence after the first night, but all week the thoughts kept coming back to him about the fight with the Aussies and about Buddy's strange attack. He could not convince himself that Bev was the root of it. There hadn't been another such incident, but Bev still tried to flirt with Kring, and Buddy was still very cool toward him. He felt pretty sure that Buddy didn't care about her as much as that. She was just a convenient excuse, and Kring was still confused. I thought I was getting to know him, kept running through his brain.

So he was alone in the house. Maury was there, of course, but might as well have not been. He made no secret that he thought Kring was in the wrong, and he didn't seem to have yet forgiven him. Anyway, Maury shut himself up in the bathroom after breakfast and played his music right through lunch.

They were long, hot, boring days and Kring spent many of the afternoons searching through Holgate for a good spot to watch the sunset. He found two or three prospective sites, but even as he surveyed them he knew these hazy July days would not end in anything but undetectable blendings of worn-out day and begrudging night.

He returned anyway one evening, to the best spot, a quiet back street with acres of salt marsh separating him from the water. He came to sit on a crumbling, rotten fence and watch the blending. It sure looked to Kring like a discount-store non-sunset, nothing like a sunrise, even a hazy one. He couldn't afford to buy any beer and he didn't smoke Spill's pot, so he just sat and watched and listened. He heard the shouts of children, he heard gulls talking, he heard the buzz of a boat he couldn't see behind the grass. It all soon bored him and he headed back to the house in the falling dusk.

There he found another party trying to impose itself on the Colony. Through the window as he approached Kring could see at least a dozen people moving around, probably milling around a hidden quarter barrel. Leaning against the wall outside, Maury smoked a Parliament with exaggerated cool. "Spill got another keg," he said with disgust as Kring walked past him with a nod and a quiet, "Hey, dude."

As he stepped inside, Kring immediately identified the booming voice of Denis coming from the kitchen, trading stories of last night's party with Spill and Crank. "Hey, man," he said to Kring when he saw him, "I thought you weren't going to join this party house."

"Yeah, well, you know how it is, Denis, I go where the women will be," Kring replied as he resigned himself to another night of noise and society and drew himself a beer at the tap. "What's that Mimi Dresden up to these days, anyway?"

Denis laughed and shook his head. "That's all over, dude! I lost her trail." He spoke from under a foam moustache. "I don't think she really exists. Don't think she ever did. That's my theory." He paused for another swallow of beer. "What are you doing tonight?" he asked Kring. "Wanna go out? I'm going to the Ketch, meeting a friend there."

Kring actually considered the offer. It might be nice to get away from this scene for a change. Although he didn't really like Denis, Kring knew that the boy could be fun to party with sometimes. It wasn't difficult to con him into buying three out of four rounds at the bar if one made a big deal out of his largess. And he often did stupid things while drunk that made for entertaining viewing. As Kring considered his options, three attractive girls walked hesitantly through the door. Kring thought he knew the prettiest one, a delicate little blond with no breasts and pouting lips. He thought he remembered her from the night before. She had been impressed with his surfing accomplishments, as he recalled. "Um, I think I'll hang out here," he said dismissively, "or wherever that little girl goes."

Denis shrugged, unconcerned. He stood by the keg for another hour, telling party tales from college. By the time he decided it was time to leave for the Ketch Club, Kring was smiling broadly and involved in a lively discussion with the blonde. Denis tried to work his way into the conversation but he only got as far as "Juliet? I'm Denis," before both parties turned away from him and found seats on the back of the couch. Kring barely paid attention when Denis leaned over and said, "I got a nice little buzz working here, dude. Now we can go out and buy expensive beers and get plowed for half the money. Sure you don't wanna go?"

He waited a minute for a response and then lumbered to the door.

Denis arrived at the Ketch nightclub with his buzz still intact, and he strode in past the bouncers, whom he knew well, with a confident "How's it going, dude." He entered a sensual-overload world of bodies, tanned and detailed, draped in expensive but casual clothes. The air was humid and flavored with cigarette smoke, perfume and loud, LOUD music. This turbulence was exactly what Denis was seeking. This was a world he thought he knew inside and out.

As he made his way to the bar he greeted people he knew slightly, and his stare made contact with the eyes of a girl sitting at a table by the blinded windows. She had short brown hair and wore a polo shirt. "Not bad" registered briefly in his mind. But this eye contact, it turned out, was a mistake of circumstance, not some magic point of convergence between two souls whose lives had been spent preparing for this one turn of Life's hole card. Without thinking, Denis recognized the moment immediately for its insignificance and looked straight past the girl. Amid the sonic assault from the band on stage, Denis scanned the room and spotted his friend Jerry at the bar, laboring to get the bartender's attention.

Denis wedged his way through the tightly bunched crowd as Jerry succeeded in placing his order. Denis reached between two people to tap his friend on the shoulder. Nods were exchanged but no words because they could not be heard without great effort. Neither Jerry nor Denis was prepared to expend that much effort. When two brown, perspiring bottles were set on the bar before Jerry, he relayed one of them back to Denis and grabbed the other. Each tipped a bottle to his mouth at the same time. The two of them stood coolly, wordlessly by the bar for a few minutes, then they wandered over to the dance floor to check out the action.

It was pretty much the same dance floor as it always was. Denis silently calculated his chances of going home with someone out there. The band thundered along, just like the band that was here last week, and the one the week before that. This band was called Casual Rebellion. Denis thought they looked bored as they played.

"No, I'm right and you know it, don't you," Denis was insisting above the tumult. He had just finished explaining to Jerry how he knew that the girl in the white T-shirt and blue denim skirt dancing below their position on the balcony didn't put out because she kept looking at her feet while she danced.

Jerry made no response to Denis's argument. He tossed back the shot of Jack Daniels that his friend had bought for him, then continued to stare into the crowd below without focusing on anything.

Denis leaned over the railing and followed the path of a lonely little punker girl below. Dark hair. Pierced nose. She looked radical, Denis thought. She disappeared beneath the balcony and a flash of movement to his left grabbed Denis's attention. A young guy in shorts and a long-sleeve, button-down shirt, a potential rival of Denis for any girl he might go home with, rolled a little spitball out of what looked like a chunk of surfboard wax. The guy dipped it into a drink someone had abandoned and tossed it onto the dance floor. He did this a few more times and he and his buddy — a guy with sculpted blond hair and horn-rimmed glasses, another potential rival (they were all potential rivals), laughed conspiratorially at their own wit. Denis sneered at them, secure in the knowledge that they were assholes. The next shot, though, landed in someone's hair and Denis changed his opinion of them as the victim waved his hands wildly, as if trying to defend himself against some flying creature. Maybe they were cool.

The spitball victim stopped flailing and just glanced around suspiciously and Denis's focus drifted to something else on the dance floor, movement at the back. It was a girl in a bright green dress with a strangely familiar presence. He watched her snake her way through the crowd, squeezing effortlessly past dancers as the music shook the walls. Denis was captivated by the way she moved. As he followed her path, one of the spitballs bounced off her shoulder and she lifted her face to the balcony and glared straight at him for an instant. In that moment he felt his stomach drop to the bottom of his groin and his soul was shaken white. It was Mimi Dresden.

The girl almost immediately shifted her gaze to the spitball artillerymen alongside Denis, and she shot them a meaningful finger. But Denis no longer saw her. His focus had been paralyzed by that instantaneous eye contact. She disappeared beneath their feet.

Quickly, Denis shook Jerry and said urgently, "Let's go downstairs! That was her!" Jerry struggled with a "Who?" as he shook his sleeve from Denis's weak grip and turned to follow him with unconsciously deliberate steps down the staircase.

As Denis and Jerry descended the stairs, the band reached a point in their show where they filled the stage with fog. The crowd at the Ketch seemed bored by it, even as it infiltrated their ranks and isolated figures from one another. The fog was thicker than it really had to be for its purpose.

Once he reached floor level Denis waded into the unnatural cloud. Jerry stumbled close behind, interested in who or what Denis was pursuing so single-mindedly. With every third step his Topsiders stuck to the floor, the surface thick with spilled liquor. Denis peered through the smoke-hidden dancers as well as he could and continued across the outer edge of the floor toward the back bar.

He stopped abruptly. There, through a break in the fog bank, he saw Mimi Dresden. She was behind the bar, serving drinks. She simply beamed through that hole for the moment it was open, the smoke parted as though just for this vision. The soft, misty gray edges of the fog window framed her face and he knew it was Mimi. She didn't smile and her eyes were focused down in the sink behind the bar, but Denis could tell. The uniform was different from the other ones she'd worn, but she wore this one, too, as only Mimi Dresden could wear it, with a grace and allure that he had previously seen only in movies. His soul once again went briefly faint, but when the opening drifted past and she and the bar were once again enshrouded, he turned sideways and squeezed his way past dancing bodies, continuing his motion toward the bar, toward Mimi Dresden.

As the fog dissipated and Casual Rebellion kicked in to their version of "Livin' On A Prayer," Denis found himself wiggling up to the bar. There was only one bartender there now, and he wasn't Mimi Dresden. Denis asked him where the other bartender had gone. As the band thundered behind them, the bartender yelled "What?" and Denis sheepishly decided not to repeat the question. Instead he ordered two shots of Sambuca and overtipped the guy. He figured to wait near the bar until Mimi Dresden reappeared.

But he hadn't figured on his companion's refusal to do another shot with him. "No way. I got to drive, man," Jerry claimed. Thus Denis felt obliged to drink both, and quickly. The first felt okay but the second, he knew right away, was a mistake. His throat and stomach objected and he burped and felt ill.

Shortly after that — he wasn't sure how shortly, his sense of time sequencing seemed a casualty of drunkenness — the edges of his vision went dark — just the edges — and he was aware of hands, or one hand, under an armpit. He was pretty sure it was one of his armpits. He was leaning on something and it bounced him a little. Moving. He was moving. The sky had lots of little stars in it.

But that streetlight glared in his face. It hurt his eyes. He had something to tell Jerry, something important. He knew Jerry was around; he could hear his voice in his ear. Just one ear, though.

But when he told Jerry what he had to tell him, he ran out of breath. He got tired before he could finish and Jerry couldn't understand the first part anyway.

He was in a car. It smelled stuffy, but he couldn't put down the window. The window was already down. His throat felt full. No, he didn't want to throw up. They passed the 7-Eleven. Then they passed another one, on the other side of the road. It looked like the same 7-Eleven. But it was on the other side of the road. Then things got dark. He didn't think

126

he got sick, though.

That was one good thing.

Kring was stepping out the door with little blond Juliet when an unfamiliar car, a late-model sedan, pulled up in the front yard and braked abruptly on the stones. Behind them, inside the house, an Artists Colony party raged.

"Is this the Artists Colony?" Kring heard a voice yell from inside the car. Before Kring could answer, the voice blurted, "Oh shit!" The driver hopped out of the car and rushed to the other side. His face was thin and his clothes draped him closely. "Hurry," he said to Kring, "he's gonna throw up. I don't want him to puke in my car."

When the driver opened the door, Kring could see his heavily browed eyes pinch shut in disgust. "Too late," he moaned. "Shit!" He reached in to pull the sick passenger out of the car and whined, "Denis, you're an asshole. I can't believe you blew chunks all over my friggin' car."

Denis mumbled a semiconscious syllable as his body was dragged by one armpit. His head fell unsupported to one side.

The driver turned to Kring. "He just went blotto on me in the bar. I don't know where he lives; I just remember him telling me about a party here, y'know, gave me directions, sounded like he hung out here a lot. I didn't know where else to bring him." He dragged Denis's slumping form slowly out onto the ground beside the car. "He didn't start to get sick until I got here," he continued as he pulled one foot, then the other out of the car and laid them on the stones. The legs were stiff, the feet crossed.

He shut the door and shuffled over to the driver's side. "Shit," he said again, inspecting the seat and floor where Denis had vomited, "now I gotta clean and vacuum and spray the whole interior. I just had it detailed a week ago." He started the car and backed away. He drove off without another word.

Kring reached his foot out in the dark and poked it at the passed-out Denis. "He's breathing," he assured Juliet. "He'll be okay as long as nobody runs over him." He took her hand to help her step over the body. "So you've never seen the beach at night, huh?"

Thirty minutes later, when they returned from the beach, the party had faded to a faint echo of its former self. By Kring's count, there were no more than eight people left in the house, and they mostly sprawled in the living room, trading smart remarks. Pink Floyd was on the stereo. Maury sat slumped in the armchair, obviously depressed. Denis was still passed out. He had been dragged inside and propped up in a folding chair next to Maury, posed in mimicry of the musician's intense posture, which had become a familiar joke around the Colony. "What happened to the party?" Kring asked.

"What do you think?" Crank said. "Cops broke it up, as usual. Made everyone leave who was underage."

Kring turned to Juliet with a grin. "How old are you?" he asked.

"Eighteen," she replied, as if unsure that it was the right answer.

"Your friends too?"

She nodded.

"Well, shit, looks like your ride left, Julie. Hey, anyone heading toward Spray Beach?"

A ride was arranged for Julie with a guy who Kring figured was sober enough to be trusted. She gave Kring a little goodnight kiss before leaving. "I love this place," she said as she headed out the door.

Within ten minutes the group had dispersed. Everyone had either left or passed out. Irrelevant Roger put a Big Audio Dynamite disc into the machine and went to bed, leaving Kring with the depressed Maury and the comatose Denis.

"Some party, huh?" Kring said as he headed toward the kitchen. "Any beer left?"

"A couple in the fridge," Maury said glumly.

"You want one?"

"No."

"What's wrong?"

"Nothing."

Kring dropped gratefully into the ratty couch with one hand wrapped around a beer can. With a start he jumped up and moved over. "Wet spot," he said with a grin. "So what's wrong, man? You not writing songs? Not having fun at these parties?"

"I'm writing, I'm having fun," Maury said with a face that under the right conditions could have turned milk sour.

"I know!" Kring said with a drunken leer. "You're not getting laid!"

Maury just shook his head.

"Well, that's 'cause you just sit off by yourself whenever there's people over and — "

"THAT'S NOT IT!" Maury exclaimed. He glared at Kring. "Why do you care anyway?"

Kring sat puzzled and gulped a swallow of beer. "I don't know, man. I guess ... I don't know ... maybe it's time I went to bed." He pushed himself up from the couch and stumbled around to head for his hammock.

"It's this place," he heard Maury say in almost a whisper.

"What?" He moved slowly back to the couch.

"Nothing."

"It's this place? Is that what you said?"

Maury said nothing.

"I know it's a shithole, but it's as much as we can afford."

"No, not the house, dude, the place." He glared at Kring. "You don't get it, do you? This was supposed to be an artists colony. And no one thinks it's for real. They all think it's an excuse to party. You think it's an excuse to party," he accused. "There are no artists here. Least of all me. We're all just a bunch of drunken bums living at the beach. Escaping from real life. That's all we're doing. And I'm the only one who thought it would be different. I thought we could do stuff here, like create and live creative lives and, and ... *do* stuff, I don't know. Spill said he was going to write poetry, Crank was gonna — I don't know what Crank was gonna do, but they were all just making fun of me. At least you didn't pretend. You said you surfed, that's the truth at least."

Kring sat on the arm of the couch as Maury spoke, as he allowed his fear and his frustration a voice in the stillness of the night.

"You guys don't care," he continued, his voice cracking a little under the strain. "You got places you can go. You don't understand; this *is* the place I could go. There's no place else. I quit my job. You don't understand, if I don't make this work, I got nothing. I got nowhere to go, man."

His eyes focused on the base of the wall, at a spot where what looked like a tomato had been splattered, but Kring could see Maury was not focusing on the mess. It was more like he focused on the emptiness that lay beyond the Artists Colony for him. Kring sensed a little bit of what Maury feared, felt the psychic cold draft that chilled Maury so deeply.

He didn't know what to say.

They sat together and listened to the faint sounds of sleeping. The music had ended and the night was so near to silent that Kring couldn't be sure that any whisper he might hear was not imagined. Maury's body had twisted slightly in his chair as he had spilled his fears, and Kring saw the desperate, foolish hope his roommate had placed in this adventure. He didn't understand its desperation, but he knew it was real.

Beside Maury, Denis sat no closer to consciousness than before but bent more surely with the effects of gravity. Almost ready to fall. His posture still approximated Maury's, but that was no longer amusing to Kring.

"So what are you gonna do?" Kring asked.

Maury looked at him with empty eyes for a minute. "I don't know," he finally said, dropping his head. "Maybe go back to the city, find another lousy job, another apartment in the 'burbs."

Kring too looked at the carpet. *Such despair*, he thought.

Denis fell to the floor with a thump and the simultaneous crash of his collapsed chair; he let out a snore and didn't stir further. Kring smiled briefly, then looked at Maury, who was shaking his head.

"Hey look, man, you can't give up; you got no choice," Kring said. "If you've given up, it's dead. But if you think it can happen, and not out of desperation but because ... I don't know.... All I know is you can make it work. You're right; I don't care about an artists colony. I just needed a place to live for a while. And right now this is just a party shack. But you're the one who's got to do it, dude. You got to get Spill off his ass and get him to write poems. Get Crank to do whatever Crank does. Show your talent. If all you do is tell people it's an artists colony, they don't care. But then you show them, and they'll start to believe it too."

Maury's head hung against his chest and he did not move, but Kring knew he listened.

"It's not just a matter of 'if you believe it hard enough' or shit like that, but you can make others believe...." Kring considered what he was going to say, as if it were a discovery for him too, "and they'll help it happen."

Maury raised his head and looked up at him, his hands still folded between his knees.

Kring took a breath and continued. "See, Spill doesn't think of this as a place for artists, he doesn't think of himself as an artist. To him and to Crank and to Irrelevant Roger, it's just a gimmick. They think it might help them get laid. *You* gotta change that, if it's gonna happen at all. If you don't, it's dead, and we'll all probably wind up getting busted for real at one of these parties, under that friggin' animal house law. You and I both know that."

They sat in silence once again for a minute, but the silence, Kring thought, had a different sound to it now, a different pitch to its breathing.

Kring stood up and looked down at Denis stretched out on the blue carpet, his skin as pale as the flesh of a pear. "He'll be all right till morning," he decided. "Mind if I turn out the lights?"

Maury assented with a nod and a murmur, and Kring went around the room switching off the lamps until the room was so dark it could have been any room, in any house. He found his hammock and climbed into it. He settled in and closed his eyes. After a time he thought he heard someone whisper, "Yeah." He opened his eyes. The faint light of the distant street lamp gave a texture to the darkness, and he heard someone moving in the room, but then the silence returned.

Chapter 14

Dreams and Visions

It never occurred to Kring, he realized later, to ask how it came about, why there were surfable waves, big waves, breaking in the bay in back of his apartment as he looked out his window, or what made the sky look like a worn canvas. He didn't stop to wonder about it, that was the cool thing. He was on his old seven-foot single fin, paddling out into the strange, syrupy green froth that rose and tossed higher than any wave he'd ever seen, even in the ocean.

The waves broke out near the channel, fifteen majestic feet high at their fullest extension. They seemed too powerful to be generated or contained in this shallow, brackish pool that sat between the island and the mainland. But there they were, arching slowly forward into near-perfect spirals of pea green and meringue, then collapsing with a slow-motion violence and an unceasing dull roar. The turbulence was awesome and the sky behind the walls of water, that canvas sky, was clotted with slate-grey clouds. A hundred dully shining suns tried to breach the weak points in the pattern but could not. This world had an enclosed feel to it as Kring paddled out. The waves were huge, but he felt no fear of them. He was unable to believe they were real or that he was going to surf them.

There were other surfers out, but none was close enough to him to be recognized. No wetsuits or riding styles looked familiar. People ringed the shore, watching in mute fascination.

These were waves in the bay, he told himself again, and still it didn't seem real. The swells washed over the buoys that marked the Intracoastal Waterway. They broke cleanly in front of his garage apartment, and down there, to the north, closer to the bridge, he saw no movement. The surface of the bay lay flat. He drove himself forward and the sky seemed to drop closer to him. The air became heavier and the water felt thicker as he pushed his way across its surface. It was warmer than the ocean and left a sharper taste on his lips.

He sensed a massive presence looming over him. He strained his neck to look up and saw he was beneath a giant wall of water about to crash down, sure to swallow him completely. The curl was already pitching out in front of the wave face, a translucent canopy over Kring and his board. The dark core of the wave was before him. He stared into it and it spoke to him, told him that it could hold his body underneath this wave, forever. Kring put his head down and paddled with all the strength he could find. He paddled straight up the face and then felt his board rise with the wave and become unweighted. He couldn't tell if he was being launched backward with the falling lip or left in the air as it passed beneath him. The split second he had expected passed and still he hung in the air, his fate uncertain. His experienced timing fell victim to these strange waves; he was still out of water, hanging in the thick, warm air, unable to place himself or the force that threatened him. Was it behind him on its way to shore or still above? Was it poised to crush and swallow him? He could not tell. He felt almost like he was swimming in those ghostly clouds that enclosed the whole bay and beach, the trees around his garage — but the beach in front of his garage looked strange; he didn't remember crossing it on his way out here. He didn't remember a beach there at all, just a bulkhead. All of a sudden he realized that his extended stay in midair must mean that he was falling down, pitched backward by the lip into its gaping maw. He had been sucked over the falls of this wave whose heart had spoken to him. And he had listened to it. Now he felt panic and took a quick breath of air, praying that he wouldn't be driven underwater with no reserve of oxygen. Just as he got that gulp of air, he flopped harmlessly on his belly, on the back slope of the wave. It had passed beneath him. He was safe.

He turned his head to call to Buddy, paddling out alongside him, thirty yards away. As he opened his mouth to speak, another wave hit him, from out of nowhere it seemed, as if atoning for the failure or the weakness of the first. Kring was flipped over like driftwood before he could react, before he could even think, and he clung desperately to his board. The abrupt taste of salt water stung his throat. He felt the board hammered against his chest by the turbulence and fury that drove him down like a pile jet. He was thrown and tumbled underneath the water, where it turned a different color — still green but murkier, more emerald. His lungs demanded oxygen but the cruel wave would not let him up. His cheeks were expanded but filled with nothing. He exhaled calmly underwater, just letting the force expend its rage against his helpless body.

Then his head broke the surface and he gulped air gratefully and coughed and gulped air again. He was floating weakly in the froth that the wave left behind on its way to the beach, the beach that Kring didn't recognize, although it was in front of his apartment. Wearily he climbed on his board and began paddling again. The board's label was under his nose. It read "Oceanside the '70." Strange, thought Kring. He hadn't used this board in six years.

He sat up on the time-yellowed Oceanside and took stock of his position. All around him the bay was churning and alive, but Kring sensed no pattern to this swell. There seemed to be no clear sets rolling in, no way to predict where the next wall would rise.

Far to the south he saw a surfer with bright orange trunks take off on a big wave. The figure was too far away for Kring to see clearly anything but the orange shorts and the surfer's path down the wave face. There was a cool ease to his glide that seemed to defuse some of the surging power, some of its fearsomeness, even as it exploded a step behind him. It was a stirring ride, a heroic ride, and Kring admired it. He heard hoots up and down the beach, from surfers in the water and from spectators on the sand. The sand, Kring noticed, looked like Hawaiian sand, honey-golden and rich, not soft and white like the sand he knew from Long Beach Island.

He felt the swells rise and fall and roll beneath him with no rhythm as he sat waiting. This is not the ocean, he reminded himself, as if it would convince him. This is the bay, outside my window.

He did not recall seeing the horizon lift with the wave. He didn't recall preparing to paddle for it as it approached. All Kring knew he was poised to make the drop into the pocket of a wall twice, three times his own height, and it terrified him. It did not look from the peak like it could be a real wave below him, and Spill was suddenly at his side on his boogie board, telling him that he should have gone to that surf movie, so he'd know what to do now, on the way down. But I did go to the movie, he thought. The drop came with a rush that forced his heart into his throat. The bottom turn was a blur but felt right and he found himself racing toe-to-toe with a great, green wall of water. He was moving with it, carried along its peeling line. Then he felt it, the place he always sought. He found the last gentle spot in all the unfolding fury, the eye of this storm. He rode in the deepest place of peace in all the watery violence that swirled around it, the wave and the whole churning bay. It was tucked in the corner of the white rushing curl, protected by it and impenetrable. But Kring *had* penetrated to it and now knew its beauty. It was fragile beyond measure and left him in awe. He looked into a wave face that mirrored him and saw only water rushing to nourish the lip spitting above.

He played with the force. He directed the Oceanside downhill and rocketed out in front of the curl to the flat at the base of the wall, then stomped with his back heel and climbed with no more effort than that to the leading lip where the wave formed out of a restless bay. He sailed there for seconds then stalled his board and slipped into a tunnel that caught up with him from behind, where he found waiting for him once again that last gentle spot, also carried along with the wave, deeper this time but always there, always calm. He left it behind, shot off ahead of it like a bullet, went low along the face, crouched for speed, and then catapulted out beyond the lip, launched into the drenched grey air. He was flying.

Seven or ten or twenty seconds later, he landed behind the wave and turned to see it sweep up on the beach, much farther than any other wave he had seen out here. People were scattered by it and some were swept away. Kring could see their figures, brightly clothed and tiny, struggling against the fierce storm tide that had washed up around them and taken them back with it, all in a flash. He was afraid for them. He worried that his garage had gotten swamped. But he had seen and tasted the last and deepest gentle spot, and it was wonderful, miraculous. He looked again to shore but could not tell whether his garage had been flooded.

It was this that occupied his mind as he awoke. He found himself dry and in his hammock, and it took him a minute to realize that he wasn't even in his garage this morning. He was in the Artists Colony and there never had been a surfable break in Barnegat Bay. He was disappointed but lay in his hammock and tried to hold onto the feeling and the magic of those waves. He found he could do it if he let them be real, if he gave them existence. He could remember them, could remember how it felt. And the feeling, at least, he knew was real.

"Hey, what day is it?" he mumbled to whoever was moving around in the kitchen.

"Um, I don't know," Crank's voice responded. "Tuesday? Thursday? Does it matter?"

"I don't think so," Kring mused as he sat up in his hammock, "but it might. Did we have a party last night? Or was that the night before?"

Crank pondered this at the counter. Spill sat next to him, silently pulling crumpled bills from the pocket of a pair of shorts he held in his hand. At last Crank gave up and said with a shrug, "I don't know."

Spill took one of the bills and stretched it out between his hands.

He raised it to his nose and drew in whatever aroma it offered. "No, we didn't have a party last night," he said to Crank disdainfully. "Broke our string, don't you remember? You went out with me to the Terrace Tavern. We met Denis there. We got wasted." He looked closely at the money, then sniffed it again. "Iced tea," he said. "I don't know what the fuck you did, Kring. You probably went drinking again with Keith and Tara."

"Who's Keith? Who's Tara?"

"That couple that were here the other night, you know, Lotion's friends from Swarthmore?"

Kring vaguely recalled someone in the past week who might fit the roles Spill described, but he couldn't be sure. The days and nights had blurred together in a strange rhythm of music, alcohol and morning hangovers just like this one, and Kring wasn't sure what it meant. He closed his eyes and clung to his surfing-in-the-bay dream with renewed conviction.

Spill just said, "Long Island iced tea," and set the bill down.

Kring pulled himself out of his hammock and strolled to the counter. "This Keith and Tara," he said, "are they maybe the type who might have slipped me a mickey?"

Spill unrolled a five, sniffed it first at one end, then the other. He shrugged and put it down in a spot of sunlight. "I don't know, man, they're your friends," he said as he reached for a stale tortilla chip that lay on the table surface. With a dull crunch he ate the chip and picked up the five again. He held the bill to his nose and said thoughtfully, "I think this was Wally's margarita."

Crank said, "Who's Wally?"

No one replied. Kring leaned on the counter and wondered why the last few days had gotten lost in his mind, how they had covered their tracks so well. It troubled him. This had never happened before, not in college, not during spring break, not even during senior week in high school, nothing like this. His dream he remembered vividly, and it seemed real, far more real than any cloudy picture of Keith and Tara or of yesterday's thunderstorm that Crank was talking about.

"Did I drink a lot the last few days?" he asked.

"Beer," Spill said, testing another dollar bill. He looked at Kring. "No more than anyone else, I guess. No, not really, because you didn't go with Crank and me to that sand bar in the inlet at lunchtime. Man, we did nothing but drink all afternoon. You didn't, as far as I know." He turned his attention to his money again. "This one's just beer," he said. "This one too," he said, placing another single on the pile.

Kring nudged Crank. "What's he doing?"

"All this money was laying on the bar last night. He's trying to figure out what got spilled on it through the course of the evening."

Kring nodded. "Anyway, I can't figure out what's happened." He jerked open the cabinets in search of something to eat. "It's weird. My dreams are more real to me than what passes for real life around here. I don't think I had a Lost Weekend or anything like that, I don't think I've been drinking that much. But I can't picture yesterday. I don't know what I did last night. All I know is last night in my dreams I surfed in the bay."

Spill looked up, his face suddenly lit. "Dude," he said, "I've had that dream, like I'm out in these big waves on my boogie board, or I'm standing on the shore and watching these waves and I'm at the bay, by the Township building. I know other guys who had a dream like that too."

"Well, I don't know what it means, but I've had it a couple of times, and it seems like those waves actually exist. And it seems like this Keith and Tara don't."

"That's pretty weird," Crank agreed.

"Jesus, someone spilled a lot of beer last night," was all Spill said as he put down another single.

"Hey, Spill," Kring said, "you working on the beach today?"

"No. But I gotta see my lieutenant about some competition I missed."

"Can you give me a ride to Ship Bottom? I need to see my landlord, let him know what happened to me. I don't want him to think I just blew him off. I feel pretty bad about just leaving like that. Besides, I got some stuff there I should get."

Spill only went as far as his morning meeting, so Kring had to walk the last thirty or forty blocks to his apartment. The day was bright and clear and made comfortable by a breeze from the south. It had been a summer of such days, it seemed to Kring, even if some of those days lately seemed to go into hiding in his mind. There were still no waves.

When Kring got to the house, he saw the pieces of his old Romantic, still lying uselessly in the yard, on the funeral bed of pine needles. They were just where he had left them — what was it now? Two weeks ago? Three? Who could tell? He went up to the front door and knocked, mentally rehearsing what he would say when Mr. Cox or his wife, Doris, opened the door. "I hit a bad streak of luck," he would say, "and I had no money to pay the rent and some friends offered me a place ..." No, best start off with an apology: "I'm sorry I just left like that, Mr. Cox, but I got caught up in something." That was better, he thought, but what was he trying to say to this old man? "Sorry I treated you like shit after all

137

you did for me"? No, not that harsh. Anyway, he'd know what to say, he figured, when they answered the damn door. But no one came, there was no stirring in the house, and Kring decided they were not home. Maybe I should leave a note, he decided, and he went into his apartment to look for a pen and some paper. On the couch sat the magazine with "his picture" in it and he could not resist a look. He flipped right to the page and for a moment almost believed it was himself; he could almost remember how it felt, that exact wave. His reality did a flip-flop as if a magnetic field had been passed over it, one pole to the other, then just as quickly back again.

"Oh, man, let me outta here," he groaned sadly to himself. He grabbed a pen and a subscription card from the magazine and quickly wrote his landlords a note explaining where he was. He stuck it in their screen door on his way out and headed back up to the beach to check the waves that hadn't been there an hour earlier and still weren't there now. He walked on to Brant Beach to hang out with Spill's partner, Googs, at the lifeguard stand and talk waves for a while. When that bored him, he decided to hitchhike back to the Colony.

Along the way he passed the Cafe driveway. Its sign beckoned to him with the torturous thought of a burger or something else to eat. Torturous because he was hungry and flat broke. He was considering a stroll down the lane to hang with Irrelevant or Victoria when a minivan pulled over and offered him a ride.

Behind the reeds that bowed gently in the breeze, Victoria lost track of how many hamburgers she had counted, and she didn't bother to begin again. "I think we're okay for now, Willy, at least until next week," she said to the cook as she shut the freezer door. Above her head the radio played "My Dream Come True." Erica Hope's hit was holding steady for the seventh week at number one. "God, I'm so sick of that song," Victoria said aloud for the thirty-fifth time this summer.

"I just thought it looked like we were running low on burgers, that's all," Willy said. Victoria heard a defensive tone in his voice and knew there was no reason for it, but she said nothing and let it pass. She turned to the counter where a customer waited to order.

"Yeah, could I get a cheese steak with onions?"

Victoria jotted down his order and ignored his admiring look. She had grown bored with admiring looks from customers this summer. The season as a whole was a little boring for her by now, and she looked forward to returning to school in little more than a month. Nothing much was happening here these days, it seemed. Just work, the beach when she wasn't working, going to the bars with her friends. The bars were getting old, too, especially the ones where the guys were most likely to hit on her with the worst lines, and it was always the ugly ones, the most boring. "I'm almost sorry I told Daddy I'd work here all season," she had confessed to her friend Trish the night before as they were driving to the Ketch. Another night at the bars. The last time she really had any fun was at that party in Holgate a few weeks back, at the place where that twerp Roger was living now. But his daily stories of their "craziness" there didn't entice her to return, and the Cafe wasn't much fun anymore either, she thought as she glanced around the deck and parking lot. No one came by just to hang out anymore. No one came by to watch sunsets.

She heard a small boat pull up at the bulkhead and thought for a moment it might be Kring. But it was only three skiers who wanted some Cokes. They thought they were really hot. She could see that right away. Their boat, at least, was nice looking, much classier than those little dinghies Kring used to bring by.

There didn't seem to be any sunsets now. She hadn't paid attention to them for weeks, and it seemed like the nights began when she wasn't looking, while she was getting dressed to go out or something. The summer days now had a quality that was not so much seamless, more just without highlights. Boring. She could hardly wait for school to begin.

It was midafternoon when Kring wandered back to the hovel. Spill was already there, sprawled out on the couch with a notebook and pen in his hands, an open bag of Doritos at his feet. When he walked through the door, it was the first time Kring was aware of what the atmosphere in the shack had become. Amid the bohemian filth of crumbs, furniture stuffing, empty bottles, used paperbacks and spent fire extinguishers that littered the room, the sound of the NOAA marine forecast droned interminably from the TV and in the air hung the mingled smells of faded marijuana smoke, stale beer and the Doritos. "What's up?" he asked as he stepped through the doorway. He noticed, also for the first time, that the door had been broken off its hinges and now stood upright against the front wall, blocking access to the light switch.

Spill looked up. "Maury finally got to me. So I told him I'd work on some poems. Just to shut him up. Hey, check this out, I picked it up at Body Language." He handed Kring a magazine on newsprint called the *Atlantic Juice Report*. Kring had seen it before. It was an East Coast surf newsletter that appeared every couple of months. "There's an article in there about us, dude. Page sixteen."

Kring opened to the middle of the paper and there it was, "Underground Ripper on LBI Cultivates Colony," byline: Fee Waybill. "Hey, this is that dude we were doing shots with the first party," Kring said with a laugh. "What a tweezer-head."

"You should read it. I think it's pretty cool. That's what made me want to write some poetry. When I read about how cool the Artists Colony sounded in there, I decided to come up with some poems about it. Of course, Maury's bitching had some effect, too."

With the article there appeared a photo of a surfer that the text identified as Kring, who in turn was identified as the phantom figure in the *Surfer* article. But the photo the newsletter published looked less like Kring than the *Surfer* picture, which wasn't him in the first place. Kring read aloud: "Recalling the legendary soul surfing days of the seventies counterculture, the Holgate Artists Colony is the center of a true underground lifestyle. It's the ultra-hip place to be on LBI. And at the eye of this swirling storm of debauchery and cutting edge-itude is Kring: the ultimate cult figure, founder of the colony and conqueror in the waves of Australian world title contender Dale Allewegen at a local break...." His voice trailed off. "This guy's an asshole," Kring said, shaking his head, feeling himself falling deeper without a struggle into the morass of surf celebrity. He rattled the paper and glanced up at Spill. "Is there anything for lunch?"

Lotion breezed through the door just then like a savior in a white T-shirt and greeted Kring with a gentle touch on his arm. Her sun-reddened hair swirled around her neck and her easy manner lifted Kring's mood instantly.

She turned an eye to Spill, reclining as he was in his uncharacteristic pose with pen and paper. "Whatcha doing, Spill-boy?" she asked as she sidled over to the couch.

"Working on some poems," was Spill's unsure reply.

"Oh yeah? What's this one about?" Lotion tapped the notebook Spill held upright in front of his face. His pen was in his mouth.

"Um, it's sort of based on *Lord of the Flies*. Did you ever read it?"

"In high school," she said.

"Well, there's this group of kids stranded on a desert island and the poem is about what if one of the kids ... like, I was wondering about the island they were on and ... well, if it had any good point breaks anywhere, if there were waves, and how it would have been different if there was a surfer in the crowd."

Lotion looked at him, then looked at Kring. He had a knowing smile on his face. "Are you serious?" she asked Spill with amusement.

"Well, yeah," he replied, rubbing his infant beard. He appeared a little hurt by her laughter. "See, I want to write poetry from the beach. Like, I'm from the beach, you know, and that's where I want my poems to come from. I want it to *mean* something, to make people think about the beach differently, you know? Besides, I got the idea from Kring."

Lotion nodded thoughtfully and glanced over at Kring. He raised his hand to claim responsibility. She laughed silently. Her hand found the Doritos bag and lifted three chips. She slipped one delicately in her mouth as she picked up a couple of sheets of paper with her free hand. "Are these more of your poems?" she asked.

"Yeah, I'm going to read some of them at our next party. Maury wants to make it a combination party/poetry reading. Maybe I'll have him play some music behind me. I think that would be cool."

"That would be fun. When are you going to do this?"

"Maybe Friday. I got to get these poems together, and plus we both work the next three nights. I got him a job at the Shellfish Company. Oh, and Crank wants to paint, wants to paint a picture of the Colony and my van and stuff to exhibit. So maybe Friday."

"Are you going to read this one, 'Never Forever'?"

"Yeah, that's one of my better ones, I think."

Lotion's eyebrows raised and her head tilted to the left, but she patiently went on to the next poem. "And what about this one?"

Spill leaned over to see which poem she was talking about. "I might give that one to Maury to write some music for it. It might make a good grunge song, don't you think?"

"Yeah, um-hm," she replied absently.

They were silent for a few minutes. From the TV the NOAA forecast buzzed repeatedly. "Marine warnings for nontropical systems: none expected," the reader announced in the same unexcited tone each time. Kring had counted four times since he'd walked in the door. He dug through the kitchen cabinets looking for food.

Lotion sifted through the half-dozen poems Spill had on the floor, and Spill chewed on his pen and stared at the pad. "Does 'broad' rhyme with 'Ford'?" he asked, then scribbled on the paper without waiting for an answer. He resumed chewing. "Man, this is hard work if you take it seriously," he said.

Lotion looked at him, sitting there in his Five-Mile Run shirt and biking shorts, turning pages with dirt-grey hands. She smiled at him but said nothing.

Kring called from the kitchen, where he was spreading peanut butter on crackers. "Hey, Lo, what have you been up to today?"

"Not much, really, but I did see this beautiful guy playing basketball all by himself — "

"That must have been me," Spill piped up. "I was playing basketball today; that's why my hands are dirty."

Lotion regarded him with amusement. "Get real," she said as she rose to join Kring by the kitchen. "No, I went for a walk this morning, down by that park on the bay, and there was this bronzed god playing basketball all alone on the court there. I didn't really pay any attention to him because I was just walking and he was just casually shooting baskets, no big deal. I went across the street in search of a Coke machine, and when I got back he was running and jumping and bouncing the ball, and so I just went over and sat down in the sand and watched him go through his games."

Kring watched her face as she imagined the basketball player. She seemed to descend almost into a trance as she described the scene. "Tell me about it," he said.

"He's beautiful, I said that before. His hair is longish and wild, finger-combed but not dirty — it's like surfer's hair, clean from the ocean but stiff from the salt. Like yours. And he's dark from the sun and he has a great body. Smooth and muscular. His sneakers are canvas, you know, classic, sweat-stained, and I can see one of the laces has broken a few times and he's skipped a hole or two in order to tie them. He's perfect. He's the guy who's supposed to be playing on every playground on days like this, all the time, everywhere, you know? Like a ghost almost, a legendary figure.

"And his face — his face, what's in his face? I mean he's got good features, nice eyes and all, but that's not where his beauty comes from. It's sort of intent, but relaxed, as if he's creating the game he's playing with each bounce of the ball and it changes each time the ball goes through the net — whish!"

"Whish?"

"Whish," she said with a smile, "just like that — whish! He smiles to himself when he makes a tough shot, I like that, I think it's cute, and he kicks a stone when three shots in a row bounce off the rim. He smiles at me when the ball rolls over against the fence by where I'm sitting and he comes to get it. I'm expecting a perfect smile, godlike and assured. But instead it's a little embarrassed. That's a bit of a letdown, but I like his face."

"So did you meet him or what?"

"I'm not finished; shut up. And he goes back to his jump shots and he's sweating, you know, it's really hot and he's jumping around. And his face is wet and running with sweat, his chest and back and arms are wet and shiny, and he looks flushed when he breaks for a minute and leans up against the chain-link fence. With all that sweat I wouldn't really want to touch him or anything, but I almost offer him my Coke. It feels like he'd rather I didn't, so I don't. I just watch him some more and I let my mind start to play around, you know, daydream. I see him, not like a potential lover or something like that, but as a symbol, an image of a certain type of man, not a real person at all but this figure of independence, a romantic loner, you know? It's like I mythologize this guy.

"I say to myself, here I am sitting here, and this beautiful, mythical figure is performing just for me and I can see something in him, an independence that drives him to play alone a game that is sometimes most beautifully played alone, playing out before me, just me, the small dramas that he's creating, and I think I'm being shown a little bit of that puzzling male psyche that I'd never been able to see before in my twenty-two years in this world. It's a little bit of that alluring, frustrating male ego, identity, dream.... It isn't any revelation, really, nothing clear, just a small understanding, almost unexplainable — it is unexplainable, really, but I know something that I never knew before."

"So what happens after you mythologize him this way?" Kring asked, suppressing a tinge of jealousy.

"Well, I'll tell ya, he doesn't seem to mind me using him like this, and the ball seems to make that 'whish' sound faster now and he's shooting as soon as he gets his hands on the ball and most of them are going in, like Whish! Whish! Whish! It's like he's winding up with a fast, furious finish to whatever league finals he's playing in.

"By this time the sun is getting really hot and my soda is gone so I get up to leave. He doesn't notice. I didn't expect him to, and I'm kind of glad that he hasn't. I have no urge to meet him. Well, I do but it's outweighed by the impression I got that he'd rather be alone and besides, I've created a beautiful vision around him, and I don't want to destroy it. But I'm glad I stopped to watch him." She stared out the window, then turned her eyes to Kring. "That's what I did today," she said, her face beaming.

Kring sat there grinning, looking in wonderment at her tanned, sculpted features and her bright eyes. "That's cool, Lo," he said thoughtfully. "You're pretty amazing, you know that?"

Lotion glanced at her watch. "Oh shit, I'm going to be late for work," she said. She jumped up and gave Kring a quick hug. "Thanks, babe,

I'll see ya later. Are you guys having another party tonight?"

"Probably," he wearily affirmed.

After she left, he mumbled jokingly, "I can play basketball too."

Spill looked up from his poetry. "What the hell was all that about?" he asked.

"Just Lotion making up her own universe, I think," Kring answered. "So who's sponsoring the keg tonight?"

Chapter 15

Buddy's Tale

The days continued to blend into one another, blurring the boundaries, removing moments from context until even the mornings did not belong to the afternoons.

"So are we having a keg tonight?" Spill asked late in one of those afternoons.

"Shit," Maury spat in response.

"What?" Spill responded defiantly. "What's up with you? I wrote poems today before my morning meeting. *I did my homework*, Dad. Don't cop an attitude."

"Besides, Maury," Crank butted in, "you got to work with Spill tonight anyway."

Maury said nothing, and Crank decided, "Okay, then, I guess it's my turn. I'll get a quarter, just in case people show up."

Kring spoke up. "Wait a minute," he said. "Spill and Maury won't be here, Buddy's not here, so we're getting a keg for me and you?"

"Buddy'll be back. Roger will be back. And you know people will stop over, just to see what's going on."

Denis walked in the door. "What's going on?" he said cheerfully.

"Just going out to get a keg. Care to contribute?"

"Always willing to give to a good cause," Denis replied as he produced a ten dollar bill and handed it to Crank.

Kring watched helplessly and said, "I'd give you some money, dude, but I'm flat broke."

"Hey, bud," Spill said, "you want a job? I can probably get you a gig washing dishes at the Shellfish if you want."

Kring didn't think too long. "Okay."

"Let me talk to the dude tonight. I'll let you know. We'll be back by eleven," he said to Crank as he and Maury strolled out the door. "I hope there's still beer left by then."

Crank and Denis procrastinated for a few minutes more, and in that time the group decided that tonight's kegger should somehow be different. Tonight, in honor of the west wind and the arrival of the mosquitoes from the mainland, they would have a bonfire in the backyard.

So while the others were gone, Kring dug a pit in the sand behind the house and gathered wood. Irrelevant Roger returned from work at the Cafe at about nine with California Bob in tow, and a friend of Bob's who lived in Indialantic, Florida. By the time Crank and Denis returned with the keg, a small bonfire was blazing and four people were waiting impatiently in the backyard. The only ones who were not constantly slapping at greenhead flies and mosquitoes on their bodies were those who positioned themselves in the wood smoke.

Denis quickly had a beer and then a refill. He drained his cup and made motions to leave. "I heard Mimi Dresden isn't working anymore. Word is she just hangs out at the Hud now," he explained.

"Back to the hunt again, huh?" Kring observed as Denis shuffled around the corner of the house out of sight.

The group traded jokes about Denis's obsessive quest for a woman that they all were sure didn't exist, and Buddy arrived on the heels of the last feeble joke. Three lifeguards followed him and they claimed that two girls were going to meet them there.

It was a low-key evening, Kring observed, with everybody alternating between scratching the day's greenhead bites and breathing the smoke from burning driftwood. There was plenty left in the keg when Spill and Maury got home from work. Buddy vanished as quickly as he had arrived. Spill drew himself a beer and told Kring, "You can start Saturday at eleven if you want."

Kring rubbed his smoke-irritated eyes and nodded. When he pulled his fists away from his face, it looked like the back wall of the house was on fire. Smoke seemed to originate from the window sill as well as from the fire itself. No one else noticed, so he shrugged and stumbled over to the keg again. He sat down on the opposite side, with the fire between him and the house, and studied the wall carefully. No, it was just the wind blowing cinders against the house. No, it really *was* smoking on its own. Who could tell? Still, no one else noticed, until a defiant little flame began licking at the window sill. "Hey," Kring asked casually, "is that the house on fire or what?"

Denis stumbled out of the Hudson House under the sign that read BAR in big, dark letters. He walked unsteadily down a wooded Beach Haven side road. Two-day-old puddles in the pavement shone a smooth, white silver in the streetlight.

Denis weaved slightly as he walked, under the influence of five beers and a bad game of pool, shadowed by unfulfilled dreams of Mimi Dresden. It was a quarter past midnight. Denis's footsteps made a slick, gravelly sound as he moved toward his car which waited for him a block away, toward the ocean. With each step his mind spun slowly from thought to thought, feeling as if it had dealt with each fully before abandoning it for a fresher, more interesting one. Most of his thoughts centered on Mimi Dresden.

I'm really getting tired of this, he thought as he moved. I know she's here on this island; I've seen her. I know she's working behind a bar somewhere and *all I've got to do is find her.* He arrived at his Camaro, fished his key chain out of the pocket of his shorts and climbed into the car. "Come on, babe, start up and take me to her," Denis implored his IROC in a whisper. He liked the idea of his vehicle not only having a soul, but also having access to a greater knowledge of certain mysteries than he did. And Mimi Dresden was one of those mysteries. He was willing to believe, as far as it meant anything, that his car would take him magically to the dream he pursued. He pushed in a tape and lurched into the nighttime traffic.

He got to the Boulevard, looked both ways, trusted his vehicle. She turned north, so that's the direction he drove.

That girl's so beautiful, he thought, *I can hardly even remember her face. But I remember how I felt when I saw her at Touché's. Just stunned. And how she froze me at the Ketch. I know she'd love me, I know she'd love to ride in this car. I could make her glad she was born a woman.*

Wow, I'm kinda drunk, really. But Spill's right, you don't really know your car until you've driven it drunk. Like you can't bond with it until you depend on it when you're wasted, really out of it, and it comes through for you, gets you home. Shit, I'm low on gas. I hope I've got enough to get to work tomorrow. I should have filled up this afternoon. Oh hell, tomorrow's Wednesday. I got tomorrow off. Cool.

It would be great, just like a cologne commercial or something. I've always wanted to live out a cologne commercial. We'd be at this pool and she'd turn to say something and I'd just dive into the pool and I'd come out of the pool fully dressed in a tux and she'd wrap around me and she'd be naked but you weren't sure — yeah! yeah! that's great — and I carry her into this big white room with a big fire going in a big white fireplace and I lay her on a thick white rug and I take off my jacket and throw it on a chair — no! Throw it on the fire — and I'd lean down to her and smoke would cover us and she'd whisper something like "It's you. I smell the fantasy" and then we'd fade, both passed out from all the sex or maybe from the smoke from my jacket ... and the only one I want to do that with is Mimi Dresden, this mysterious woman that no one can pin down. I never felt this way before, that there is only this one girl for me. This is bizarre. I bet she's, well, I bet she's this brilliant painter, and she got fed up with the art scene in L.A. and found New York was worse or something and she's just looking for the right studly guy to restore her inspiration. Hey Mimi, I can inspire you! Give me a chance, stop running away. Damn.

Denis awoke from his dream world and was relieved to see that his IROC was still on the road, going pretty well straight. He stopped at the light by Nardi's Tavern behind a black Mercedes with white New York plates. "Fucking rich New Yorkers," he sneered. "I wish they'd stop coming down here. Why don't you stay in New York, asshole! Or at least learn to drive."

I bet she's great in bed. I bet she probably knows some tricks that even I've never thought of. And I'm some stud, Janine would vouch for that. Or Maureen will. I have a feeling I'll meet her tonight. That's all I need, just to see her and say something. I just know she'll be at Joe Pops. I just know it.

He mouthed the words of the song on the tape through the wait at another stoplight, and when he got into Ship Bottom he parked in a bank parking lot and jogged across the street to Joe Pops Shore Bar. He chatted familiarly with one of the bouncers for a moment, then entered another loud, hot, crowded club. He liked the sound of the band onstage. Denis was sure Mimi Dresden was here someplace; it was the kind of place he could see her being. He felt himself absorbed into the crowd, like they wanted him here. When he found a seat at the bar, he felt himself being absorbed into the vodka-and-grapefruit that he ordered from Donna, a barmaid he knew.

148

Another barmaid came by. This one he did not know. He liked her looks and flirted with her. She seemed to try to be too clever, but he got what he judged to be a good response and he asked for her name and phone number. She said her name was Alison, and then just smiled as if she had a secret. Denis pressed her, trying to get her to reveal her number, or tell him where she lived, or even acknowledge that she had a phone. But she just smiled and kept her secret. She served him his next drink and made change at the register. On one of the dollar bills she returned to him she wrote "Alison" with her number beneath it. She lay that bill on top of the thin pile with a sly look, but Denis was watching the crowd, not her look. When he turned around he thanked her and said, "So you aren't going to give me your number or what?"

"No," she said, teasing. Denis turned away again to watch the band. He had one more drink after that and when he got up to leave, he left Alison a three dollar tip. One of the dollars was the bill on which she'd written her number.

As he walked away, Denis wearily mumbled "Bitch" under his breath.

He stumbled out to his car, and when he opened the door he said, "You let me down, babe. I told you to take me to Mimi Dresden and you failed me. She wasn't there. Just some frigid chick who wouldn't give me her phone number." On his way home he passed a movie theater and he puzzled over the films listed on the marquee. None of the titles seemed to have real, complete words in them, just shorthand abbreviations.

When Alison saw that Denis had left her her own number as a tip, she scribbled out what she had written and slipped the bill back into the register.

Three blocks past the movie theater, the world outside Denis's car lit up with a red glow, then a blue one, then a red one again, alternating at closer intervals until they seemed to merge. There were flashing lights right on his tail, and he pulled as smoothly as he could to the side of the road.

A Township cop stuck his head in Denis's window, demanding his documents. When Denis handed them over, the officer examined them and said, "Have you been drinking tonight?"

"No, sir," Denis replied as convincingly as he could.

"You were driving with no headlights, Denis. Would you step out of the car please?"

In the sand of the Colony's backyard, the keg was empty but the bonfire still burned, glowing now within the bowl of earth that Kring had

149

dug hours earlier. The back wall of the house was blackened in a pencil-tip pattern or, as Kring had pointed out to Spill, in the shape of a surf-board nose. The renegade flames had scorched the exterior before Buddy returned and heroically found a fire extinguisher that had not been fully spent in their Bring-Your-Own-Fire Extinguisher party of two weeks back. He exhausted the device on the siding, then dramatically reported that Denis had gotten busted for DWI in Brant Beach. The news took no one by surprise.

Now, at three in the morning under a moon nearing full, a debate raged around what was left of their primal celebration fire. It was more properly a string of debates, changing subjects almost as often as one of the participants squashed a mosquito on a bare leg. The tone oscillated between heated and facetious, fueled by a bottle of tequila, some crushed Vivarin tablets, and the growing conceit of the Artists Colony as a haven for bohemian intellectual intercourse. This conceit was held most strongly by Spill and Crank, but they spread it aggressively among the others.

The bottle of Monte Alban passed around the circle as Buddy sat on the ground and plucked aimlessly at Maury's guitar, pretending to croon for Bev. She sat behind him on the sofa, which had been dragged out-side for the evening. Spill slugged a gulp of tequila and slapped at Crank's arm, barking, "Dude, American Indians are being *complimented* when they're used in commercials! It's a sign of respect, dude."

"Bullshit," Crank retorted. "It's just to sell blue jeans or perfume or some shit."

"That's right," Bev added. "It's just exploitation."

Kring interrupted Bev's ideas on exploitation, which he saw coming and wanted to avoid, when he looked to the sky and said, "That moon's incredible. Anyone up for night surfing?"

Buddy's eyes flashed, betraying interest, but he continued to pluck at the guitar and said nothing.

Crank said, "No, man, we're having this really heavy discussion about … what were we talking about?"

That was a stumper. It stopped everyone in their tracks and prompted another round of shots.

The yellow liquid sloshed against the walls of the bottle as it was passed around, and the dead worm inside swam frantically from side to side. It gradually came to rest after Kring put the bottle at his feet, his face contorted after swallowing his shot. "Whew," he said, "that just didn't taste good."

"No, but just think of the strange and wonderful things it does to

150

your brain," Buddy said absently from behind the guitar.

"That's for sure," Maury responded with a grin that was not his own.

"Just what *does* it do to your brain, in your opinion?" Bev asked as she poked Buddy's shoulder.

"We-ell-l, no one's really sure," he began with mystery, "because once you sober up, you're never really sure what happened. But it's different from other forms of alcohol. I mean it hits you different from whiskey or vodka. It's almost an hallucinogenic effect. It, like, doesn't just mess with your perception or your emotions, it's like it messes with your *soul*. Anyone who has drunk tequila, or mescal, will tell you it makes you think and act like nothing else will. It comes from the same place as mescaline, after all. It's how the Indians of Mexico got back at the white man, by making this liquid." Buddy reached for the bottle at Kring's feet and held it up in the firelight. The wavering, reddening shadows threw his face into dramatic relief, and the worm in the bottle looked like it would have been fluorescent, if it weren't so thoroughly soaked with alcohol. "They made this liquid," he continued, "out of cactus juice that would really fuck with white men, like our whiskey did to them. That's my theory."

Bev was amused but unconvinced. "Well, what does it do? I want to know."

"I don't know. It's like, say your soul was oriented to the north, it was pointed that way in normal life. Well, tequila just twists that a little bit so that it's now facing, instead of twelve o'clock, maybe twelve thirty or twelve forty-five. Then when you sober up you're back at twelve o'clock."

"Well, maybe twelve-oh-five until the hangover clears," Kring added.

"Granted," Buddy said with a nod. "And whiskey," he continued, "if it affects the soul at all, maybe rotates it to eleven fifty."

Bev looked at Buddy suspiciously, then narrowed her eyes and said, "Just who are you that you know all this stuff? Where did you go to school? Where did you get these ideas?"

"I'm just an experienced drunk, that's all."

Bev wasn't satisfied. "What do you mean?" She gave his shoulder another shove. "Why don't you have a driver's license? Why won't you tell me your real name, after we've *slept together*? Where do you come from?"

Buddy said nothing, didn't move his head. He let her talk to his back. He stared into the fire and sighed. He asked Crank to cut up a Vivarin tablet for him and with a violent sniff he inhaled the coarse yellow dust in preparation for the telling of his story. The caffeine's effect was predictably awful. Buddy's eyes watered and he shook his head in reflex.

"I don't remember much before I came to this country," he began.

"I was only like seven when I came here. My mother was a mountain Indian in Nicaragua. My father was American, but I never knew him. He may have been a missionary. He may have been a mercenary. I don't know. My mother didn't want me there in the mountains with her, so she sent me by boat to Miami where her sister Inez lived."

"By yourself?" Bev interrupted.

"Yeah, by myself. My mother was scared and a little loony," he explained. "I believe that she was killed after I left. I never saw my Aunt Inez, she never showed up to get me in Miami. The immigration people were trying to figure out what to do with me, so I slipped out of there while they weren't looking and hooked up with this Cuban grocer in Little Havana. His son had died not long before, and he let me do little shit jobs for him and let me eat and sleep there. He was a freak, but I lived with that dude, Augusto, for like four years. Then when he was drunk one night he tried to rape me and I knocked him out cold with some big vegetable. I don't know what vegetable it was, like a huge eggplant or zucchini or something, but it did the job. I took like two hundred dollars from the cash register and lit off for someplace else. I ended up in Mobile, Alabama. I hung out there for a year, just living in the streets, scamming meals when I could, going hungry when I couldn't. That got old in a hurry, so then I hitchhiked to New Mexico and lived in the mountains all summer, like I remembered from Nicaragua."

Buddy looked around at this point and saw an audience spellbound. They were absorbed in his story; they were his to do with as he chose.

"When the snows came that autumn I couldn't deal with it, and I went into the desert. That's where I ran into Piquon, this Indian mystic, and I lived with him for a while. I ate magic mushrooms and drank tequila and learned about, like these voyages through the soul and hidden places of the mind that could be unlocked by faith, y'know, and mind-freeing chemicals."

"That musta been cool," said Crank.

"Awesome," Maury added.

"It was bullshit," Buddy said. "I just hung around with the dude because his hut was warm and I had something to eat and I got high. That much was great."

"That does sound great," Bev observed. "Why did you leave?"

"The shrooms really tasted like shit, and I got tired of humoring this old stoner Indian who wanted me to be his disciple. It was a drag. I left. I headed west again, hitched to L.A. I learned to surf. I lived in Venice Beach, I had a few little jobs, got involved in some burglary and shoplifting.

Then I used some of the Indian's secrets that he'd taught me and I grew shrooms in this little room I rented. I sold them on the street. It wasn't a big income, but it kept me from starving on the street. One of my clients was a young actress, whom you've all seen in movies, but I can't tell you who it was. We eventually started doing it — "

"Doing it?" Bev interrupted, "Doing what?"

"Doing it. You know — the wild thing. *The nasty,* sharing sweat, penetration — we became lovers, okay?"

"Oh, gross," Bev said.

"What? You think it's gross that they were lovers?" Crank asked.

"No, all those names for sex are gross."

"Anyway," Buddy continued, "we'd both eat mushrooms and trip out in the hills above L.A. We'd get naked and go on these long, surreal sexual-hallucinogenic adventures. The lights would move around below us and spell words we couldn't read and the sky would fall at us in waves, changing color a little bit with each wave of the night sky, and the stars would spell words, just like the lights of the city, and we couldn't read them, either. And our bodies would float together in the air, imprisoned between these two fronts of inconceivable language, and then we'd float apart from each other, even though we were still touching, even though we could *feel* our bodies touching, we'd be miles apart. It was weird. She loved it. She begged me not to leave."

"Who was it?" Bev asked. "Why did you leave?"

"I can't tell you who it was, dude. I promised her when I left. And I left for the same reason that I ever left any other place, the same reason I ever did anything in my life. Because I knew — something told me it was time to move. The thing that set me off was this: I was at her house for like a week, one time, and then I went back to my room in Venice. There was someone else living in it, and the landlady told me that some-one had been there asking questions about me, someone who didn't look so nice, she said. I have no idea who it was, maybe a cop, maybe my father whoever the hell he is, maybe the grocer from Miami. It may have just been someone who wanted shrooms. But I wasn't into answering questions no matter who it was. So I left. I went back to the hills, gath-ered the little bit of stuff I had there, and left."

"How did you end up on Long Beach Island?"

"Well, I had read an article in *National Geographic* about the Chesa-peake, on how people made their living from the bay, and I thought that would be a good, healthy way to live, free of questions from strangers and paper identification and shit. I was in need of some health at that point. But I also wanted to surf, and I knew Jersey's waves are better than Maryland's and that the bays are closer to the beach here. So now I clam for a living. I just go out and gather clams and sell them at the Cafe or to one of the dealers, and it's all I need. I don't need much money to eat, I have this place to live in for now, and no one asks me any questions."

"Until tonight," Crank said with a slowly exposed wild grin. "We've got the story finally! The mystery man reveals all! Call *The Beachcomber*! Call the TV news! Buddy unmasked!"

Buddy turned his face to Crank and registered shock. His head dropped in defeat. "Shit. It's true," he said quietly. "I tried so hard to keep my past from anyone else, keep it to myself, and now I get drunk and blow it just like that."

Bev put her arm around his shoulders. "But it's such a great story, you've experienced so much, why would you want to hide it?"

"I don't know; I thought people wouldn't believe me, that they wouldn't understand...." Buddy's voice trailed off and he appeared to be near tears. Bev moved over to him, as if he needed something and she could help. Buddy shrugged her off. He stood up and took another shot of Monte Alban from the bottle.

"So why *did* you tell us?" Kring asked, unconvinced of what his senses told him was going on here.

"I don't know, man. I guess I can't handle this stuff like I could when I was fourteen growing up in New Mexico. It must have made me talk, I think." He looked at the bottle. It was almost empty. "You bastard," he said to it. With that he drank the last of it with the worm and tossed the empty bottle to bounce on the sofa.

He strode purposefully away from the group and disappeared around the corner of the building. The rest of them sat in stunned silence, not sure what to say.

After a minute Bev rose and followed Buddy around the building. The fire burned low and gave off no heat now, just a feeble orange light from its embers. Kring leaned forward and stirred the bowl, and a small flame leapt from a coal for a moment. It had died already when Bev came back, distraught. "I can't find him," she said. "His car is gone."

Poetry Party

Something was different the next morning, something basic, fundamental. It wasn't Kring's discovery upon waking fully clothed, that Bev was curled up with him in his hammock. And it was nothing really to do, he thought, with Buddy's disappearance the night before. Buddy had been away from the Colony more often than he'd been there, and under pretenses as mysterious. But it could have been that this time Buddy would not return. Kring knew that somehow.

While he lay in the hammock, trying how to figure how to get his arm out from under Bev without disturbing her, Kring heard Crank make the observation that it was now August: "And not August the first, either, it's like a few days into the month, man. Why didn't anybody tell me?" That could be the difference too, Kring thought. He had seen in years past how the whole atmosphere of the island changed color when the last month of the summer swept in from whichever direction it came.

Whatever, whether it was Bev or Buddy or the calendar, the morning stillness sounded different in the Artists Colony this morning, and the sunlight seemed to come from a strange angle through the window. Also, Kring noticed, the smell of charred siding drifted in from the backyard every once in a while on shifting air currents.

The morning peace was interrupted by the clatter of a noisy automobile rolling into the front yard and the nervous exchange of grommet voices outside. Kring could tell they were grommet voices by their high-pitched tones, the characteristic rhythms. "Is this it?" he heard one of them ask. "You sure?"

"I think so. I was only here for that one party and it was at night, but I think so."

"There's a board in the shower. This must be it."

A tow-headed sixteen-year-old peered from the doorway that had no door. He looked at Kring and said over his shoulder to his companions, "This is it, dude. He's here." Three boys shuffled uncertainly into the room, trying to look as cool as they could. Kring recognized them, at least he recognized the tow-headed leader of the group. He and his buddies had squeezed their way into one of the early parties here and worshiped Kring for a bit and tried to convince him to enter the island surf contest. This morning they all wore identical T-shirts, with a stylized shark design where a breast pocket would be.

"Hey, man," the tow-headed one began hesitantly. The others mouthed equally hesitant "heys" to Kring and to Crank across the room.

"Hey," Kring replied laconically from his hammock, "Tyler, right?" The towhead nodded as Kring added, "Nice shirts."

Tyler's face brightened and he said, "Yeah, dude, aren't they awesome? Check out the back." He turned around and displayed the "LBI True Classic" surf contest logo. "You get one when you sign up for the contest. It's today. The contest I mean. Aren't you gonna enter, dude?"

One of the others, with a sunburned lip and a peeling nose, added, "You gotta enter, dude. Otherwise that Australian dick Roddy is gonna win. That would *suck*, dude."

"So what?" Kring challenged. "Big deal if he wins; so what does that mean? He's a good surfer."

"But he's a *dick*, brah. And he's Australian. No one has ever won this contest but islanders. Not even anyone from Pennsylvania ever won it."

Tyler added, "You're the only one good enough to beat this guy. You gotta."

The third, a tall redhead, mumbled, "Yeah, maybe shut him up for once."

"The pride of the whole island is at stake, dude. We can't let that Australian puss win."

Kring said, "Wait a minute. *You* guys live in Pennsylvania."

Tyler quickly stepped up. "Yeah, but we're locals too, you know? We don't just come down on weekends. We're here all summer. And we *need* you. I *hate* that guy Roddy! He cuts you off and thinks he's so hot. You have to beat him, dude. You have to."

Kring had heard all this before, and from others besides these grommets. He'd heard the idea that he must enter the contest, and he had been rejecting it all summer. He couldn't be bothered. But these grommets had such an urgency in their voices and such faith in their eyes that he felt the obligation they claimed for him might be real, after all. Their emotional vigor, their energy swept him into their camp, where the purity of the LBI True was important. He believed for those moments that he could win the goddamn contest and, more than that, that he had to win it, for all of Long Beach Island.

He struggled to extricate his limbs that were pinned under Bev's body and climbed out of the hammock. Bev stirred and looked at him with half-awake eyes pained by the sudden daylight. "Where are you going?" she squeaked. Kring looked at her and then nodded to the grommets. "I'll do it," he said.

The grommets jumped up as if they could hardly believe it. "All right!" they shouted and slapped each other's upright palms. "We did it, man! He's gonna do it!"

Tyler's face suddenly grew as serious as a sixteen-year-old, platinum-haired surfer can look and he said, "Dude! We better get going so you can get there in time to sign up, brah. I got my mom's car. Let's go!"

Kring changed into some surf shorts that this summer had seen no laundry other than the swirling waters of the Atlantic, then followed the grommets outside. He found a spot in the car for his surfboard, a prime spot in the back that forced two of the boys to sit practically on top of each other so the board could rest comfortably.

On the ride up the island to the contest site, Kring shifted uneasily in his seat and stabilized the board on top of the back seat. He was discomforted not with his brand new board stuffed in the grommet's mom's car, but rather with the responsibility these kids had piled on him. It felt wrong. He was no contest surfer. He knew he probably wasn't as good as everybody thought he was, and all the reasons he had refused to enter the contest all along reargued their cases inside him. This conflict, this rivalry that had sprung up between him and Roddy was accidental, superficial and hollow, and he was uneasy about his little-deserved fame as a surfer on the island. As for the contest itself, the hints about a local-favored bias in the judging bothered him. In every suggestion that he enter there had been the implication that all he had to do was show up and ride the minimum number of waves to be declared the winner, no matter how well the Aussie surfed.

But the thing that disturbed him most had nothing to do with his rivalry or the judging. It focused instead on the contest itself. This just isn't my fight, he told himself over and over. It belongs to them, and I'm not even interested in the nature of it. Surf contests might be cool. They're just not what I surf for. This is not what I seek when I paddle out.

As he rode down the Boulevard in Tyler's mom's station wagon, he listened to the kids' amped-up chatter whipping back and forth, and pictured himself as he was at their age, a thoroughly stoked surf rat when surfing was all that mattered. He knew he couldn't disappoint these grommets. That would be a heinous thing to do. He smiled and settled back in the front seat, decision finally made. He did, however, make the effort to eject the thrash-metal tape grinding in the stereo. "Who was that?" he asked Tyler.

"Ned's Atomic, dude," was the reply from the back seat. "Put it back in!"

Kring ignored the plea and simply tuned in something less anarchic on the radio. Pearl Jam. The kids let him get away with that. He was entitled. They knew it. He was going to come through for them.

On the beach, a judges stand of sorts had been erected: a table, chairs and a banner. The white sand was crawling with surfers, but Kring was dismayed to see the ocean patiently tapping the shore with two-foot waves. Occasionally a three-footer would roll in outside. The conditions were barely surfable, but there was a contest heat going on, and out in the water the color-vested surfers scrambled after anything that might carry them toward shore.

People on the beach took notice of Kring as he marched down the dune with his board, brand-new, never-waxed and unblemished. Guys came up to him, faces he recognized, and they all asked the same questions: "Are you gonna enter, dude?" "You gonna beat that Aussie bastard?" Kring could see the word of his arrival spread across the beach like electric current over a power grid. He could almost trace its path to the waterline.

He did not see his rival, that diabolical Australian, Roderick Thorp, but he was keyed up about the confrontation. "Is this how all surf competitions feel?" he wondered as he dropped his board in the sand to stretch his muscles and a small knot in his stomach began to bounce.

His grommet escort buzzed proudly around him, basking in the glow he shed as he approached the judges stand.

The judges were all well-respected members of the local surfing establishment. There was the owner of the Hurricane Surf Shop, and an independent shaper from Harvey Cedars, and the guy who wrote a surfing column in the paper. None of them showed any signs of recognizing Kring.

"Can I still sign up?" he asked the journalist.

"What division?"

Kring looked over the list of categories. "Senior Shortboard."

"Yeah, you can still enter. Fill this out."

Kring handed his board to the red-headed grom and picked up a miniature-golf scoring pencil.

"What size T-shirt you wear?" the writer asked.

"I don't know ... large, I guess."

"We're out of large. Here's a medium. Fifteen bucks."

Kring stopped short, with only a "K" written on his entry form. He looked at the judge. "What?" he asked.

"How are you going to pay your entry fee? Cash or what? You can use a credit card if you want."

Kring looked at the grommets, then back at the judge and straightened up. "Fifteen bucks?" he asked. He put down the scoring pencil and tore his entry form in two pieces. "I don't pay to surf," he said simply, and he took his board from the redhead and calmly strode away.

The shocked grommets looked at each other, then chased after him, leaving the journalist with a size medium T-shirt hanging from his outstretched hand.

"Dude!" the towhead called. "Dude, what's up? Where are you going?"

Kring said as he marched, "I don't pay to surf, man. It's that simple."

"Dude, it's not that much!" the redhead exclaimed. "It's only fifteen bucks."

"Brah, it's not like you're paying to surf," Tyler insisted with a hopeful face. "You're just like paying for the T-shirt, really, and you get to surf for free."

Kring stopped and faced the grommets. "In the first place, I don't have any money, not even for the T-shirt. I'm broke."

"We'll give you the money. We'll pay your sign-up fee, brah. Come on," he pleaded desperately.

Kring shook his head sadly. "I don't pay to surf, dudes," he said. He pointed toward the small waves. "And I sure don't pay to surf that slop." He walked on another few steps, then turned to the motionless grommets and said, "So I guess I gotta hitchhike back home, huh?"

The grommets turned sadly as one and headed toward the water.

Kring walked from the contest site to the Cafe, which was only five blocks away. There he spent most of the day hanging out and eating the food that Irrelevant Roger placed in front of him at no charge. Kring was amazed that he hadn't thought of this free-feed racket before today. When Victoria showed up to take over, Roger offered him a ride back to the Colony. "She didn't seem so suspicious of me this time," Kring mentioned to Roger as they rode out of the parking lot. "Not that she said anything, but she smiled nice at least."

"Ah, she's a bitch," Roger replied.

When they got to the Artists Colony, Maury was rearranging the furniture, and Crank was hanging a canvas to which he had applied paint that morning. "What do you think, dudes?" he asked, indicating his abstract creation. "I got two more just like it. They're out in the backyard drying in the sun."

Kring looked at the painting without seriousness. "Does it have a name?" he asked.

"I call it 'Abstract Kiosk.'"

"Ah, the moral ambiguity factor."

"Exactly." He adjusted the canvas on its nail. "Hey, how did the contest go?"

Before Kring could answer, Spill burst through the door with his lifeguard gear slung over his shoulder and yelled, "He pussied out!"

"I didn't pussy out, dude! I took a moral stand."

"Yeah, well, word on the beach is that you backed out because you didn't want to face that Aussie. The locals are all pissed off."

Kring snorted. "I don't give a shit. I didn't surf because I'm not gonna pay fifteen bucks to surf. Just because a bunch of misguided grommets decide I'm the one to save the world from one dickhead Australian ... I'm not a contest surfer. I never had any interest in surfing in contests, and I'm not gonna pay fifteen bucks — fifteen bucks that I don't have — to ride shitty waves that I wouldn't bother with if they paid me."

"Yeah, well, don't worry, I saved your ass." Spill tossed his gear down on the couch. "Get this. I was relieving a late lunch on the next beach down from the contest, and my lieutenant comes by on the ATV and says that the Aussie was leading his heat. So I called a shark sighting and pulled everyone in from the water!" His own laughter mingled with the finish of his story. "They never finished the heat! The Australian, what's his name, Roderick, he wouldn't go back in the water, and they postponed the rest of the contest until tomorrow! Is that great or what?"

The story went over big among the Colonists and laughter rang through the open rafters of the house. It helped Kring feel less traitorous. He knew the whole episode would probably cost him his cult hero status. And he *would* miss it. It was kind of cool, that whole scene, feeling like he was important. He was beginning to like it. Now it was history and he felt sad a little. But it was a lie all along to go with the grommets, to pretend to be their hero. The first few times that anyone had suggested the contest to him he had considered it, and each time he decided that it wasn't what he wanted. He didn't want to surf for judges, he didn't want to surf for other surfers. He didn't even want to surf to please the little girls like Juliet on the beach.

Whatever compelled him to spend his money on a new surfboard instead of rent when his old board snapped, it wasn't one of those reasons. It wasn't the expectations of other surfers or a need to impress them that drove him to get out of bed on cold mornings before the sun rose, just to check the waves. There were no young girls on the beach in midwinter when he encased himself in neoprene head to toe, protected against forty degree water.

He knew that the challenge others wanted him to accept was not a real one. It was vapid, meaningless in the face of what surfing meant to him. Surfing was a source of some magic in his life, some enhancing, pulsing power that fed him, that reminded him of the wonder so much of his life seemed to have lost in the process of growing up. Why that was so important to him he could not describe, why it was necessary for him to resist the onset of mundane adulthood that his classmates at college — it seemed so far away! — had so quickly accepted. Surfing and all it added to his life was vital, kept him alive, in a way that even he couldn't explain.

And Kring didn't think many of the surfers who were so pissed off at him now would understand that. The ones who surfed for the same reasons as he did would understand it without being told. And they were out there, may even have been in the contest. But they didn't give a shit if the title went to an islander or an Australian or a Pennsylvanian, because it didn't matter. It didn't change the waves. It didn't change the feeling, or who they were.

Spill cleared his lifeguard gear off the couch and the Artists Colony resumed its preparations for the poetry reading. Kring helped to rearrange the furniture while Irrelevant Roger went to light the grill for the bluefish fillets he had stolen from the Cafe.

When Lotion walked in, she was on her own, and she sat down with Kring in front of the area they were calling the stage. Maury tuned his guitar for them. Off to the side, Spill shuffled through his pages.

Lotion remarked to Kring, "This will be fun, won't it, boy?"

"It'll be different, you gotta say that."

Crank came through the room carrying another painting.

Maury's guitar hummed delicately as he tuned each string and then strummed some warm-up chords. "How's it sound?" he asked his audience.

"Sounds okay to me, dude," Kring assured him.

Maury nodded and strummed once more.

"Dinner's ready," Roger announced as he marched in with a platter of grilled fish, sizzling on aluminum foil. The group gathered around for a pre-exhibit communal feast.

Spill nudged Maury as they ate. "Nervous?"

Maury looked composed but unconvincing. "Nah," he said, "I know it'll be cool. They'll like my songs; they'll dig your poems."

"And how could they not like Crank's paintings."

"Really, dude. Such artistry."

Maury had pride in his voice as he said, "And we're finally a real Artists Colony."

"Absolutely."

"No doubt."

Spill finished his fish, crumpled the remaining skin into a golf ball on his plate and went to the stage with his poems in hand. "Let me know what you guys think of this, like how it sounds, okay?

> *Strangers trapped in unknown hells*
> *Friends and lovers ringing sad bells*
> *Today is the last thing I expected*
> *Tomorrow I expect to be lost*

"Whaddaya think? Sound okay?"

Lotion glanced at Kring with a gentle smirk on her face. Kring met her look and decided to comment on Spill's projection rather than the content. "Sounds good, man, real clear. Maybe a little louder."

Maury showed more enthusiasm. "That's really good, dude! All right!"

"Thanks. Okay, I'll try another, just to be sure, y'know, that my voice will have impact on the audience.

> *Sex is my homeland —*

"No, I don't want to do that one yet. Here's one:

> *The sun sinks slowly before my eyes*
> *My lover, my lover*
> *Don't leave me now while my eyes can't see*
> *Don't leave me 'til breakfast lover*
> *Please, lover, please."*

Maury jumped up from the table. "Wow, that is great, dude! Really wild!"

Roger joined him. "Yeah, dude, that's amazing! How do you think of that stuff?"

"I don't know, man, it just comes to me when I sit down to write it."

"Is that the whole poem?" Kring asked.

"No, there's more, you wanna hear it?"

"No, no, you'd better save it for the real audience. You don't want to peak too early, y'know."

"Yeah, you're right. By the way, dude, do you have a copy of *Lord of the Flies*? I want to make sure I got this one character's name right, y'know, before I read this poem out loud."

"Yeah, I got a copy but it's at my old pad. Somebody's got to run me to Ship Bottom."

"Hey, I'll tell you what," Roger suggested. "You can take Crank in my car, drop him off to get the keg and pick him up on the way back."

"There's one problem: I've got a suspended license."

"Oh yeah, I forgot."

"So what?" Spill broke in. "Buddy's been driving on this island since March with no license, in an unregistered car. What's the big deal?"

Lotion had been silent but now spoke up from the table. "Look, Kring, you take Roger's car and go home; I'll take Crank to get the keg. That way Crank won't have to wait forty minutes for you to get back."

"But why don't we—"

"No, this will work, this'll be better. Let's go, Crank."

Kring was puzzled by Lotion's insistence on this arrangement, but he didn't argue, and he looked forward to driving the length of the island with a suspended license. Except for taking Spill's van for that one wave check in July, he hadn't driven a vehicle. He didn't want to take the chance. But now Lotion seemed to think it was the thing to do, and he felt her power to bend things her way when they were important. When she described the plan, it sounded logical. When he thought she winked at him, it seemed inevitable.

On the way to Ship Bottom he drove cautiously. He stopped at yellow lights. He signaled every lane change. Roger's Chevette was a little sluggish and hard-steering, but it felt good to Kring to be behind the wheel, in traffic, for the first time in months. When he finally made the turn into his driveway, the sun was low in the west and he realized, as he shuffled in bare feet on the pine needles of his yard, that he had not seen a sunset since he left this place. In Holgate, the Artists Colony was surrounded by newer houses on pilings that blocked any type of view and, too, July and August were never the best months of the year for sunsets. But still, he thought, not even one.... He again turned to the sky stretching over the bay. It looked striking. It looked very good. Maybe I'll stick around to catch this one, he thought.

He ducked into the apartment and found a couple of beers still in the refrigerator, still cold. One of them he carried out to the bulkhead, where he sat on the old, tar-stained wooden wall. Some of the creosote softened by the afternoon sun stuck to his leg and his shorts, but he didn't care. He threw off his shirt and just let the sun's last, hazy glow warm his almost naked body. He drank his beer. It was not a mystical experience. The sunset turned out to be unspectacular, incomplete, but at the same time it was gradual and unpressured and Kring found it relaxing to sit there and watch it soak into the low haze coating the western sky.

When the daylight was almost spent, Kring got up and went into the apartment to search for the book Spill wanted. When he flipped a light switch, he was a little bit shocked with how familiar everything looked under the yellow lamplight. Yet at the same time, it seemed like more than just three weeks since he had lived here. It looked somehow different, even from when he had stopped to leave Mr. Cox that note. The note! He had forgotten to even check if his landlord was home. He peeked out the window and there, across the yard, he saw the folded slip of paper still wedged between the screen and the door. His landlord, apparently, hadn't returned since Kring left it there.

Turning back to his apartment Kring reacquainted himself with the space. He went to the fridge and threw out a few items that had no business being left in there so long: lettuce, a chicken leg, some macaroni and cheese growing fuzz. These he fed to the couple of gulls hanging around outside.

Back inside, he picked up a T-shirt that was on the floor by his sofa bed. "Hey, my Romantic Surfboards shirt!" he said as he held it up. "I was wondering where this was." He strolled over to the makeshift bookshelf and pulled out his copy of *Lord of the Flies*. This was a book he hadn't read in years, and as he flipped it open to the middle, a young cricket began its early-season song-chatter in the bushes outside. Kring read a couple of lines in the book and soon found himself enmeshed in the story and the style of the prose and he lost himself in it. When he finally remembered what he was supposed to be doing, he had read pages sixty-three to eighty-five, and it was almost nine-thirty and pitch-dark outside. Spill was probably finished reading his poems by now and wouldn't even need the book. The party was probably in full swing. He didn't have much trouble visualizing it — pretty much the same thing as almost every other night of the past three weeks: plastic cups being filled with beer, music getting turned louder every ten minutes by someone different each time, teenage kids inviting themselves in and lining up at the keg. Maybe the poetry reading made a difference this time, he thought. But he didn't think it likely.

Kring looked at his sofa bed against the garage door. It invited him to sit down and he did, automatically. He stretched his legs out before him and inspected the cluttered, small room. He was surprised at how reluctant he was to leave. This place felt like home to him, much more than the Artists Colony did, and it was almost painful to try to convince himself to return to Holgate. He just felt like staying. Spill no longer needed the book. And Roger would probably be better off without his car, as he'd only get wasted and be tempted to drive under the influence.

"To hell with the party," he said aloud. He shed his shorts almost defiantly and stretched out on his sofa without even opening it up. He covered himself with the familiar-smelling blanket, now a little more musty than he remembered, and listened to the cricket. It felt like the first early night he'd had all summer. It felt very good. I'll talk to the old man tomorrow, Kring thought. I'll tell him I've got a job now, and I can pay him the rent. He stretched his muscles in a long, slow arch on the couch. I'll explain things to the old guy, straighten out any problems. Then he remembered the note he left, still sitting there. If he's around, that is.

Chapter 17

After the Colony

T he air in the garage was the first thing Kring noticed when he awoke. It was different than the Colony. Cooler, he thought, though it must be seventy-five degrees already. Fresher, though the windows had not been opened for weeks. Here somehow he could breathe more easily. The couch beneath him smelled musty, but this air was free of the scent of degradation that had soaked into the Colony walls. The stale beer that had been spilled on the carpet there, the indistinct food rotting in the kitchen, the muggy heat of August conspiring to imprison the place with its own odor, that was all absent here in Kring's garage. Here that muggy heat of August had done nothing more than bake the settled dust to his table.

It was early in the morning, much earlier than he had gotten used to waking at the Colony. The humidity of the young day clung to his skin like a shirt two sizes too small, but he liked it and crawled eagerly off his couch. He would observe the ritual of the wave check though he knew he would find nothing there. He stepped out into the sun in his yard, and he saw M. Cox's Oldsmobile in the driveway, loaded with luggage, damp with shaded dew.

"I don't know where they've been, but I guess they're home," Kring said to himself as he mounted his bike.

He pedaled past familiar houses, up to the familiar beach. There he found waves. From where he stood on the dune they looked small, no more than three feet, but they might be surfable. He raced back to his bike at the head of the street and hopped on it. He pointed it down-hill toward his garage, and it was only then that he realized that his brand-new board was still at the Colony. And that he had Roger's car. And that he had a job waiting for him at eleven this morning.

Kring weaved his way freely, rolling through the streets that narrowed as they closed in on the bayfront. When he came in view of his place, there was Mr. Cox. The old man was slowly, deliberately unloading his car. He wore Bermuda shorts and a short-sleeve shirt. On his feet, as usual, were socks and sandals.

"Morning, Mr. Cox," Kring said cheerfully as he glided up, his feet extended away from the pedals.

The old man looked up in surprise. "Oh, I didn't expect to see you, young man. Not after that note we got last night. I'm sorry you're having trouble. A boy your age should be having fun in the summertime, not struggling to support himself."

"Let me explain. I wrote that note a few days ago. I didn't know you were away."

"Oh, yes, Doris and I were in Florida for three weeks, visiting her sister." Mr. Cox then lowered his voice as if taking Kring into his confidence. "I would have told you we were going, but you seemed to be always out surfing or on a date or something of that sort. Always having fun, eh?" he said with a wink.

"Florida, huh? Well, that must have been nice. How is Mrs. Cox — Doris?"

"Just fine, just fine, although it was miserably hot down there. The weather in Florida this time of year doesn't do her arthritis much good. She's making breakfast right now. Would you like to join us?"

Kring considered the offer and thought of the nakedness of his own cupboards. And there was the explanation he still had to deliver. "I'd like that, thanks," he said. "Can I give you a hand here with this luggage?"

Over a bowl of wheat flakes and a glass of grapefruit juice, Kring subtly pleaded his case to the old couple, and they made a sympathetic jury.

"You see, I lost my job and I couldn't find another one," he fibbed, "you know how the economy is, and I was embarrassed that I couldn't pay you my rent, and then I snapped my surfboard in two while I was surfing."

"Oh dear," Doris broke in, "were you hurt?"

"Not really. I was okay, but it was scary. It was on a really big wave and I almost drowned. Actually, I hurt my foot and couldn't walk," he lied again, "and some friends took me right from the beach to their place. I stayed there until I could move around. And I guess by then you had left for Florida." It sounded like a pretty good story to Kring, and it looked like the kindly old couple were buying it.

"But when I came back here to get a book," he continued, "it just felt so good to be back that I stayed the night. And I've got a job now. I start today, and so I can pay my rent and then maybe replace my surfboard before the good autumn waves hit." He allowed himself this one last little fib, a reordering of the truth about his surfboard. But it was worth it to both parties if his landlords saw him as an energetic but responsible young man.

"Well, son," Mr. Cox said as he got up to pour more coffee into his wife's cup, "we're certainly not going to kick you out. You pay us your rent whenever you can. Go ahead and replace your surfboard first. Doris and I know you're a good boy; you wouldn't try to cheat us. And it helps us to know you are around. It was good to know you were here while we were away, that you were keeping an eye on the place. Of course, we weren't aware that you weren't here," he said with a knowing wink, "but that's okay. Nobody broke into the place. Everything's just as we left it. As far as I'm concerned, you never left."

Ten minutes later Kring was back in his apartment, and as he was blowing dust off of counters and taking stock of his food stores, he decided that breakfast with his landlords had gone pretty well. Not only were they not mad at him, but he had feared that he'd have to hide his surfboard until he paid his rent. That's cool, he thought. But now I've got to work because I *have* to pay them what I owe, after that guilt trip they laid on me, however sweet it was.

He killed some more time in his apartment, then drove the Chevette to the Cafe to find out when Roger was working today. Kring did not really want to return to the Artists Colony right away and have to explain to them that he had split for good.

A new girl, one he didn't know, was working the breakfast counter, and she told him that Victoria was on the schedule for the afternoon and Roger wouldn't be in until seven. Kring knew he couldn't get in touch with Roger before then, to have him bring his board to the Cafe, unless he went to the Colony. He imagined an even exchange with Roger, surfboard for automobile, but no, he decided, he would drop the car off tonight, after work, as a good-faith gesture. He was still curious about the party that he missed, too.

Then he went to work.

Spill wasn't working at the restaurant and neither was Maury, but Kring met the boss, a guy named Phil, and got thrown immediately into the routine. He was elbow-deep in warm, soapy water when he overheard a couple of the busboys mention the party of the night before. He didn't hear much, but one claimed that he left when things "got too crazy." Kring heard no more details. The workday with all its newness flew by, even though the kitchen was stifling hot and at times things moved so quickly that Kring felt his head spinning. But when he was done at six, he climbed into Roger's car and cautiously drove it to the liquor store to pick up some beer, then headed to the Cafe. He didn't anticipate a sunset on this typically hazy August day, but while he was in the car, a thunderstorm that had been gathering all afternoon finally broke over the island. When he got to the Cafe he had to duck quickly under the awning to avoid getting drenched. It was one of those crazy, freak summer storms that sometimes rushed across from the hotplate of the mainland, the kind of storm that clears out the still, heavy air with rain that falls so heavily it rumbles on the ground. The sky had gotten very dark very quickly and it just opened wide, letting all the rain out at one time, it seemed. It lasted no longer than twenty minutes, and Kring sat it out at the counter alone with Victoria. They sipped on beers and talked about nothing important while the rain poured around them, both of them waiting for Irrelevant Roger to show up.

After the rain passed the puddles quickly disappeared into the dry, thirsty earth, and Kring moved out onto the deck, into the sunlight that returned as the storm clouds swept over them to the east. The ripped-open cardboard of a twelve-pack sat between his feet, and the wood surfaces of the deck and the tables were shiny wet. Kring sat on a beach towel that Victoria dug out of the Lost-and-Found box and he passed the time by urging Victoria to change the radio station each time she complained about the songs that she heard over and over, every day.

Since there were no other customers, Victoria walked out from behind the counter and sat next to him on the picnic bench. She made him share the beach towel with her and asked for a beer. They relaxed and talked about people they knew, about the Artists Colony, about the parties. Their talk turned to the Cafe, to the sunsets. She listened to him describe the sky to her. He was touched by her attention, intrigued by this interest she had never shown him before. The cleansing storm had left clear blue in its wake, taking the haze with it out to sea or turning it to rain and pouring it down on their heads, and he talked about the consciousness the sky had, how it must be satisfied with its day now. "That's nonsense," she said, though gently, as if it were beautiful nonsense, like none she had ever heard before. Maybe it was the beer, Kring thought, softening the edges of her opinions, but she seemed happy sitting here, and he felt like the reason. He knew, of course, that the evening must have something to do with it too, so fresh and sweet after the muggy heat of the day — clear and colorful and bright.

Victoria threw her head back and looked at the sky as he described it. She murmured that it was like none she'd ever seen before. Kring looked up too, straight up at the sky and behind them, to the east, where the still-expressive storm clouds were sweeping out to sea. Directly above, the pale blue sweet sky seemed out of place, and the setting sunlight before them didn't fade, but instead glowed with a gold-orange that touched everything with magic, like spilled cinnamon powder. It spread its hue on everything that would catch and hold it: on windows, on the Cafe walls, on the water, on their own tanned faces as they watched. Kring pointed out all of this in one expressive sweep of his hand and a few words.

While they were huddled on the bench, Irrelevant Roger pulled up and got out of a car Kring didn't recognize. Roger greeted them with some mention of his own car, then said nothing more when they acted as if he weren't there.

Kring had been taken by surprise when Victoria sat beside him, and he talked in a rush, it seemed, without really thinking, only talking, and feeling, and talking some more. They were blessed with a brilliant rose and orange and purple sunset and his mind buzzed, his body tingled because he was discovering that he liked Victoria and was turned on and he suspected that she was discovering something similar. He felt the change in air pressure or static electricity or whatever it is in the air that follows a violent storm, and she appeared fascinated by it. He told her how he saw the colors interacting, pointed out the purples framing the deepening rose, the orange turning to pure gold on the surface of the water.

Behind them Irrelevant Roger washed some utensils and listened to the same songs on the same radio station that Victoria had listened to all afternoon. He paid no attention to the sky. Kring was only vaguely aware of Roger's presence, but he had no interest now in hearing any stories of parties. He suspected that Roger wanted him to offer a beer. But Kring would not interrupt this moment for such trivia.

The sun dropped ever closer to the horizon without the appearance of motion, until it slipped behind an ash-purple cloud and they could see the two bodies move as they slowly passed each other. And they were both moving. Victoria claimed to be freaked out by it. She had never before seen the sun actually move, she told him in an excited voice. Kring felt the same thing every time he saw a great sunset and had learned the subtleties of the feeling. The feeling, he believed, was wonder.

The sunset seemed to be signaling something, but, Kring thought, that was one of the great things about sunsets. If something important was happening, then a spectacular sunset, or even an ordinary one, could appear as portentous as the Archangel Gabriel. And if nothing significant was going on, you could easily ignore the portent. You could concentrate on the metaphor. Or just the colors. Tonight Kring tried to concentrate on the colors.

When it was dark, Victoria offered to drive him home. Kring tossed Roger's keys to him behind the counter as he strode past to the parking lot. "Bring my surfboard up when you come to work tomorrow, okay?" he called. "It's in the outdoor shower." Victoria had a strange little smile on her face when they climbed into her car.

When they pulled up at Kring's place, she shut off the engine and got out along with him. "Look at all the stars that are out now," she said, gazing at the darkness above. "It's such a pretty night."

"Do you want to go for a walk?" he asked quietly.

"Um-hm."

They walked together along the bulkhead and helped each other maneuver around waist-high fences that extended to the water's edge. They picked a path to a small marina a couple of blocks away. They talked while they wandered. They talked about what summer meant and not about how soon it would be over. They talked quietly, and laughed at silly things. The two of them wandered out on one of the docks of the marina, listening to the soft pap-pap-pap of the water tapping the white fiberglass hulls docked there, and the occasional sting of a halyard on a sailboat mast. The stars shed no light, though they gave a delicate backdrop in which to wander, and the dock lights were spread out along their path.

They saw no other people on their walk, and when they got to the end of the pier Kring sat back on a waist-high piling and Victoria leaned her folded arms on a railing. He looked at the stars. She watched the play of the dim lights on the water beneath them. "What is surfing like?" she asked innocently.

He pondered this while he stared at the faded grid of pinprick lights in the dark sky. "It's hard to say," he began. "It's nothing like stuff you might expect. You ever water-ski?"

"Yes."

"Well, it's nothing like that."

She laughed. "That's a big help."

"Well, it's a little bit like that, but you're not pulled by anything, you're *carried with it, with* the wave. And you work with it. That makes all the difference in the world, y'know?"

"But what does it *feel* like?"

"When it's right, when the wave is good and you're right there, right where the wave wants you to be, it feels like ... all tension just drains away, it's like you were born to find that spot, it's like that wave would be un-fulfilled if you hadn't ridden it. The feeling is a little like ..." His voice trailed away into the warm air around them.

"Sex?" she asked with a smile almost hidden by the darkness.

"Yeah. What made you say that?"

"I've heard that comparison before. I have a hard time believing it."

"That's because you've never surfed."

"Maybe you're right. It sounds wonderful."

They fell silent for a time, and the space between them seemed to grow warmer, more comfortable, almost more comfortable than the rest of the August evening air. Kring found himself talking easily with this girl, with little of his usual self-containment. He found it intoxicating, and she met his eyes warmly with her own each time he looked to her. What was it that was different tonight, with Victoria? He searched her face trying to figure out if that's where the difference lay, in her face, the difference between Vic and any of the girls he met at the Artists Colony; they were fun, but none ever inspired anything passionate in him. They were just fun.

Tonight he was excited, he felt the thrill, the thrill of discovery. He didn't want to let on, though. He didn't want to scare her off with anything so special as the thrill of discovery.

Hours passed on the dock, and Victoria seemed to be growing tired of the uncomfortable railing on which she now sat. Kring felt the imprint of the piling crown on the seat of his own shorts and he hopped down to the planking.

"Are you ready to head back?" he asked with a gentle hand on her arm.

She nodded and they reversed their earlier path, back to dry land. After a few steps, Victoria put her arm through his. His muscles stiffened and he felt a slight hesitation in her touch. When she left her hand there anyway, he felt relief, and the fibers in his back began to thaw. They passed a few more tied-up boats and he reached for her hand, his heart racing. Why? he asked himself, why was his heart racing? He'd been here before, in this position with other girls in his life, other girls even this summer. He sensed her breathing was a little unsure. At least she was off balance too, he thought.

This didn't seem like it should be happening. It was a wonderful surprise, but it didn't fit in with the rest of the summer, so far, for him, and it probably didn't for Victoria, either.

They got to the end of the dock and stepped onto the dark, noisy gravel of the yard. In the light of a Pepsi machine he grabbed her arm and stopped, turned her to him. Their lips met, tentatively at first, then they kissed gratefully, relievedly, passionately in the white fluorescent glow from the vending machine. They kissed like the sky had rained, furiously, releasing pent-up humid emotion as quickly as they could. It was wet and warm and delicious in its surprise.

The few hours they had spent together this evening made them feel like they knew each other well, and made yesterday, when they weren't so close — when they weren't even friends really — seem like ages ago. They devoured this passionate closeness that had grown between them, each hungrily tasting it in the other's mouth. It tasted good, it satisfied their souls momentarily and so they drank it as a cat drinks its milk, tongue touching and drawing in, touching and drawing in.

They stood there locked in an embrace until a car rolled in, braked in a cloud of dust and briefly spotted them in its headlights. They pulled self-consciously apart with embarrassed smiles as the headlights burned themselves out and the engine went silent. They could hear the radio for a second before that too burned itself out. They couldn't tell what song had been playing. They turned away from the car. From a deck above them, a dog's deep *woof* sounded in the night. They headed back along the bulkhead the way they had come.

At Kring's garage they kissed again, this time tenderly, this time good night, because Victoria seemed to know he would not invite her in. Kring believed she wouldn't accept such an invitation tonight, either. It might have fit the rest of his summer, spending the night together, but would not have fit this night. It would not have been ... *poetic*, this night. And this night was where they lived, where they chose to stay.

She got in her car and he watched her go with a smile on his face, then he pushed open the door to his dark apartment and disappeared inside, already wondering when he would get to see her next.

Their Own Music

Kring rode by the Cafe on his bike the next day after work. Victoria was behind the counter.

"Hey Vic," he called as he rolled to the counter, "what's up?"

"Hi, you," she said with a smile. "I've got something for ya."

She carefully lifted his surfboard from behind the counter. "Roger brought it in this morning," she said.

His eyes grew wide. "Careful, Vic," he urged her, "it's brand new, you know." He gasped when she bumped the board lightly on the condiment shelf. When he got the precious instrument in his hands, he inspected the area for damage.

"I didn't hurt it, did I?" she asked anxiously.

"No, no, it's okay. Not even a scratch. This is great!" he said with a smile. "I got my board back! And there are decent waves today."

"Waves? You mean you're not going to stay and talk to me?" she said in a teasing pout.

"I'll be back in a couple of hours, Vic. Before you're off work. There's only like an hour and a half of daylight left. I'll stop by when I'm done and talk to you."

She dropped the pout and said agreeably, "That's okay; you go surfing. I've got to leave soon anyway. I'm going home for a couple of days to set up my apartment for school."

"You're going home tonight? When will you be back?"

"I'm just going to sign a lease and move some of my stuff in. I'll be back maybe tomorrow, maybe the next day. I was only teasing about staying to keep me company. You go surfing if there are waves. Wouldn't want you to miss *that*."

Kring wondered if her tone was a subtle reference to his comparison last night of surfing and sex. He studied Victoria. Something had happened while they walked together under the stars, but he wasn't sure yet what it was. Was it a summer thing or more real? Hesitantly he sat down at the counter with his surfboard standing beside him. Victoria smiled and gave him a Coke.

"What's this about an apartment?" he asked.

"My roommates and I already found a place; we just have to get all the legal stuff taken care of, and we want to get moved in before school starts."

"You go to Villanova, right?"

"Yep."

"When's school start?"

"Like a week and a half."

"Hmm." He finished his soda with one last gulp. "Hey, Vic, you got any Sex Wax in that lost-and-found box back there?"

"I think so." She reached for the box, then eyed him suspiciously. "Why? What for?"

Kring feigned innocence. "No reason."

She plunked down an orangey, half-hockey puck of wax on the counter. "That's orange-flavored, isn't it?"

"I'm not sure if it's orange or tangerine. I could never figure it out. Thanks, Vic." He rubbed a layer of wax on the fiberglass of his board and a vaguely exotic citrus scent rose from the deck. He drew it into his nostrils with his eyes closed. "First time it's ever been waxed," he noted with a grin.

"This mean you're going surfing after all?"

"Yeah. I'm sorry, but ... it's been *weeks*, Vic. If you're gone by the time I get back, I guess I'll see you in a couple of days, okay?"

"Sure, surfer boy. Have fun."

The waves breaking up the street from the Cafe were a welcome relief from the month-long flat spell that had gripped the Jersey shore. They were about chest-high on Kring and clean, but they had no power. Summer trash. The beach was deserted, the break empty. He realized, as he crawled his way over the swells and sat up to wait for his first wave, that it felt really good to get wet. While he waited his thoughts turned automatically to Victoria. He thought of her voice and her eyes and her walk. He got a warm flush, renewed with each thought, and he replayed the scenes of their walk on the pier the night before, but it all dissipated when a wave approached and he paddled furiously to let it catch him in its bowl. He hopped up as it broke to the right with a clean, sloping line, and his movement on the rushing face almost mimicked the wave's motion. He threw his body radically into the wave, but he felt a harmony, an instinctive feel of working with the flow of the water, not against it, like a salmon following a river's currents. It was an instinct that guided his legs, his upper body, his vision. His whole body fell into the rhythm that existed between it and the wave. When he saw that the wave unfolding ahead of him was about to die, he quickly climbed the short face and launched himself off his board into a high backflip. Under the water, the twirling flash of a brilliant blue sky and an inverted horizon flashed again, behind his closed eyelids.

When he surfaced, exhilarated, he heard a hoot from a direction he couldn't identify. He paid no attention to it, didn't even look around and just paddled back outside again. A brown pelican cruised by, inches from the restless surface of the water. Kring's mind jumped back to Victoria again as he sat up and gazed out to sea.

He heard the splashing of another surfer's approach across the water, and he turned to see Buddy paddling toward him. Kring, who had not seen Buddy since the night he had rushed out of the Artists Colony's backyard, said nothing, just nodded.

"Nice swell," Buddy observed.

"First time I've been out in a month," Kring answered.

"Me too."

No further words were exchanged between them. They watched the swells roll by in silence until a suspicion that Kring had held for a few weeks forced itself to be voiced. "That story you told that night, about your history, that was fiction, wasn't it? It was a crock of shit."

Buddy sat quietly for a minute. He looked hurt, but then a smile broke across his face. "Yeah, I made it up, just to keep those guys happy." He grabbed a jellyfish floating by and threw it at nothing. "How did you know?"

"Well, for one, the Spaniards are the ones credited with developing tequila, not the Indians. Anyone who has ever bought a bottle of Monte Alban and read the little booklet knows that. Also, I don't think you can grow magic mushrooms in a shoebox." He spun around on his board in anticipation of a wave but it proved too small and he let it pass. "Good story, though."

"Yeah."

They surfed and sat and paddled and sat and paddled and surfed and sat and were joined by two other locals when the sun was deepening its color, falling near to the rooftops above the beach. They stretched the daylight as far as it would go, and when the sun finally settled out of sight and the ocean was growing darker all around them, when they could barely see the waves approach, Kring and Buddy shoved off from their vigil and paddled in to the beach.

There they settled on the sand, looking out to sea, to the darkness-concealed swell they had just surfed.

Buddy said, "I hear there's a tropical storm in the Atlantic, east of the Caribbean. If it moves north we may get some waves from it."

"That would be cool. Nice early-autumn present."

It was dark enough that Kring could still see Buddy next to him but couldn't see his expression or tell what color his shorts were. Finally he said, "So what's the *real* story? Where are you really from?"

"I've tried to leave it behind me," Buddy began slowly. "That's why I tell everyone something different. It's not that it's been so painful, although some of it has, it's more that so little of what I remember makes sense."

"Like what?"

"Like, I can picture a dull orange sky, and it must have been a cold winter day because I can see bare, black trees in my mind. Or I remember big men with no faces coming to my house and talking low with my father outside. I remember Illinois, and eating breakfast in a diner with my mother. But I don't remember what my mother looked like. Does that make sense? And I remember very clearly being very scared in a big, ugly, cold building, and running out in front of a car. But I don't know what any of those images mean, where to place them or even which came before the others. I do know that the bit with the car came after the others and that the next thing I remembered was a hospital bed and me not being able to move my leg."

"What happened then? Do you know?"

"Yeah, from then on it's clear, but really unpleasant. It's what I tried to put behind me. The driver of the car was a very rich woman who adopted me. I don't know how this came about or whatever happened to my parents. But this lady — Sylvia, her name was — adopted me because she felt guilty for running me over, even though it was my fault. And she felt guilty because she hated herself. I lived in this mansion and I had lots of toys to play with, but I never had a birthday, didn't know what one was. It was a miserable place, that mansion. She hated men and treated them like shit. And here I was growing up and becoming a man, another man for her to abuse. She treated me worse and worse each year. So I split when I was, I don't know, I would guess I was about fifteen...." His voice trailed into silence.

Kring sighed in resignation. "You're not going to tell me the truth, are you?"

"You didn't buy that story either, huh?"

They sat next to each other in the sand, in silence, for a few more minutes. It was dark. Victoria had surely left for Philadelphia by now, Kring thought.

"Well, I guess I better get going," Buddy said.

"Yeah, that's what it's all about, isn't it?"

"What's that mean?"

"I don't know; it's just something to say."

Kring thought about Victoria constantly over the next few days. All day while he worked in the restaurant or as he sat on his surfboard in the ocean, he daydreamed and imagined her in bed with him, and at night in between his dreams he wondered how she would feel sleeping on his chest. After the first few daydreams he could no longer recall her face. He could see her mouth, and the tiny dimples that appeared at its corners when she smiled, but the rest of her face refused to come out from hiding in the shadows of his fantasies. The way she wore her hair helped him recall her, but then that became a stereotype, a reflex for him, and soon became useless too.

Kring didn't see her for four days after they'd gone for their walk. She was in Philadelphia getting ready to move into her apartment at school in a week, and it was during those few days that he lost her face from his memory. Can she really like me? he wondered dozens of times each hour. He was ready to decide it was all a waste of energy, that even if she slept with him that would be the end of it, and it would briefly satisfy him but ultimately leave him disappointed again, like the others. Kring was aware he had grown cynical about the virtues of sex, and of romantic love too, because they never lived up to the ideals he had been led to expect. He let Rebecca float downstream out of his grasp, and Lissa before her, and then the girls from the Colony because he just didn't care enough to pursue them. Their various charms weren't enough to overcome his pessimism, his feeling that, beyond a certain point, love was all a waste of time. Surfing, he thought, never left him feeling that way, not even during a long flat spell.

Victims of a flooding, a familiar stain of animal desire, he and Victoria were drawing together for an encounter — he hoped, anyway — that would make them drunk with the intimate feel of another's warm body. But Kring didn't look forward to the hangover that would follow, the "shy apologies and polite regrets" of which Elvis Costello sang. Kring had seen too many of those regrets this summer, and they would surely remain unspoken, as always. Maybe Lotion was right when she said he wanted too much from sex. Maybe he should try to see it differently, since he asked so much of it.

He wanted Victoria, though; he knew that. He wanted her to like him, he wanted to taste more of her skin. And even as he puzzled and worried and wondered, even as he insisted that a night, or a week, with Victoria would disappoint him, he knew that this realization would have no effect. It was as if he had no choice. He knew that it would happen and he could do nothing about it.

The next time he saw her was the day he left a message at the Cafe for her. "Tell her to stop by my place after work!" he had directed Irrelevant Roger, and that evening she knocked on his door. She had only a week now before classes began, and it was amazing to see her. She looked fresh and bright and more desirable than he even remembered. She told him excitedly about the apartment she had found and about her roommates and she mentioned three times how she couldn't believe the summer was almost over. But they were strangely distant with each other, as if unsure that their walk the other night had really happened, or that they had kissed like lovers. Kring made spaghetti for the two of them and they drank from a bottle of merlot that he had gotten.

They had finished eating and he was stacking the plates in his sink when he said, "How about a walk on the beach?"

"Okay," she said quickly.

Kring splashed some more wine in one of the glasses and offered it to Victoria. She sipped from it and pushed it back to him. He took his sip and set the half-full glass on the table. They walked out the door and headed up the quiet, dark street toward the ocean. He took her hand. He nervously let go of it a minute later, as they raced across the Boulevard, but they both began to breathe more easily.

As they crossed over the dune, they passed from the sporadic streetlight to a strange darkness. As well as he knew the beach by day, under night's cover it always took on an alien look, Kring thought, more secretive. They were concealed here, the two of them together. The soft sand was cold now under their bare feet and damp in the evening dew. The ocean was out there, they could hear its restless rolling, but the froth of the small breakers appeared out of nowhere and evaporated on the shiny, dark sand at the tide line.

It was in this magic world that Kring walked with Victoria. He didn't know her thoughts, barely knew his own, but he trusted her affection. They walked alongside the water's furtive movements, past two rock jetties. They came to the third, this one a waist-high wooden wall half-buried in the sand, and they turned back. They talked about nothing as they walked, nothings that filled the silence, nothings that opened up the night sky to them both.

As they strolled along the water, past the dune where they had entered the beach, Kring led Victoria with a gentle hand on her back up to the higher sand, where it was darker among the dune grass, out of the lights of the houses. There they sat. They held each other and kissed with the same fury and from the same famine as before, the other night, in the spotlight of the Pepsi machine. That night, Kring and Victoria had been asking each other something and answering yes with each kiss. But here, this night in the shadowy sand crucible they dug for themselves, deeper with each unconscious kick, they both offered something precious to the other and were too busy offering to take what was placed before them. They lost themselves in the taste and wetness of their mouths, in the feel of another's body responding to the touch. They rolled and breathed and explored necks, ears, shoulders, and backs, breasts and loins. They worked themselves into a frenzy, a breathless dance in the sand. There was nothing that could be wrong, nothing that could not be good. When he offered his hand to the whiteness of her thigh, she exhaled open-mouthed, then said softly, "Not on the beach. I don't like it on the beach."

He tried to sound patient when he said in a whisper like hers, "Let's go back, then."

They walked quickly, awkwardly in each other's arms, and Kring liked the way Victoria's face looked in the streetlight. It looked washed-out and different, but he liked it because he felt he knew her enough to recognize even this different face as her own. Her smile too had a new quality to it. Not as cool. A little uncontrolled.

On the way back they passed a house that sounded like it had a party going. Kring knew the house. The music pounded its way out into the evening air, a muffled reggae escort for their walk, and Kring almost let himself dance in the street at her side. Almost, but not quite. He didn't know her *that* well. His feet skipped once in response to the impulse.

When they reached the garage, he turned off the lights before she was even inside and they kissed hard, swallowed all they could. When they had to break apart to breathe they flung off their shirts and she

knocked over the half-full wineglass with her arm. It spilled onto the floor
as Kring searched in the dark for a tape to play. "This'll be good," he said,
looking closely at one cassette as he slipped it in his player and punched
a button. He helped her undress and stepped out of his canvas shorts,
naked in the darkness. An indistinct sound of surf and sea gull's cry
whispered from the little speakers, overlaid by guitar curling around it
like cigarette smoke. "Oh ... what is this?" she asked.

"*Dreamboat Annie*," he said. "An old Heart album, I think you'll like
it." He opened up the sofa bed and spread a blanket across it. He guided
her down to lay alongside him and the uneven mattress seemed to embrace
them in its characteristic valleys. Kring enfolded Victoria's naked body in
his own and they gripped and soothed and touched each other's skin and
they kissed with increasing fury as the music seemed to match their rising
tempo with its own. Kring was again amazed that this was she, Victoria,
Victoria Tanner, here in bed with him. He stopped and looked at her with a
smile. She seemed a bit puzzled. "What?" she asked.

"Nothing," he said,

"*What?*"

"Just glad. And a little amazed."

"Yeah. Me too."

The music played on, but after a couple of minutes its direction was
lost on them. They swam in warm pleasure of other senses and cared
for nothing else. They moved together in subtle, imperfect, primitive
rhythms and breathed and whispered and she grabbed at his back and
he wound his fingers through her soft, tangled hair. They were joined there,
and they were joined when their feet curled around each other and when
they kissed and when he entered her, and before long they grew accus-
tomed to the intoxication and the frenzy slowed, lost its urgency. They
were no longer in such a hurry to taste all that they had dreamed of. Kring
was enjoying all of Victoria: her laugh, her warm breath, her attention —
her presence. Not just her body. He didn't get past the bodies of the girls
at the Colony, or Rebecca either for that matter. He had tried, but not
until now, with this girl, did it happen, with this girl who now looked at
him as he lay still and who whispered to him, too low for him to understand. But it didn't matter what she had said. She was just whispering
to herself about him, and he watched as she closed her eyes and took
him again to dance. When she opened her eyes once more to look at him,
he thought he saw in them a liquid glimmer, the tiny play of light on water.
Maybe it was a teardrop, maybe it was his own imagination. Whatever,
he knew there would be no hangover tomorrow. There was something

here, with this girl, something that felt close to something he had been seeking for a long time. It made him believe that it may all be worth it after all. This revelation amazed him, and he wanted to share that amazement with her. He didn't speak. He just took her fully with all his muscles and limbs, and their imperfect rhythms rocked them until the drug of his own body seized his brain and his senses and he released himself to its flood and she clutched at his back, and he collapsed on her chest, weakened and out of breath.

That was it, he thought. She stroked his hair and murmured and ran her palms over the muscles of his back and the music played behind them, above them, in their ears. Then the player ate the tape with an insidious little hiss. Kring paid no attention, but Victoria struggled from beneath him to reach the stop button with the back of her hand. The machine saved her the trouble, shutting itself off with a click, and the two of them lay together in silence, happy to remain so for a while.

Later, after they had fallen asleep alongside each other, sharing his cotton blanket, later, long after the thin moon's secretive rise in the east, Kring found himself half-awake, blinking through confused eyes, ready to fall back asleep again, unsure what had stirred those eyes to open. He looked at Victoria next to him and touched her hair. Then he heard it again, and he knew what had disturbed his sleep. Outside his window, in the still island night, a mockingbird was calling with its bird-jazz song. Its sweet music seemed out of place in a morning heavy with dew and darkness, undisturbed by a sun yet to hint at rising. The soft-sound rhythms of the island's deepest hidden hours were split by the forlorn medley, and then those rhythms of those hours washed around again where the song had been, once it was gone.

Kring lay on the mattress with one hand under his head and heard the mockingbird's voice, and he listened. When it sang he turned to look out the open door but saw nothing through the screen. Victoria slept on beside him, comfortably, beautifully, he thought.

From out of nowhere, it seemed, a fragment of a song ran through his head, just the tune at first. The words would not come to mind. He hummed the tune to himself and then he heard the words: *Blackbird singing in the dead of night.* He remembered the Waterboys doing it in a song they played, but it had sounded strangely familiar when he'd first heard them do it. The Beatles, maybe? He could not remember. He wondered why he had never thought of what the words evoked before. It sounded nice, sure:

Blackbird singing in the dead of night,
Take these broken wings, learn to fly,
All your life you were only waiting for this moment to arrive.

The words were sweet to sing, but strangely they had never called any image to his mind before. At least nothing like the image that the early morning birdsong evoked for him now that had awakened him this four A.M. of a mid-August night. He had never tried to imagine that blackbird or what it might sound like as its song burst from the silence of that night's deadness.

He waved the blanket off his body and slowly swung his legs over the side of the bed. The weak springs creaked with every movement. Victoria still slept. He pulled a pair of white shorts over his legs and quietly crept over to the window in his bare feet. The mockingbird sang a short burst. It must be sitting on the antenna of the house, he thought. The aroma of wine spilled on the floor hung in the air, and it smelled sweet.

The sight that greeted him through the window astonished him. Through the cedar bushes that crowded his garage and framed his window, he saw a small, bright moon only an hour or so away from disappearing in the west. Its grey light settled in broad streaks on a bay that was black and nearly still. There were night-dark clouds with pale outlines scattered in the sky, and the peace of the hour flooded his sleep-dulled senses. He stood at the window a minute, silently intoning *Wow*, his own prayer of thanks, perhaps to the mockingbird whose song had awakened him.

It was beautiful, but something nagged at Kring, some voice that mumbled deep inside his soul, mumbled something Kring could not hear. He glanced over at Victoria. He smiled. She was sweet and she liked him, and it had been good.

Then his gaze returned to the scene outside his window, to the moon on the water, and he thought of the waves he had surfed out there in his dream. They were magical; they were as real as his memory and he wanted to see them rise. He wanted to ride them. It made him ache just a little to think that they existed nowhere but in his imagination, in his memory.

Still, it was a beautiful scene before him this night.

He returned to the side of the bed and lightly shook Victoria. "C'mere, Vic, you've got to see this," he whispered. He whispered though he had no reason to whisper, except to avoid stirring the peace-filled silence. He didn't want to drop a pebble into a still pond and suffer its ripples on

183

the surface. Victoria awoke confused and wrapped the blanket around her body as she followed Kring's lead to the window. Then she, too, whispered. "God, that's beautiful." They stood in front of the view, she wrapped in a soft blanket and his arms, he in simple white shorts that separated his muscled torso from dark legs, both of them tanned and bathed in the listless spot of moonlight. Kring felt like they were the ghostly reincarnations of a pair of lovers of Iroquois legend who live and love forever but only when the moon is bright. And when they are seen the hunt will be a good one, is the tradition he imagined. But perhaps they always appear, every night like this one, and sometimes go unseen. Or, he wondered capriciously, do they need earthly eyes before which to display their eternal love?

He shook his head to stop its drifting and he gripped Victoria's body tighter.

Kring liked having Victoria in his arms, and she smiled at his arms around her. Her face was tired. Her eyes were swollen and her hair tousled, but he recognized this as her face too, and he adored it tonight. Her mouth turned up in a crooked smile and he rested his face in the cup of her shoulder. Then the mockingbird from a new perch sang again clearly and she was startled, and she laughed, delighted at having caught her breath at its sound. She turned to him and he kissed her and they crawled back onto the creaky, stabbing bed where they curled together and made deep-morning love like those Iroquois lovers, ignoring the waves that would not be surfed in that bay, and the only music they heard was the strange, clear, intermittent song of that mockingbird.

Chapter 19

The Colors Change

That week went by quickly for Victoria and Kring — too quickly, it seemed, for them to arrange anything in it. On Monday Spill had quit work at the Shellfish, and Kring was given more hours, mostly at night, when Spill had worked. Victoria worked days, so in the afternoons Kring hung out at the Cafe. He had to be at work before the sun went down, however, and there were no good sunsets that week anyway. Kring knew that because he paid attention to the sky from the back door of the Shellfish kitchen.

He refused to get obsessive about her. Although she was on his mind constantly, he made an effort to maintain a casual appearance when they were together, and Victoria, possibly taking her cues from Kring, acted likewise. Before they knew it, the day they had ignored all week arrived, and Victoria had to leave to begin her senior year at Villanova.

They were unsure how to say goodbye on this day, so they ignored that, too, by making plans to get together over the weekend.

"So you'll be down Saturday?" he said.

"Yeah, Daddy wants me to work Labor Day weekend at least."

"Cool. So how about if we get together on Saturday night? Go to dinner, spend some time together ..."

"That sounds really nice."

That week they were apart went easily for Kring, everything considered. He surfed small waves and washed dishes and kept a careful eye on the approach of Labor Day weekend which was the traditional close of the summer season on Long Beach Island. He saw none of the gang those few days. Buddy had vanished again after his one appearance in

185

the surf, and all Kring heard of Spill and Crank were sketchy rumors of some cataclysmic Colony party. When he met Lotion at the Gateway bar on Friday evening, she had heard nothing of the Colony either.

"I haven't been by there since you left," she confessed over a beer. "Haven't heard of any parties, and I don't know what went on at that poetry reading." She toyed with the cardboard coaster under her mug. "I left early too that night. Didn't feel like staying around. You know, when you left, I was *hoping* you would stay at your place."

"Why was that?"

"I don't know, really, it just seemed ... poetic."

"Yeah. It felt right, I guess, that night, to stay in my place," he mused, then glanced up at the TV above the bar. "Goddamn it, what a bunch of shit."

Lotion turned her head to see what he was cursing so violently. "What are you watching?"

"One of those beer commercials — you know, where smug, pretty people meet each other with no effort and drink that glamorous domestic beer. Or they buy it, anyway. They never actually drink it on-screen. And no one ever actually takes a bite out of a McDonald's hamburger. They just fake it, and no one ever notices."

"So why does that bother you?"

"I don't know. I guess ... 'cause it's fake. And they assume we can't tell the difference."

"Sometimes I don't think I can tell the difference," Lotion said. "Sometimes I think it's better when I can't." She delicately sipped her beer. "What brought on this tirade, anyway? Tough day at work?"

"No, not really."

"Tough day in the waves?"

"I don't know, yeah, I did get a ding on my brand-new board yesterday. Some little twerp dropped in on me. That pissed me off. I recognized the kid too. He was one of the grommets who wanted me to enter that contest a couple weeks ago." He took a drink from his mug. A tiny beer drip slipped down his chin. "I don't know; I'm just a little on edge."

"How come?"

"I think it's, like, everything's gonna change after this weekend, Lo. I don't know what to expect, what's gonna happen."

"Do you mean with Victoria?"

"Well, yeah, but also with work, my apartment — I live in a garage for Chrissake — my friends, the whole island. Everything around here will be different when summer's over, and I'm realizing I don't know what the fall will be like. It's a little bit unnerving, Lo."

She nodded. A waitress came by with bar menus. Kring ordered a basket of french fries.

"And it shouldn't happen like this," he said suddenly.

"Happen like what?"

"I mean summer shouldn't end on September first. Just because it's a holiday and school starts the next day. It's artificial. What the hell? Leaves won't start falling on Tuesday. It won't get cold overnight." He rapped his knuckles on the bar once and looked at her. "You'll still be around."

"Yes," she said assuringly, "I'll be around for a while."

"So I'll just let summer live on, that's what I'll do. My summer won't end on Monday. It'll just go on until it's ready to end. And then I'll greet autumn. Happily. I'll be happy with it. I'll be ready. I'm just not ready for it this week, you know?"

"Well, good for you." There was amusement in Lotion's voice but she also seemed pleased, and Kring felt good about it. It felt like he was finally learning how to control his world, how to make it his own. His summer would be longer and fuller than everyone else's on Long Beach Island, just because he decided it would.

The french fries arrived and Kring poured a puddle of ketchup in one corner of the basket. He dipped a fry and bit one end of it. "Fries're hot," he said. He looked at Lotion. "So what are you doing this weekend? Anything?"

"There are a few parties I could go to. Rebecca's having one, a big barbecue on Sunday. You feel like going?"

"I don't think so. I haven't talked to her since July — since that morning. I'd feel awkward."

"I wonder what the Artists Colony is doing for Labor Day. They must be doing something big."

"I don't know. Haven't heard a word. I'm probably so far off the grapevine now that nothing reaches me anymore."

"What about that Withoutniks show at the Tide tomorrow? You going to that?"

"Probably not. I pick up my first paycheck tomorrow and I don't know how much money I'll have. Anyway, I think I'm going to take Victoria to dinner."

"Really." Lotion seemed surprised. "So is that going okay?"

"What? The thing with Victoria? I don't know, Lo. She's really cool, one of the best things about this summer, but she's like going to school now and probably won't be down here many weekends even, once it gets cold. I can't get up there to visit her until I get my license back and that won't be 'til October. But I like her," he said with an air of assurance. "I do like her."

Lotion nodded and pushed away her empty mug. "Look, I've got to get out of here. I'm meeting someone at Tuckers." She stole one last fry. "Have fun at dinner tomorrow."

Kring sat at the bar after she was gone, trying to finish the french fries. The faces scattered around the Gateway all belonged to strangers tonight. He saw no friends at the bar, nor at any of the tables. He thought he saw Ricky Van Floyd in the liquor store, but he ducked out before Kring could be sure. There were still half a dozen french fries left in the basket when he emptied his beer. He got up and strode into the men's room, still holding his mug. There he addressed the urinal with his feet apart, rested the glass on the porcelain. Suddenly he lifted the mug and slammed it into the plumbing on the wall. It shattered and the sound rang off the tiling and quickly died, left him holding a disembodied handle of clear glass. The broken pieces of the mug cluttered the urinal drain. He fixed his fly, dropped the handle in the trash and quickly left the men's room and the bar without looking at anyone.

Saturday Kring had the day off. He picked up his check before lunch and cashed it right away. It wasn't much but it was cash, and he treated himself to lunch, at the Water's Edge Bath House, right on the beach. He sat at a picnic table in the indistinct August sunshine and watched people stream over the dune onto the sand beyond the tall grass. He couldn't hear the surf over the shouts and screams and lifeguard whistles, and without much effort he was able to imagine that the people arriving were marching forward with no clear idea of where they were headed, led by some unseen Pied Piper to the sand. It amused him to project blind, unthinking momentum onto each face that passed as he feasted on his cheese steak. A herring gull landed on the deck next to him. Kring tossed him a chunk of his roll.

Then Buddy was behind him, standing there silently, hand on the table, waiting to be noticed. Kring pretended that he had seen the direction from which Buddy had come.

"What's up, dude?" Kring greeted him.

"Not much. You on lunch or what?"

"No, I'm off today. What you been up to?"

Buddy looked off in the distance. "Stuff," he said. He took one of Kring's potato chips and crunched it. "What are you doing this weekend?"

"Trying to figure things out still. I'm going to dinner with Victoria tonight. Beyond that I don't know. How about you?"

Buddy said nothing for a minute, just sat at the table, squinting at the sun. "Ah ... I'm thinking I'm gonna leave the island tonight, maybe."

Kring tried not to look surprised, because after all he had expected this for a few weeks. Actually he had not really expected an announcement, just assumed he would never see Buddy again after one of his mysterious disappearances. A couple of times he thought that it had already happened. "For real?" was all he said.

"Yeah, for real, brah. For good." Buddy just stared at a point in the distance, in the sky beyond the dune grass. "It's just time to move on. I wanna beat the traffic," he joked.

"Gotta move on, huh? Where you gonna go?"

"I'm not sure yet. Maybe Wisconsin, or the Poconos. I don't know, dude, I can't tell ya."

"But why?"

"Why am I going? Aw, man, this island is just getting too small. It knows me too well. Too many people know me from the Colony or whatever, and it makes me uncomfortable. It's only gonna get worse."

Kring looked at him, puzzled, then just shook his head.

"Besides," Buddy continued in a lower voice, "I just got in an accident on the Boulevard. I had to leave my car there."

"You just left your car at the scene and split? Where? When?"

"Just a couple of minutes ago. In front of the Ship Bottom police station." Kring could see the anxiety on Buddy's face now that he looked for it, and it was something he'd never seen before. "I only found you by a lucky accident, man," Buddy continued, and Kring could hear a tremble in his voice. "I was looking to get lost on the beach."

"Shit," Kring said as he thought about the spot Buddy was in all of a sudden. "Anyone hurt? Was it bad?"

"I don't know, man; I ran a red light and slammed into a minivan. I wasn't going fast, but I still hit my wrist on the dash and my shoulder on the wheel. I just opened the door and took off on foot." He sat down with a pained effort. "So now I got no wheels. And I gotta get out of here, gotta start a new life somewhere where people don't know who I am, where I can be anonymous, where I can be free ..."

"Free? Free of *what*, for god's sake? Well, free of traffic citations I guess, but who knows you at all on this island? No one knows where you come from, no one even knows your real name! All anybody knows about you, and that's just a few people, is that bullshit story you made

189

up that night."

"Yeah, well, sometimes that's enough, that they think they know who I am. Sometimes that's enough." He grabbed Kring's soda and stole an ice cube.

"Enough for what?"

"It's enough to be like a limit on my personality, y'know, a restriction, and I don't want to deal with that."

"What do you mean, 'a restriction on your personality'? What kind of shit is that?"

"Hey, we become what others think we are. Like, if someone tells you you're good-looking, then you become a good-looking person in your own mind, right? If someone believes you're a madman then you start to live it. Well, man, I don't trust people enough to let them tell me who I am, right? So by the time they begin to figure me out, I'm gone. It's been that way my whole life, man. I don't give them the chance to create me for themselves and then impose that on me. I've seen shit like that happen too many times. It's a tragedy."

"But what about those times when other people help you find good in yourself, something greater than you thought possible — it's a part of living with people, man. Part of society."

"Part of living with people who know you too well."

"Same thing."

Buddy did not reply as the holiday crowds swarmed around them. He just kept grabbing Kring's cup and eating ice cubes. Kring was annoyed by this behavior, but more deeply he was struck by the absurdity of such a discussion with this person who had just wrecked his car and abandoned it in the street. Buddy was in some real trouble if he got caught. He knew it. That's why he was so anxious and upset. But Kring also knew that he was serious about his reasons for leaving, that he believed this shit he expounded here.

Yet Kring sensed there was something else, something more behind Buddy's escape than just his precious virginal personality, his *tabula rasa*. His flight was made more urgent by the accident, but it was driven by something else, a force that he did not or could not acknowledge. Kring didn't know what it was, but he didn't feel moved to argue with Buddy about it. There was a spirit of some sort to Buddy's nomadic ideal that Kring found stirring, that he didn't want to see destroyed, no matter how futile it was.

"So you're leaving sometime today?"

"Tonight, probably. I'll hitch, get a ride off the island, ride all night in some direction and find myself gone tomorrow."

"That's really fucking romantic."

"Don't get offended or anything, dude."

"Nah. I know you're in trouble. I don't suppose you'll write."

"Probably not."

"Yeah, well, that's cool. Hey, I gotta be getting back. Got a ding to repair. So take it easy, dude. It's been cool."

Buddy said nothing for a minute, then grabbed Kring's arm.

"Hey, you think you could lend me some money? Like a hundred and fifty bucks maybe? I know it's a lot but I'll send it back to you when I get a job, I promise."

"Then you *will* write, at least once," Kring observed.

"I guess I will. If you lend me the money."

Kring knew that it defied all logic to give Buddy this money which was a good chunk of what he had earned since getting a job, money he was intending to give to Mr. Cox for his rent. He wouldn't see another paycheck for two more weeks, and he needed to buy food too. But he knew he would hand over the cash that lumped in his pocket. There was something about Buddy and his absurd experiment that appealed to Kring. It was as if a bizarre frontier were being explored, and Kring was intrigued, almost enough to offer to go with him. But that would have defeated the experiment, corrupted the frontier from the start. No, he wouldn't follow Buddy's path, but his friend was desperate and Kring guessed he would help finance the expedition. He was sure he'd never see the money again.

Kring reached into his pocket and pulled out a thick bank envelope. He counted out the money and did some quick calculating. "Dude, how about one-twenty? It's all I can afford," he said as he handed it to Buddy.

"I really appreciate this, dude. You won't be sorry."

Kring just nodded. He stood when Buddy did, but he didn't move from his place while Buddy walked away without a backward glance. Kring remained at the picnic table while his mystery-shrouded friend limped downhill, away from the sea, and was swallowed by the throngs of people streaming to the beach.

That afternoon, after he had explained to Mr. Cox about a friend in need and given him a hundred dollars against the rent he owed, as he waited for Victoria to arrive so they could go to dinner, Kring grew more and more bothered by his final meeting with Buddy. The exotic coating of lone-wolf heroism was thinly spread on what Kring now saw as Buddy's cowardice, and it wore threadbare in the heat of the afternoon the more Kring thought about it. Victoria drove up a little after six, and he climbed into her car. As they rode to the restaurant, his mind was occupied with why he had given Buddy the money, but more than that, why he had been so ready to dismiss him from his summer, from his life.

"That's not like me," he insisted to Victoria as they settled in at their outdoor table. "It's not like me to blow off people that easily, I mean people that are part of my life. I know he was in trouble and all, but even so, I just handed him the money knowing I would never see him again. That's not like me."

"Isn't it?" she asked pointedly. "I'm not sure I could see you really making an effort to get Buddy to stay around. Seems like that would be out of character for you."

"Ah, well, you don't know me that well yet. Friends are pretty important to me. It's just that with Buddy, when he told me that he didn't trust other people to tell him who he was, it wasn't until later that it struck me that I was one of those people that he didn't trust. Why? Why would he distrust me? I never gave him cause — unless you count that fiasco with that chick Bev, and that was stupid anyway."

They ordered their dinner and as they started on their salads, Victoria said, "I don't know. I always thought you were kind of a loner, like you didn't really hang with anyone in particular. It actually kind of surprised me when you asked me if I wanted to go to dinner this weekend." She plopped a cherry tomato in her mouth. "And who's this 'Bev chick'?"

"No one, just some girl Buddy brought to the Colony who liked me. Nothing for you to worry about." He waved a fly away from their food. "You know, in a way you're right about me, I guess, but I'm nothing like Buddy. Jesus, he's afraid to even tell someone his real name. That's a little over-the-top, don't you think? A little paranoid or something. How could he have any real friends when he doesn't even trust them with his *name*? But yeah, there is something about his anonymity that is appealing."

"What do you mean?"

"Like he's in hiding, but he's not exactly in exile. Or maybe he's permanently in exile, and that's the point. Of always moving, I mean. There's something extreme in it. But it can't be healthy, can it?"

He buttered a roll, and their dinners arrived.

"So how was your first week of classes?" he asked, changing the subject.

"They're okay, I guess. I've got this one public speaking course that should be fun.... Hey, you *are* going to visit me at school, aren't you?"

"Of course I'll visit. I'm not sure when, but I'll get up there. After I get my license back."

They talked about school and how soon the summer would be over on the island, and Kring told her of his determination to let it last as long as it wanted. The idea tickled Victoria, and Kring was about to laugh it off when she said, "I wish I could do that. But I have to go to school." When they were ready to leave, Kring left a generous tip with the check. He had money. It felt good to be liquid — for a change. As they were walking out of the restaurant, however, for a second he considered going back to whittle down some of his generosity, because he discovered that after Buddy, his landlord and dinner, he had left himself with three dollars. But he took a quick mental inventory, and he had enough food to stretch it out for two weeks. He had lived in poverty most of the summer, after all, and he thanked God that he worked now in the food service industry. He was grateful that he had a place to sleep.

He shared that place with Victoria that night, and they fell asleep, talking quietly together. They never even undressed. In the morning, they agreed that it was nice to do that. Then they had sex. Then they had breakfast. As Victoria showered in his tiny bathroom, Kring began cleaning the breakfast dishes. He recalled his financial situation and checked his wallet. The three single dollar bills were huddled together there as he remembered. He looked at them, at the paper. One bill was worn and faded, another missing a corner, the third folded, creased in quarters and with numbers scribbled on its back. Each took on an identity now, something that had escaped every other piece of money that he had earned or spent all summer long. He could treat these bills as friends almost, as long as they were around, and when the time came to spend one, he would choose carefully among them, and his choice would have meaning. He would no longer be spending an anonymous dollar bill, he thought, but a familiar one, more precious than is usual in a conventional consumer/legal tender relationship. He appreciated the difference, understood its intrigue. But that didn't mean he was very happy about it.

After Victoria left for work at the Cafe, the three single dollar bills kept Kring company all the way to the Shellfish, where he was able to grab a flounder sandwich for lunch. He was just finishing up the noontime rush of dishes when Maury poked his head in the back door of the kitchen.

"Hey, man," he said. "I'm glad I caught you here. I wanted to say goodbye before I left."

"Hey, music man, what's up? How's the Colony? Where you going?"

"I'm going back to advertising, man. That's where I belong. I was just fooling myself with this bohemian songwriter bullshit."

"What do you mean? I thought your songs were pretty good. You just need to believe in yourself a little more." He leaned on the doorway, catching a breeze on his arms and neck. "What's gonna happen with the Colony?"

"The Colony's dead, dude, didn't you hear? And besides, believing in myself would only work if I *were* a songwriter. Which I'm not."

"What do you mean the Colony's dead? What happened after the party?"

"There was no 'after the party.' That party destroyed the place. Walls fell, windows broke, cops all over the place, man — it was crazy that night. I've been staying at Spill's for the last couple of weeks, and I finally found a job with a newspaper in Trenton. I gotta go; I'm getting a ride with a friend of mine, this guy Dan — I don't think you met him. Anyway, I'm heading out. I just wanted to say goodbye, thanks for everything, y'know? So take care, dude, keep surfing, and maybe I'll see you next summer, okay?"

"Yeah, you too, man, it's been fun. Good luck."

They shook hands briefly without vigor and then Maury ducked out of the door into the grubby alley, stepping over some flattened cardboard, off to find his friend Dan. Then he was gone too.

Damn, Kring thought as he drifted back into the kitchen, Buddy's gone, now Maury, Victoria will be leaving and I'm sure she won't be back — shit, this damn summer is organizing itself all of a sudden into something splintered and melodramatic. It's like they're all panicking because it's Labor Day and they think everything is gonna change and so it *does* change. But it doesn't have to. Dammit, I *know* that.

And still Kring knew this day felt different now, a little more precious because next Sunday wouldn't be a summer Sunday, and people were letting things change because they felt they had to or because the calendar told them to, and there wasn't much time left now. Kring felt betrayed as he plunged his hands into the sink full of dishes.

Chapter 20

Labor Day

L abor Day morning dawned cloudy with a breezy chill in the air.
Once out of bed, Kring threw on a sweatshirt for the bike ride up
to the beach, and his wave check revealed sweetly curling, chest-
high surf in a green-gray and frothy white ocean. His arms felt the chill,
but his feet were warmed by seventy-degree seawater.

He returned to his garage for his board and an impatient breakfast
of corn flakes. Then he hit the still-deserted beach, edgy with anticipation.

Once he was out in the water, though, he found the waves frustrating and deceitful. Their looks were good and clean, but they rolled flatly
through the ocean until they hit a sand bar. There they jacked up steeply,
hollowed out and broke in a rush. Kring charged after several inviting
waves and watched them all roll underneath him, until he began to take
more risks, to paddle longer and drop in later, as they pitched forward
onto the bar. He suffered four or five brutal wipeouts on waves before he
made one, and then he rode gratefully until the curl closed on him. It
wasn't anything special, but the one ride redeemed the frustration of all
those wipeouts.

After an hour of surfing, Kring noticed there were others in the water,
but they were all in the distance. There was a clutch of surfers four blocks
to the north, and a couple of guys in wetsuits the other way. A group of
dolphins swam by him heading south, and Kring paddled a couple of
strokes toward them. He wondered if the surfers they had just passed
had noticed. He'd had no clue that there was anything there until he caught
a fleeting glimpse of a fin submerging, and in the choppy conditions and
cloudy seascape, he couldn't be sure what he had seen. He looked hard,
paid close attention to the surface beyond him and was soon able to count

at least a half dozen different dorsal fins breaking the surface every couple of minutes in a deliberate parade along the shoreline. Kring let two ridable waves go by as he paddled cautiously toward the dolphins. They frightened him, with their abrupt reminder of how much that he could not see lay below the surface of the ocean. Yet at the same time they charged him with energy, with a live awareness of how close he was to these creatures. He was part of their environment. He felt connected to them in some way this morning, some way wild and real.

An assault came across the water, a shrill whistle from a black-shirted lifeguard who waved his arms frantically from the stand. He seemed to be signaling for Kring to come in. Kring ignored him until he was sure the last dolphin had surfaced, ten minutes after a shining fin disappeared just thirty yards from where his feet dangled in the water. Then he said aloud, "What the hell does *he* want?" and stroked toward shore.

"Tomorrow at least," he thought as he paddled, "the waves will be here, the sun will be here, the dolphins will be here, but the damn lifeguards will be *gone*. The crowds will be gone. I'll have the beach back, back to myself." He smiled at the thought and he smoothly caught a steep backside wave and rode it into the shallows, almost to the band of crushed shells that swirled in the shorebreak.

Once he was on the sand, he recognized the lifeguard as the same rookie who had hassled him earlier in the summer. That simple face had also been in the crowd at a couple of parties at the Artists Colony. Kring never learned his name, and never cared. The kid seemed agitated as he hopped off his elevated chair. "Dude!" he yelled. "Didn't you see those sharks go by? They could have attacked you! That's why I called you in."

Kring just looked at him. "They were dolphins."

"I know a shark when I see one, dude, and they were it."

Kring just laughed.

"Besides," the guard continued, "there aren't any dolphins around here. They only live in, like, Florida. I know there's sharks here. They called the surf contest 'cause of a shark!"

Kring shook his head. He laughed again out of frustration and turned his back on the kid. He had to be at work in an hour anyway. At least, he thought as he left with a glance over his shoulder at the kid, you'll be back in high school tomorrow, and not on my beach. How could a *lifeguard* be so clueless? he wondered. For some reason, despite the cloudy skies that symbolized the disintegrating summer, Kring was cheered. He felt good.

He went to work at Shellfish and when he was done around four-thirty, he smelled like crustaceans and seafood. The sky was still overcast, but he saw that out over the mainland it was trying to clear. He headed back to his garage on his bike, pedaling leisurely, though he knew Victoria had said she would stop over before she left. She might be there already.

When he turned the corner onto his short street, Victoria's car was parked in his yard. He found Victoria waiting by the water. "I'm sorry, Vic," he apologized, "I just got off work. You been waiting long?"

"Just got here."

They embraced, and kissed long and thirstily.

Kring pointed to the thin band of clearing sky on the horizon and observed, "We just may get a sunset out of this."

"Maybe. I don't think I'll catch it, though. I promised my mom I'd be home by eight."

Kring looked surprised. "Oh. I thought we'd have some time together tonight before you left."

"We have some time," she said with a ready smile, which Kring returned, and they reached for each other again as they turned to head for the apartment.

The slam of a car door echoed from the other side of the building, followed almost immediately by a second identical sound. Kring and Victoria broke apart, and Spill and Crank appeared at the side door, knocking. It took a second for Spill to notice the couple out by the water. He walked toward them.

"Hey!" he called. "I heard rumors you two hooked up. Cool deal. What's going on?"

"Hanging out," Kring said cryptically.

"Yeah, well, we're not gonna stay long. Just wanted to stop by, see what you been up to since that last night at the Artists Colony."

"Doing okay. Working at the Shellfish. Hey, what's this I hear about the Colony? Someone said it was destroyed?"

Crank stepped around Spill with a six-pack in his hand and gestured to Kring and Victoria. "You guys want a beer? It's imported, so we need an opener."

Spill grabbed one of the bottles, delicately positioned the lip of its cap on an edge of the aluminum screen door, and slammed his fist down on top of it. The cap dropped off, but the bottle foamed up at the mouth and spilled over his hand. "Who needs an opener?" he said triumphantly, ignoring the scar that he left on Kring's screen door.

"Here's an opener," Victoria said as she handed Crank her key chain.

"So anyway," Spill continued, "about the Colony. Well, that night you split we trashed the place for good. My poems went over big, and everybody dug Maury's music, but the party afterward got pretty out-of-hand. I think the naked passion in my poetry had something to do with it, personally. But it was great. There was a real weird crowd that night, all these freaky people — like there was this one chick, real earth-head type, probably into the Grateful Dead and recycling and all that — remember her, dude?" He looked at Crank and chuckled. Crank nodded and laughed as he flipped the top off another bottle and handed it to Victoria.

"She was such a freak," Spill continued, "and so Crank goes up to her and he's all, 'That's a funny accent you got, where ya from?' and she all, like so serious, 'I'm from Earth.' Just like that, real plain, 'I'm from Earth.' And Crank's all, 'Oh, I have a friend from Earth, this guy named Oliver, do you know him?' " Spill broke up with laughter at his own story and Kring pictured a drunken Crank confronting an earth-mother type. He laughed too.

"Well, anyway," Spill went on, "something crazy got started, some sort of group destruction binge, and by like one o'clock the TV screen had a fire extinguisher through it, the one wall by the ugly green house, you know, on that side, the whole wall was caved in and the roof was held up I think by the telephone lines or something, and all the windows were broken 'cause people were throwing like cakes of Sex Wax and potatoes through them. And Roger, he dove head first into the plumbing under the sink after a mouse that I'm pretty sure he imagined, and so water was gushing out like a fountain in Rome or something. You should have seen it at sunrise, dude, because a few of us were still partying then, and it looked like some IRA bomb site in Beirut or something from a bad Chevy Chase movie." Spill told the story with intent to elicit more laughs from the others. "I wrote a crazy free-verse poem about it and I'm gonna try to get my poems published. I'll wash dishes and live in New Jersey and write poetry. It'll be great. And *The SandPaper* is going to do a profile of me and of the Colony. Is that cool or what?"

"Sounds crazy," Kring said, "a fitting end for the legend that is the Artists Colony. So why did Maury split? Did the Colony really mean that much to him?"

"No, he got scared about going to prison because we all got arrested after the party, and besides, he decided he wasn't really a songwriter, I guess."

"You got arrested?"

"Yeah, no big deal. The dude who owned the place didn't press charges but that didn't make any difference to Maury. He's all, 'This crazy artist's life isn't for me, dude.' He didn't like being on the lam. Went and got a job. But he's like twenty-six or something anyway. It's kind of hard to maintain that youthful zeal that long, y'know?" He took a long drink of his beer and then said to Victoria, "Don't your classes start soon, Vee?"

"Last week. I had a statistics class today, but I blew it off for the long weekend at the shore. I figured, I'm a senior, I can afford it."

"Cool."

She turned to Kring. "I ought to get going," she said quietly. She asked Crank for her key chain and then looked at Kring with a melancholy smile. "Come visit me, okay? Soon."

Kring just replied helplessly, "Yeah, I will. And — "

She stopped and looked at him again, with eyes that expected something. Kring wanted to tell her what he thought she had come to mean to him in the last few weeks of her summer, that she was special and that he would miss her, all things she wanted to hear him say. But the small crowd around them was not part of the world they had created in the last part of August here. It was a block to Kring, even though Spill and Crank wouldn't have thought twice about what he wanted to say, or about the kiss he and Victoria should have shared. The world he shared with Vic should have transcended this other. And he knew this, but still all he could say was, "Um, drive carefully. Good luck with your classes. I'm going to miss you, Vic."

Victoria looked at him for a moment, then leaned up and kissed him lightly and said, "I'll miss you, too."

Kring watched her walk away, thought he saw a hesitation in her walk before her steps quickened toward the street. He saw her without the power to decide for herself when her summer would end. His own power to do this seemed a little bit smaller, a little bit more hollow than he had believed, even that morning.

She almost bumped into Denis as she tried to hurry around the corner, and Kring knew that the next time he saw her, they would be different people to each other, no longer part of the same world. She would be a college senior, he an undefined beach boy trying to find his way. They would always have been lovers — however brief — summer lovers and bound by something more special than just a cliché. But would they never go beyond that, Kring wondered. Would that be the end of this story? He liked Victoria as she was, in his life, and it saddened him to see her leave. He hoped that maybe she knew what he wanted to tell her, but one thing he knew already: He would regret his silence.

"What's up, dudes?" Denis said as he stepped out of Victoria's path. She disappeared around the corner. A minute later Kring heard her start, then fade quickly into a sad, distant silence.

"I heard what happened to the Artists Colony, man," Denis said.

"Hey, Denis," Crank replied, "what's up with you? You kind of disappeared there for a while. You catch up with that barmaid and get lost in her thing or what?"

"No, man. I got busted DWI. And my dad is pissed. My court case is next week and if my lawyer can't get me off, my dad won't pay for me to take the real estate course. But I think I'll get out of it," he said confidently as he took the beer Spill handed him.

"Why? What'll get you off?"

"I don't know exactly, but this guy is supposed to be good, like the best DWI lawyer in the state. So what are you guys doing tonight? Me and some guys were sitting in front of the old Freedom shop waving goodbye to all the tourists leaving."

"When are you going back home, Denis?" Crank asked.

"Not for a couple of weeks. Unless I lose my license."

Kring finished his beer and held the empty bottle in his hand as he gazed west across the water. The cloud curtain had lifted a little farther from the horizon, and the distant sky it revealed seemed to have a soft glow about it. The sun was still behind clouds, but it would make it to the clearing before it set today.

Lotion bounded around the corner to join the party with a loud "Hey everyone!" She took the last beer when Spill offered it. "Anyone got an opener?" she asked breathlessly.

"Inside," Kring answered, his empty bottle still in his hand. Lotion ducked in the door. He was glad to see her, but was still bothered by his inaction, his impotence at Victoria's departure. He had left too much unsaid, hadn't even kissed her as she was leaving, like he wanted to.

Music came alive inside the garage, a song from a Spin Doctors album that Kring knew Lotion liked. She poked her head out the door and called, "Hey, Key, do you have any Elvis Costello tapes? I want to hear this one tune I heard earlier this summer. I know how it goes but I can't remember the name of the song."

"Yeah, I have a couple Elvis tapes. You want me to help you find them?"

"No, I'll handle it." She slipped back inside.

When Kring spun back to face the water, Buddy was standing there silently at the bulkhead.

200

Kring had to look twice to be sure he was really there.

"What the — ? Where the hell did you come from? Why are you back? I thought you were outta here."

Spill and Crank and Denis now saw him for the first time too and moved toward him. "Hey, dude," Crank said, "I wondered what the hell happened to you. I was waiting to read in the newspaper about them finding your body."

Buddy just shook his head with no real expression and said nothing. Then, quietly, he replied, "I had to take care of some things." He tapped his closed fist against Kring's arm. "Here, dude," he said.

Kring shifted the empty bottle to his other hand and took what Buddy offered him. It was a roll of bills. It was a lot of money. "What's this?" he asked.

"The money I owed you. Plus a little interest."

"How much interest?"

"There's a little over three hundred here altogether." Buddy met the astonished stares with the explanation, "Some of my *investments* matured." He said no more than that, and neither did anyone else. The music stopped.

After a dumbstruck minute Kring managed to mumble, "I didn't expect this."

"It's just to save me having to write you."

They heard from inside the garage the outcome of Lotion's music search, as the voice of Elvis Costello burst out of the shadows for a few seconds, then silenced again. When "Peace Love and Understanding" rang in the air Kring figured she found what she was looking for and she came dancing out into the yard. "I love this song. Hey, look who's here!" she exclaimed when she saw Buddy. "What are you doing these days, that you're so out-of-sight?"

"Oh, I'm just here to deliver some news to Denis."

"To me, dude? What is it?

"I found Mimi Dresden for you, brah."

"No way! Dude, where is she? Is she here?"

"She's in New York. Bad news, though, dude. She's living with Lloyd Hubris. Lloyd quit the band. He's gonna make a solo album, and Mimi Dresden's his new bass player."

Denis stumbled backwards a step, shocked and unable to reply. Spill and Crank fell on top of each other laughing at the news.

Kring squeezed the roll of bills in his hand, then tossed it in the air, caught it and said, "Well, if this is gonna be a party, I'd better go get some beer. Now that I got some money."

Spill offered to drive him but Kring declined. "I'll just take my bike up to Lang's," he said.

When he emerged from the liquor store Kring balanced two twelve-packs on his handlebars and steadied them with one hand. The two-hundred ninety or so dollars that remained made an awkward lump in the pocket of his shorts. As he pedaled down the street toward the bay and turned onto Central Avenue, he saw that the light all around him had changed. It seemed he felt it before he saw it, but there was a new tint to the houses, to the sand along the sides of the road, even to the asphalt surface itself. He had turned toward home but his attention was drawn instead in the opposite direction, to a public dock on a small cove that reached in to the edge of Central Avenue. There he stopped, and he had a clear view of the western horizon spreading under the thick, dark clouds. The edge of the sky seemed to burn like ash without flame, glowing brighter and hotter as its material grew scarcer and more precious. Down the street an elderly woman walked toward him, her terrier tugging at its leash. She stopped with her face to that wester sky and she gazed at it. She seemed to be enraptured for a moment, then continued her walk back the way she'd come. The other way, Kring watched two children climb onto the roof of a parked car to get a better look. He mounted his bike again, steadied the twelve-packs on his handlebars and pedaled toward the kids. He slapped the car they were on when he passed it and they shouted "Hey!" after him. He laughed. He came to a cross-street that ended abruptly at the bay, stopped there and stood straddling his bike. He watched the source of that light emerge beneath the clouds, and the orange was so intense that Kring could almost see it released in waves from the glowing ball of the sun. He had no sunglasses and so could not stare for more than a few seconds at a time, but he saw its light explode and burn on the underside of the cloud cover above him that extended out to sea. Trapped between that water and those clouds, spilling onto the island on which he stood, the light raged silently against its prison walls, vibrated off every surface it touched. Kring could feel its vibrations penetrate his body when he closed his eyes, could see the spots it left on his vision, and feel the warmth on his face and on his legs. The sun was fully free now of the long, imposing, solid cloud front above, not yet in contact with the treeline of the mainland. It hung in the narrow neon sky it made, and glowed with a fury and a heat that brought it alive. It was only light, but it was a light of such intensity, a light so seldom seen, that it cast all of the familiar landmarks of Kring's world in new tints, new shadows. He didn't even try to see it, but Kring took his hand away from his eyes and stared, and what he saw was morning. It was a sunrise before him — bold and vibrant — and a landscape, a whole world, was suddenly reversed: a bay was to the east, an ocean to the west, and the sun inched upward before him. The separation between its bottom rim and the treeline widened as the seconds passed, and Kring saw it move. "Cool," he said.

But the light burned his retinas. Involuntarily he clenched shut his eyes and covered them with his forearm.

When he dared again to look, the lower rim was down, touching the horizon. That didn't matter to Kring; he knew he had seen it, he knew it was real. It was as real as his knowledge of it, it was a part of his experience, part of what made him who he was at that moment, and that person, he sensed already, was a bit different than the one who had left to get beer for his friends ten minutes before. He closed his eyes again.

His eyes had not yet recovered from the burn when he again opened them another time, unable to resist the magic. The bottom curve of the sun was already settled beneath the horizon and the orange light had lost a touch of its vibrancy, and Kring could stare at it longer now. Something in this sunset, or in him, told him that yeah, he'd been right all along, that summer did not end tonight — though it had changed. It was the difference. He knew it. He could live the rest of the summer now, love the rest of the summer and be ready for autumn when it came. He felt more than lucky — blessed, maybe, that it would be later for him than for most. Autumn would be special too, and when it showed up, he'd be ready, just as he had learned to be ready for the waves, to be there when they broke and to take their energy as his own.

He watched the last orange sliver absorb into the distant earth, achingly, slowly, and then it was gone. He closed his eyes and saw again its blue imprints behind his eyelids, on his vision itself, and he pushed his bicycle into motion toward home.

The group was still hanging out there, Buddy included, when Kring returned with the beer, and they tore into the top box, stripping it of half its stock. Lotion went inside to tend to the music, which had stopped playing. The boys talked about this final night of their summer, and Crank suggested they all meet later at the Ketch Club. Kring declined the invitation, then he looked around and noticed Buddy was gone. An open beer can sat on the bulkhead. The yard grew darker and the bay reflected the colors still gathering on the underside of the clouds.

"Anyone know where Buddy went?" he asked.

"He was right here," Spill said.

"There's his beer, on the bulkhead," Denis observed.

"Yeah, I know he was here when I got back. I remember him taking a beer. Now he's gone. Again."

"He's a freak. He'll be back," Crank declared. "I'm hungry. I'm gonna go home to get something to eat. Nice sunset, dude. Catch you later." He looked at Spill. "You coming, brah?"

Spill cradled his unfinished beer and grabbed another. "Yeah, I'm coming," he said, then to Kring, "I'll probably be around. I'll catch ya. I'll see ya in the fall," he joked.

Denis put down his beer and reached to shake Kring's hand. "I gotta get going too, bud. Maybe I'll see you later at the Ketch, or the Tide."

"Maybe."

That quickly Kring was left alone in the hurried evening darkness. The sun was gone, and the band of sky where it had burned not even a quarter-hour earlier was now a rapidly deepening purple beneath the clouds. Music began again inside the garage and Kring watched Lotion emerge from one darkness into this other. He could not see much of her features, just the outline of her face and the shining whites of her eyes as she gazed at the slowly mutating sky.

"I have a secret, Lo," he said quietly.

She looked at him.

"That sunset ..."

"It was amazing, wasn't it?"

"I saw it rise."

"What do you mean?"

"How do I explain it? It was morning, Lo." He pointed to the blue streak over the mainland. "That was the east. The bridge was south of us. I spun the world around for a moment. I saw the sun rise in the sky. I watched it move. It was real. It was so cool."

Lotion smiled. She closed her eyes before speaking, then turned her look on Kring. "I know," she said. "It's not so different after all, is it?"

Kring looked at her and said nothing.

"I've got a secret too," she said.

"Oh yeah? What's that?"

"Nothing big. Just that I saw Buddy leave."

Kring's mouth fell open and formed into a grin. "You didn't!"

"He took a couple of sips of beer from the can he had just opened, then he tried to slip out through the bushes while he thought no one was looking. But I saw him from the garage."

204

"You caught him." He laughed, and his laughter seemed to startle the reeds and pine branches in his backyard. But it was just a lone breeze blowing from the south, stirring them into a whisper. "That's great, Lo," he said. "That's perfect."

He touched her elbow and pointed toward the apartment, and they could hear the tape Lotion had put in the player, the music drifting through the bushes. He hummed along with the song, "Oliver's Army," and Lotion put her hand inside his arm as he sang, "Call Careers Information, have you got yourself an occupation, Oliver's Army are on their way, Oliver's Army is here to stay ..." They started to sway with the music, a slow unrehearsed dance on their way to the door. "And I would rather be anywhere else than here today ..." Kring stopped singing this line. "Not this time, Elvis, old man. I love your work, but I don't want to be anywhere else today."

"Me either, surfer boy."

They walked slowly toward the garage as behind them the sky drained itself of light. When they reached the corner of the building, Kring looked back and he could no longer tell where the sky met the water. The transition was complete. There would be others, but right now he liked the way this one looked.

B ruce Novotny was born in Atlantic City, New Jersey, just before the legendary coastal storm of March 1962. He graduated from the University of Notre Dame, where he co-founded the campus humor magazine. While doing a year of post-graduate work at Cambridge University, he represented the school in the British universities soccer tournament. A local on the sands of Long Beach Island, New Jersey, he surfed the island's beachbreaks, paddled his surf ski on Little Egg Harbor Bay, managed the family's marina business, and wrote a contemporary culture column for the summer weekly *Beachcomber* in the late 1980s. After contemplating Jersey Shore sunsets for many years, he now lives in southern California where he is pursuing a carreer as a screenwriter. *Tales From an Endless Summer* is his first book.

Down The Shore Publishing offers many other book and calendar titles (with a special emphasis on the mid-Atlantic coast). For a free catalog, or to be added to the mailing list, just send us a request:

Down The Shore Publishing
Box 3100, Harvey Cedars, NJ 08008